Also available in the Dance Legacy Series:

The Legend of L'Esprit

DANCE LEGACY SERIES

Chasing the Spotlight

— A NOVEL —

DORIS GREENBERG and PANDRÉ SHANDLEY

Ten|16
PRESS

www.ten16press.com - Waukesha, WI

Chasing the Spotlight
Copyrighted © 2021 Doris Greenberg and Pandré Shandley
ISBN 978-1-64538-223-2
First Edition

Chasing the Spotlight
by Doris Greenberg and Pandré Shandley

For information, please contact:

www.ten16press.com
Waukesha, WI

Edited by Jenna Zerbel
Cover design by Kaeley Dunteman

Cover Imagery:
Malte Schmidt - unsplash.com
Paul Green - unsplash.com
David Hofmann - unsplash.com

Dedications

For AMS and RMS

No day shall erase you from the memory of time

Virgil

DAG

For my Michael
Ryan, Brittany, Ryleigh and Connor
Kahlin and Bryan

The blessings of a loving family outnumber the stars

PAS

A Note from the Authors

Chasing the Spotlight is a reflection of our love for New York City: its people, sights, sounds and vibrant energy. We are especially captivated by the historic theatre district. The immense and varied trove of talent and creativity found there is second to none.

Written pre-COVID-19, we drew from our many visits to the greatest city in the world. Whether exploring with family and friends as tourists or chaperoning studio dancers, the city always offered new experiences around every corner and exciting places, like hidden treasures, waiting to be discovered.

New York City, we eagerly anticipate your robust return to . . .

Restaurants and hotels filled to capacity,

Crowded delis,

Busy sidewalks,

and noisy streets.

Most of all, may every theatre box office window feature a prominently displayed SRO sign.

We ♥ NY!

Doris and Pandy

Prologue

"Stairway to the Stars Dance Convention," New York City

"*Shut up you spoiled diva*, or I swear you'll never dance in the spotlight again."

The teenager's eyes dart in terror. She tugs desperately at the ties that constrict her wrists and ankles. Each frantic movement binds them tighter.

"Relax, babe. You're not going anywhere."

The attacker swings a small handgun dangerously close to the girl's head and roughly yanks her hair. She moans when he covers her nose and mouth with a chloroform-soaked rag; her fear fades into unconsciousness. The man slaps his victim's face to make sure she's out cold then presses his lips to her ear. "That's it, Sleeping Beauty. Sweet dreams."

The kidnapper removes his disguise. He peels off fake eyebrows and a faux mustache, careful to place each piece along with the stolen hotel uniform inside an empty garment bag. Satisfied with his work, he sends a single word text on his recently purchased burner phone. *Done*.

COME FLY AWAY

Come Fly Away is a dance revue choreographed by Twyla Tharp (an American dancer, choreographer, and author) incorporating the songs of Frank Sinatra. The show premiered on Broadway at the Marquis Theatre in March of 2010. It received awards for best choreography and outstanding male dancer. Although one *New York Times* critic deemed it "an undramatic, clubland non-event," colleague, Charles Isherwood, called it "a sleek, energizing mixture of Sinatra's inimitable cool and Ms. Tharp's kinetic heat." The musical, set in a New York City nightclub, follows four couples as they look for love.

Three Days Earlier
LaGuardia Airport

My excitement of catching a glimpse of the Statue of Liberty as we bank for our descent nearly matches the rush of the jet's powerful engines. As the tires hit the tarmac, I listen to the captain's welcome to New York City with unabashed glee. After seventeen years of dreaming, I, Libby Nobleton, a self-professed dance-nerd, have finally arrived.

I giggle when Danny, my handsome French seat partner who moved to the States at an early age, pretends to pry my white-knuckled fingers from the armrest. The flash in his warm, brown eyes hints that he wishes we could stay among the clouds a while longer. If he asked me to come fly away, I'd be sorely tempted. While I'm overjoyed at the thought of spending the next week with him at the STTS, Stairway to the Stars national dance convention, he reminds me in his charming accent that he's competing for the title of the male DOTY, Dancer of the Year. I can hardly wait to see his body in motion. I'm suddenly embarrassed when I catch my dad's sharpening eyebrows; I'm grateful he can't actually read my mind.

Ignoring the pilot's order to stay seated and belted until we arrive safely at our gate, most passengers jam the narrow aisle grabbing bags from overhead compartments. I poke Danny when I notice the same greasy-haired creep who's been obsessed with my fellow L'Esprit (Le Spree) Studios dancer since the beginning of our flight. We watch him eyeball Cynthia Cunningham, fondly known as C.C., while he pushes his way forward.

"I swear he's up to something."

"Me, too," Danny says.

I hope we're wrong and do my best to forget about the stranger. After all, now is not the time for stress; our many hours of rehearsals are finished. We can't possibly be more prepared. I'm sure everyone's thinking the same thing; let's get this party started! I'm amused by the inquiring looks from my favorite dance pals: the highly-spirited C.C., a tall, redheaded tap dancer, sweet Brooke Allen, a petite, blonde ballerina known for her crushing hugs, and Jarrell Jordan, a young Will Smith doppelganger. He's our studio's most versatile male performer who excels at everything. I know they're itching for me to spill the tea on what Danny and I talked about during the flight.

Having only been a student at L'Esprit for the past year, I'm thankful for the special bond we share. I remember thinking my life was over and regret the tantrums I threw when my dad took a job as a featured columnist with the *Chicago Tribune*. My family's relocation to Illinois forced me to abandon my Wisconsin studio and beloved dance teacher, Miss Dana Greenly. But when she referred me to L'Esprit, her best friend's Chicago dance studio, I fell instantly in love with Miss Aimée Harris, its owner and artistic director. Although I'll always hold a special place in my heart for Miss Dana, I'm blessed to be part of L'Esprit's success and unique history.

When Danny and I slide into the aisle, I don't mind that we're pressed together during the slow shuffle to the exit. His body, so close to mine, gives me a thrill. We enter the terminal where C.C., Brooke, and Jarrell stage an impromptu welcome. They jokingly pretend as if I'm a famous diva arriving for her starring role on Broadway.

"Miss Nobleton," Brooke shouts, gathering the attention of curious onlookers, "can we get an autograph and picture of you tossing your lustrous, chestnut locks?"

I play along and swing my hair from side to side. "You're such dears for this splendid greeting, but my schedule simply won't allow me to honor any requests at this time."

"I think I've just seen the future, and it's not pretty," Jarrell quips. "And who's your friend, Libby?"

"Hey everybody, this is Danny, umm, I didn't catch your last name."

"It's Landry," Danny says.

"This is C.C., Brooke, and Jarrell," I say. "Danny's from Star Struck Studios in L.A., and he's competing, too."

"Great! Nice to finally meet you, Danny. I remember you from past nationals, but I missed seeing you here last year," C.C. says.

"You're right," Danny admits. "I had to take a few months off. A severely sprained ankle with a partially torn tendon kept me from dancing. It was the worst. I was forced to stay home and undergo a strict regimen of physical therapy. I hated every minute that kept me away from dance."

Danny doesn't miss our sad glances aimed at Brooke.

"Did I say something wrong?" he asks.

"No. Not at all," Brooke says. "It's just that I can't compete this year because, although fine now, I was a pretty sick puppy last year, and my doctors won't clear me to dance for a few more weeks."

"Oh man, that's rough. I'm sorry, Brooke," Danny says.

"It's okay. Really! In my opinion, I'm completely recovered," she says. "Besides, I get to run music for Trent Michaels. I'm actually looking forward to it. No pressure of competition, no crazy makeup or clingy costumes. It'll be fun."

"I give you credit, Brooke. You always know how to put a positive spin on things," I say.

"I'm impressed," Danny says. "Being sidelined isn't easy. But wow, Trent Michaels is my idol. He's a Tony Award winning dancer and choreographer! How do you know him?"

"Mr. Trent's at L'Esprit all the time. He's engaged to our teacher, Miss Aimée. They've been sweethearts forever," Brooke says.

"That's awesome. I'm taking a bunch of his classes, so I guess we'll be seeing a lot of each other," Danny says.

"All righty then," I say. "Pleasantries aside, let's find our baggage carousel and get out of this airport. I'm dying to see New York City!"

Loaded with costume bags and suitcases, we scramble aboard the hotel's shuttle. As the cityscape grows closer, I contently listen to the excited chatter of my friends and our parents. Everyone's here except the Allen family. I imagine Brooke's happy for the freedom but misses them nonetheless.

"Honestly, Libby, is this your first trip to New York?" Danny asks.

"Yup," I say, "unless you count the times I've been here in my dreams."

"Well, there's nothing like the real thing," Danny winks. "Don't look now, but your dreams are about to come true."

My jaw drops as the full expanse of the city swells before our eyes. Chicago's big, but *this* stunning sight is one I'll remember for as long as I live. Danny squeezes my hand and I squeeze back. I'm in heaven. What can possibly go wrong?

GRAND HOTEL

Grand Hotel is a multiple Tony Award winning musical with book by Luther Davis and choreography by Tommy Tune based on a 1929 novel and play, *Menschen im Hotel* (People in a Hotel) by Vicki Baum. It subsequently became a 1932 MGM feature film. The musical premiered on Broadway at the Martin Beck Theatre in November of 1989. It focuses on events taking place over the course of a weekend in an elegant hotel with intersecting stories of its eccentric guests including an aging, prima ballerina.

Chapter Two

*I*t's *early evening by the* time we arrive at the five-star Broadway Center Hotel. I wish I had a trained voice, because I literally want to break into song. New York City exceeds my every expectation. Not a single picture I viewed or article I read captured the immensity of the Big Apple. Our luxury hotel towers in the skyline with forty-five gleaming floors of reflective glass and steel. Evidently, their website's extensive photo gallery wasn't enough to prepare a first-time visitor like me. The lights of the city and this grand hotel, rooted in the middle of neon-lit Times Square, magically shine.

"It's so much bigger and brighter than anything I've ever seen," I say. "Chicago makes me feel like a small fish in a big pond. Here, I'm not even a minnow."

"Don't let it scare you," Jarrell laughs. "In the immortal words of Dory, your favorite Pixar character, 'Just keep swimming.'"

Our driver pops open the back of the van while the hotel doorman pushes through the oversized revolving door.

"This is insane!" I say, peering upward.

When we step out from the shuttle's air-conditioned comfort, the lingering July heat greets us like a sticky hug. "The weather app warned this week's temperatures would be blistering," Jarrell fans his face.

"It doesn't bother me," I say. "I don't care. I'm here!"

"Yes, you are, Miss. Welcome!" The doorman offers me his hand.

"Broadway's bustling for you, Libby!" Danny flashes his smile.

Gosh his teeth are dazzling. How flawless can one boy be?

Crowds push in every direction while cabs by the dozens race to avoid missing the next light. People of all ages and backgrounds speak in every language imaginable. But most noticeable are the constant, howling sirens.

"Is the city on fire?" I ask.

Danny and the doorman chuckle.

"No, that's normal Manhattan noise," C.C. says.

New York pulses with non-stop electricity. Immense, blinking billboards illuminate the evening sky, and I'm dizzy with sensory overload. The smell of hot dogs and pretzels from nearby vendors wafts in the air. Unfortunately, it's followed by the pungent odor of recently deposited trash bags that line the sidewalks.

"Phew, I wasn't expecting that," I rub my nose.

"Oh, you'll get used to it. With millions of people passing through Times Square each year, garbage has to go somewhere," C.C. says.

"Wait. Did you say millions?"

"That's right." Jarrell laughs. "You're only one of five-hundred thousand tourists a day on these famous streets."

C.C. touches my shoulder. "It's all good, Libby. We've got your back. Anyone's first visit can be both exhilarating and intimidating."

"But trust us, you're going to love it," Brooke says.

"Especially," C.C. whispers, "if your French hottie is with us all week." I practically choke on my gum.

As instructed by Miss Aimée, we gather our suitcases and enter the hotel. The massive marble foyer sparkles. The lobby, adorned with magnificent modern art, is furnished with a sleek reception desk. Colorful vases of lavish flowers greet us along with an attentive staff dressed in crisp, red-trimmed, gray uniforms. While our parents handle the check-in, L'Esprit's dancers tweet and post images of the fabulous Broadway Center Hotel on social media.

I'm pleasantly surprised to learn L.A.'s Star Struck Studios has rooms just a few floors below ours. Danny jots his room number on a piece of paper and gently presses it into my palm. *There's his mind-blowing touch again. God, he's special.*

"Danny wants to be the first to show me the city," I say. "Can we all go together?" Mom approves, but my dad's frown is unmistakable.

"I'll meet you right here in an hour, Libby," Danny says. "Call my room if your plans change." When he heads for the elevators, I admire his athletic body, fitted impeccably in faded jeans and a white shirt. His muscular arm pulls his suitcase, and I note the shooting star tattoo he showed me earlier on the plane. I love that its French inscription, *Ayez la foi*, means *have faith*. When he faces me from the distance of the elevator's closing door, he runs his fingers through his silky, dark hair, and his half-cocked grin tickles my stomach. I'm embarrassed by my intense fixation, but then his wink tells me that he doesn't mind.

Jarrell pats my back, "You can close your mouth, Libby."

"And wipe that drool off your chin, too," C.C. laughs.

"Leave her alone, you guys. He's dreamy. She has every right to drool," Brooke says.

When Jarrell throws her a sideward glance, Brooke detects an uncharacteristic hint of jealously. "Jarrell, stop. You know we'll always love you best," she says.

We make a mad dash to our rooms on the thirtieth floor to drop off our bags and freshen up. First to the door, I scan the keycard. Like magic, it unlocks. Our home-away-from-home is stylishly designed. Brooke throws open the sheer curtains with a flourish. "I'm in love with the skyline of this city," she says. "This floor-to-ceiling view never fails to take my breath away."

I jump through the air and flop onto one of the double beds. The fluffy duvet hugs me like a billowy, white cloud. "This is unbelievable," I sigh, making a pretend snow angel. I throw my arms in the air. "I love New York City! I couldn't be happier." Snatching a pillow to cover my mouth, I scream, "Ahh! Thank you, Lord!"

"Amen to that, Sister," Brooke says.

"Personally, I think it's her new crush that's got her acting all C-R-A-Z-Y!"

"No way, C.C.! That's not it. Oh, maybe a small part," I smirk.

C.C. pulls the pillow from my grasp and smacks me over the head, "Hang on tight, Miss Happy Pants. I think someone named Daniel Landry has bought you a one-way ticket on the roller-coaster of love."

Our hair combed and makeup reapplied, we head to the lobby to find L'Esprit's faculty and our parents waiting. Although it seems impossible, Danny stands next to Jarrell looking more attractive than even an hour ago. Before we make our way onto the sidewalk, I thank my mom and dad for bringing me to New York and letting me finally attend my first nationals. I always understood that our many years of caring for my ailing grandfather was our family's priority, and although we miss him terribly and mourn his loss, I'm grateful to be here now. I sense they study Danny when I leave them to join him and the rest of our group.

"Will, I think something's happening to our daughter," Kate Nobleton says with a twinge of enthusiasm.

"What do you mean? What's happening?"

"Libby and that boy. Don't you see the spark?" she says while snapping views of the city through the lens of her professional-grade camera and gifted photographer's eye.

"Oh, no! Not if I can help it. That boy's from L.A. and he's French!"

"Shocking! There's a newsflash for your column."

"In my opinion, he looks like a West Coast player, a real quick-stepper."

"Of course, he does; he's a dancer."

"Hardy-har-har," Will Nobleton wrinkles his face. "I know that Miss Aimée likes him, but it's just that he's . . ."

"He's what?"

"He's too . . ."

"Too what? Polite, handsome, loves dance as much as Libby?"

"No. I don't know. He seems nice enough I guess, but, well, don't you agree he's too old and worldly for our daughter? For Pete's sake, Kate, he's completely unchaperoned."

"Will, he's a recent high school graduate. He's maybe eighteen; Libby's seventeen. You have to let her grow up sometime."

"Like I said, not if I can help it," Will pouts.

Kate takes his hand. "It'll be fine, honey. Just look at your leggy Libby. She and her friends are having the time of their lives."

"Well, I'm keeping a sharp eye on him all the same."

In the distance, a stranger follows. He discreetly takes bursts of photos, but none are of the cityscape. Each click of his camera focuses on just one unsuspecting target.

BRIGHT LIGHTS, BIG CITY

Bright Lights, Big City is a rock musical with music, lyrics, and book by Scottish composer Paul Scott Goodman based on the novel of the same name by Jay McInerney. The piece premiered Off-Broadway at the New York Theatre Workshop in February of 1999. The story follows a week in the life of a successful young writer who loses himself in the chaos of New York City in the 1980s.

Chapter Three

*B*rightly lit, giant ads of every color bombard Times Square. Ten at night looks more like noon. Rolling newsflashes scroll across the front of ABC studios, and glitzy screens featuring celebrities and half-naked models vie for our attention. Most thrilling are the Broadway billboards promoting the latest shows on the Great White Way, which I learned from Miss Aimée became the nickname for Broadway in the late 1890s when the street was first illuminated by newly installed electrical lights. Today, its blinding glow has to be seen to be believed.

As we keep pace with the mobs of tourists soaking in the sights, I politely ignore the pushy vendor who tries to sell me a pair of knockoff Gucci sunglasses and the others who wave I ♥ NY T-shirts, purses, and watches in my face. At another table, an artist sketches a caricature of a little boy who should be in bed by now. Like the old Sinatra song says, this truly is the city that never sleeps.

I'm relieved to be out from underneath my father's overprotective scrutiny when our teachers and parents stop for coffee at an all-night diner. We promise to meet them in an hour at the top of the staircase above the TKTS discount ticket booth on 47th and Broadway in Duffy Square.

"You guys, there he is," C.C. yelps and points.

"Who?" I ask.

"It must be her boyfriend from last year," Jarrell sighs.

C.C. sprints to have her picture taken. Brooke shrieks, "O-M-G, it's him! The Naked Cowboy!"

When I view the scantily dressed man through the horde of pedestrians, my eyes open six miles wide. Wearing only a cowboy hat, boots, and a pair of tighty-whities, he sings, strums his guitar, and periodically stops to pose for photos for cash.

"Libby, try not to act like you've never seen a man in his underwear before," Jarrell teases. "You don't want to startle old Danny boy."

With a closed fist, I slug his shoulder. "I danced with you in your leopard loin cloth, didn't I?"

Both Danny and Jarrell grin.

"I have news for you; on these streets, anything goes," Danny says.

I give Jarrell a second pop for good measure.

After C.C. finishes her photo op with the local celebrity, she drops a few dollars in his open guitar case. With an exaggerated wink and her best Texan drawl, she circles one arm above her head and hollers, "Yee haw, ladies! Save a horse, ride a cowboy."

Everyone within earshot laughs, even The Naked Cowboy. Oh, how I wish I could be more like C.C.

A short distance away, another street actor stands frozen atop a simple wooden platform. He's completely covered in a second skin of silvery paint. His piercing, dark eyes remind me of Daniella Devereaux's whispering statue. She's the patron ballerina of our studio, L'Esprit, who died a fiery death in 1926. The mysterious eyes of her legendary sculpture eerily resemble those of this street performer. It's a long story. Maybe someday, if I explain our junior detective skills and the unraveling of the truth behind Daniella's tragic end, Danny won't judge me too harshly. *Will he believe in the Legend of L'Esprit and how her statue came to life? Doesn't every girl talk to ghosts and travel through time?*

A propped sign in front of the metallic man reads, "To see me dance, empty the pockets of your pants." When a small boy takes a five-dollar bill from his mother and places it in the tip jar, synthesized music plays. The automated dancer comes to life and moves robotically for several minutes before freezing in a new position.

"That's so cool. He's mesmerizing," I say.

"So are you," Danny says. I suddenly realize he's been centered on me the entire time. "I love the way your eyes light up, Libby. You're pretty when you smile."

"Hmm. Only when I smile?" I struggle to act casual.

"You caught me. I have to admit, I think you're pretty all the time. And if I'm honest, since we met this morning on the plane, I've thought of little else." With an endearing shrug, he laughs. "Did I just say that out loud?"

His words cause my pulse to skip. My legs weaken like Miss Aimeé's did when C.C., Brooke, and I once witnessed Mr. Trent, thinking they were alone, hotly pursue her at the studio. Except now, I'm the one someone wants. *Is the most gorgeous guy I've ever met flirting with me? Am I flirting back?* Jarrell taps me on the shoulder, and I snap back to reality. "There's the TKTS booth. Are you coming?"

While the rest of our group charges up the red-lit plexiglass staircase, Danny and I pause at the Duffy monument located in front of the steps. It portrays fearless Father Francis P. Duffy with a helmet at his feet and the Bible in his hand. He stands in front of a Celtic cross. I learn that he was a Roman Catholic priest and military chaplain that served in many wars. He eventually pastored at Holy Cross Church in Hell's Kitchen, a rough area of Manhattan. According to legend, after his death in 1932, he joined the thousands of men in Heaven that he served on the battlefields of France. Although Irish, he was decorated by the French for his devotion to his men under fire during World War I. The line on the back of the bronze effigy reads, "A LIFE OF SERVICE FOR GOD AND COUNTRY."

Just like Daniella's memorial plaque at L'Esprit, the monument is overlooked by most. I, however, can't ignore my goosebumps. I'm reminded of Miss Aimée's predecessors, A.J. Dalton and his beloved wife, Daniella, whose untimely death inspired him to rebuild L'Esprit Dance Studios.

The forlorn look on my face prompts Danny to ask, "What's wrong?"

"Please don't laugh. I'm awed by those who dedicate themselves to serving others and the sacrifices they make."

"Who are you?" he says. "Beautiful and perceptive." Together we climb to the top of the stairs where we take pictures of the spectacular site. I'm ecstatic when Danny asks Brooke to take one of the two of us. When Brooke returns his phone, Danny studies the image. "We look great together," he smiles.

"We do? Can I see?"

Although it's not my best picture, it's certainly not my worst. He, of course, looks like a world class model. "You wouldn't mind forwarding me a copy, would you?"

"Now there's a clever way to get a guy to ask for your number," he says.

My face turns a deep shade of red.

"Libby, please. I've wanted to ask for it all day."

When he pulls up his contact list to add my information, I notice what seems like a thousand names in his address book. Many are girls. I'm suddenly insecure and doubt his intentions. After he sends the photo, I change the subject.

"This town is nothing but lights, lights, and more lights!" I say.

"Not to mention people, people, and more people," says Brooke.

"Look at the endless stream of taxis," Danny says. "Everybody in this city is headed somewhere."

I wonder if that includes me and you. I bite my lip. "It's like we've been transported to another dimension. Everything on this planet is made of LED liquid walls," I say.

"Be careful that a creature from outer space doesn't get you," Brooke teases.

"It's true," Jarrell says as he slips his arm around me. "They do like nibbling on the newbies."

"Ha ha, Mr. Comedian of the Year," I say.

Jarrell flashes a playful grin. "No, that's Mr. Stairway to the Stars."

"We're mighty confident tonight, aren't we, your royal highness?" C.C. says.

"More like your royal pain in the –"

Jarrell quickly covers Brooke's mouth, "Don't say it, babe. You know you love me."

"You do remember that Mr. Daniel Landry has a reputation

for being a great dancer, too. Don't you?" Brooke says.

"Of course, I do. He can be my wingman. I'll even let him polish my trophy." Both boys share a good-natured fist bump.

"You two clowns behave," C.C. says. "But you're right, Libby. No matter how many times I've seen Times Square, it never gets old."

Although I'm not quite sure what to make of me and Danny, I'm impressed with how easygoing and relaxed he and Jarrell are with each other. There's none of the obvious animosity you'd expect between high-level competitors. They don't behave anything like my nemesis in high school and dance, Whitney Ruthers. She's the meanest girl I know. *Gosh, I hope I don't meet more like her at nationals, but mostly, I hope Danny isn't toying with my emotions.*

Turning my attention from the top of the staircase to the tourists below, I spy a man peering from behind the Duffy monument. The telescopic lens on his camera blocks his face.

"Do you see him?" I ask. "That guy has his camera pointed at us."

By the time everybody follows my extended finger, he's gone. "Seriously, C.C., he could be the same creep that was checking you out on the plane today."

"What are you talking about?"

"We didn't want to upset you, but Danny and I saw a strange man observing your every move during most of the flight. He left in a hurry and disappeared into the busy terminal. I forgot about him until now."

"It can't possibly be the same person. Your imagination must be running away with you," C.C. says.

I refrain from reminding her that the dancing ghosts of L'Esprit were real. "C.C., I'm telling you, something's off."

"Well, he's not there now, and our parents are here."

Before we reach the bottom of the steps, a sun-kissed blonde appears out of nowhere and wraps her arms around Danny's waist. Another, a black-haired beauty, strokes her fingers through Danny's thick mane and affectionately rubs his back, but when he's not looking, she glares at me. While a small group of Star Struck dancers rush to welcome Danny, the four of us are rudely pushed to the outside of their circle.

"Hey, Skylar," Danny says to the cute blonde, "it's great to be here in the Big Apple again, isn't it?"

"You made it, Bud!" Another male dancer slaps Danny's shoulder.

"Glad to see you, hot stuff," says the raven-haired girl with a hotter-than-hot attitude and over-the-top flair for Hollywood glamour. She bats her heavy, false eyelashes before leaving an imprint of her lips on Danny's cheek.

"And here's the enchanting Mercedes Slade. You're as captivating and full of surprises as ever." Danny kisses her hand.

"We missed you today," Skylar pouts.

"I'm happy you made it safely. My flight was downright boring," Mercedes says.

"Thanks a lot," Skylar scowls.

"I worry when we're not together, Danny," Mercedes says.

"Oh, you shouldn't," he glances at me. "I'm in good company."

Mercedes' face screams that she doesn't appreciate me or his comment.

"So, tell us Danny: since you were delayed in L.A. by your audition, what are your chances of landing the job?" Skylar asks.

"You never know. I think it went well, but I won't hear anything until I get home," he says.

"I guarantee you'll soon be dancing in an Old Navy or Target commercial!" Mercedes says. "No one believes in you more than I do."

As their conversation continues, I'm disappointed that Danny, so preoccupied with Mercedes and his Star Struck friends, barely notices that we've been separated.

"Does that chick have a major crush on Danny and stink eye for you, or what?" C.C. whispers.

"She actually makes Whitney Ruthers seem human," Brooke adds.

"I'm warning you, Libby, she's got a *thaang* for your Danny. She's a dark temptress, that one," Jarrell says.

Brooke gives him a shove, "C'mon, leave it alone."

"Yeah, don't make things worse for her," C.C. says.

"I don't mind. Danny and I just met. We're only getting to know each other. His studio friends are naturally happy to see him," I say, not convincing anyone—not even myself.

With the influx of tourists filling Duffy Square, Danny and I eventually lose sight of each other. I return to the hotel with my parents, annoyed with how quickly he forgot me and how pleased my dad seems that he did.

In my room I want to call or text Danny, but I don't. Worse yet, he doesn't contact me. I mindlessly scroll through his Instagram account. Fortunately, he has no privacy settings, and I view his life in photos. Of course, he's pictured with tons of friends, and always somewhere in the frame is Mercedes Slade. Frustrated and hurting, I refuse to be blinded by the bright lights, big city. I have dance in the morning, and no boy will ruin that for me. Drifting off to sleep, I wonder about Mercedes. *What's her story?*

At the same instant, Danny uploads his most recent pictures. Although a few are with his Star Struck pals, they're mostly of Libby. Under the picture Brooke took of the two of them, he posts the comment, "New York's incredible, so is Libby Nobleton." He ends it with a smiley face emoticon, the one with two hearts for eyes.

Somewhere else in the hotel, a stalker sits in the darkest corner of his room. He examines the images he took of Libby and her friends and bides his time.

CITY OF ANGELS

City of Angels is a multiple Tony Award winning musical comedy set in Los Angeles in the late 1940s with book by Larry Gelbart and musical numbers staged by Walter Painter. It premiered on Broadway at the Virginia Theatre in December of 1989 to mixed reviews but mostly lavish praise. "There's no end to the cleverness," wrote Frank Rich of the *New York Times*. Yet the *Variety* reviewer amid his praise complained, "the second act gets itself tangled."

Chapter Four

☆

Several Days Earlier
Beverly Hills, California

*M*ercedes Slade and her BFF since middle school, Skylar Wilkins, stand on the corner of Wilshire and Rodeo after a day of shopping and sushi at the acclaimed Urasawa Restaurant. While awaiting the Slade limousine, Skylar excitedly rambles about their upcoming trip to New York City. "Mercedes, this year's dance convention is gonna be fan-freakin-tabulous. I mean like totally unbelievable!"

"Why wouldn't it be? *I'm* competing, aren't I?"

"We both are!"

"Of course, Sky," Mercedes sneers.

"All of Star Struck's top dancers will be there. We're the best L.A. has to offer." Skylar strikes a ta-da pose, earning the sideward glances of more than a few passing pedestrians.

"Who's the best?" Mercedes lifts her professionally shaped brows.

"I know it's you, but I've got style and moves, too."

"Agreed. But just so we're straight on the matter."

"I get it. It's your senior year and time for you to own the spotlight. I can hardly wait to compete again. I just love winning, don't you?"

"I wouldn't have it any other way," Mercedes says. "Chasing the spotlight and becoming a star are all that matter in my household."

"That's not true," Skylar insists.

"Really? Do you know who my parents are?" Mercedes shakes her head. "My dad simply can't breathe unless he's surrounded by success, and my mother left us so she could sparkle on Broadway." After another limo drives past, Mercedes adjusts her Dolce & Gabbana sunglasses perched high on her cosmetically sculpted nose. "Where's that stupid driver?"

"Chill, Mercedes. Hunky Vinnie Wilde will be here any second. He told you he had to get the car washed and waxed. For now, let's focus on NYC and the fact that our studio is superior to any of those others, except for maybe the one out of Chicago." Skylar scrunches her face. "What's the name of it again?"

Peering from above her diamond-rimmed frames, Mercedes rolls her eyes. "L'Esprit, you bubblehead. I've told you a hundred times it's LE SPREE. The one named after that dead ballerina, Daniella Devereaux. It's French and means *the spirit* or something idiotic like that."

"Oh, you mean Le Giant Spit." Skylar waves her arms and mimics a ghost, "*BooOOOoooaah*. What a bunch of crap!"

The two friends giggle.

"Their dancers are full of it, too," Skylar says, "maybe a few are decent but certainly not as talented as us. We both know there are way too many losers in the dance world."

"Yeah, especially that redhead, C.C.," Mercedes snaps. "I still can't believe she placed higher than me last year."

"Lucky for you the little prima, Brooke Allen, isn't competing. She beat you, too, didn't she?"

"Shut up, Sky!"

"No wait! All I'm saying is you could win your coveted ticket to stardom. You're the real deal! So what if your nose and boobs aren't," she laughs. "You know what I mean; you could take it all. Can't you see it—your picture on the cover of *Dance Star Magazine*? In your interview, you'll have to thank *moi*, your dearest dance buddy. How excellent would that be? I heard Disney hired some of the previous winners to dance in their theme parks and movies."

Lost in her own world and oblivious to Skylar's mindless prattle, Mercedes imagines the applause as she's crowned the female Dancer of the Year. The press coverage and accolades to follow will certainly secure the future she's always craved.

Although she loves her father, Carter Slade, a big-time Hollywood talent agent, she wouldn't mind getting away from the bimbos that chase him. He is, after all, athletically fit, ruggedly handsome, and loaded with cash. But being Broadway's sought-after-sweetheart like her mother, the gorgeous and talented Olivia Hampton-Slade, is practically all she thinks about.

"I've got to get out of L.A., Sky. I'm sick of living with Daddy and his constantly changing entourage, not to mention his latest girlfriend, Avery Harper, the flirty tennis pro from our ritzy country club. That gold-digger prances around the mansion's pool in her lemon-yellow, thong bikini like she owns the place."

"Gross!"

"I know, right? I despise her! I have to win. My dad's too busy to notice me. He's always entertaining clients and casting agents, or worse, parading about town with Avery. I simply can't let this chance of winning the national title and earning a scholarship to train in New York slip away."

"Poor baby. Stop complaining. Be glad your parents are divorced. Mine tolerate each other until cocktail hour when all hell breaks loose. Even the staff runs for cover. You dance to get out of L.A.; I dance to get out of my house. Our trip to New York can't come soon enough to suit me."

Leaning against a streetlamp, rocking her pedicured, sandaled foot over the Old-World cobblestones, Mercedes' mind races. She swipes her tongue across her perfectly bleached teeth and forces herself to think of something more pleasant. Gazing beyond Skylar's jabbering, orange-blossomed lips, Mercedes studies her reflection in the nearby window of a trendy boutique. She twirls a long strand of hair and imagines herself on stage beside the male Dancer of the Year. Everyone says the guy she's danced with since fifth grade and pined after forever, Daniel Landry, is a shoo-in for the male DOTY title. Mercedes, accustomed to getting almost everything in life she wants, can't accept the fact that he dated her briefly but broke it off to pursue his performing arts career. At least that's the polite excuse he hid behind.

Skylar accidentally bumps one of Mercedes's shopping bags while listing the Broadway shows she plans to see. Mercedes nods as if paying attention but secretly wonders if the lacey panties, black Versace dress, and strappy, size six Jimmy Choo's purchased on Daddy's credit card will get Danny to notice her again.

For months, Mercedes has been consumed with thoughts of Danny, especially since seeing him rehearse his solo. She can't stop obsessing over every detail of his chiseled chest and six-pack abs. When she's not fantasizing about Danny, she imagines her parents remarrying and doing what other parents do—supporting their child's ambitions. She envisions her father cancelling his appointments for the week and cheering for her at nationals. Mercedes can't recall the last time her father saw her dance. Oh wait, a year ago, when she finished behind Brooke and C.C. His disappointment stung when he barely stayed for a congratulatory hug. She speculates about what it would be like to see real tears of pride roll down her mother's cheeks, unlike the fake tears offered during her weekly live performances. If only her parents would love each other and her as much as they love their brilliant careers. Will they both make an appearance at the convention this year to see her win? Danny, of course, will have his muscular arms tightly wrapped around her tiny waist. "I'm so glad it's you. I was a fool to ever let you go," he'll whisper. Mercedes has no doubt that Danny's destined for greatness and that sharing the spotlight with him is her destiny, too.

Skylar taps her fingernail on the lens of Mercedes' sunglasses. "Hellooo. Are you in there? Why don't you check your cell phone?"

The text from the Slade's chauffeur reads, *Almost there.*

"What does it say?" Skylar asks, trying to grab the phone. "Is it from my dreamboat, Vinnie?"

"Knock it off, Sky. You know he's too old for you."

"He's only twenty-seven, and he's such a stud. Who cares?"

"My dad, for one! Don't let Vinnie's leading-man face or smoldering eyes fool you. You don't want to get mixed up with an actor. Trust me, I've met plenty. Besides, he reeks of cheap cologne."

"I love the way he smells. And, since when do you pay attention to anything your old man thinks?"

"I don't, but you and I both know Vinnie's only interested in two things: fame and money. He's just waiting to be discovered. That's why he drives Daddy's limo. He wants my dad to give him a break in show business. Get it through your thick skull. He's not interested in you."

Skylar undoes another button of her form-fitting blouse. "We'll see about that."

"This may be the city of angels, but you, Sky, are definitely not one of them."

GREASE

Grease is a multi-nominated Tony Award musical with music, lyrics, and book by Jim Jacobs and Warren Casey, choreography by Patricia Birch. The show was originally produced on stage in Chicago. It opened on Broadway in June of 1972 at the Broadhurst Theatre before ultimately moving to the larger Majestic Theatre in 1980. Considered the 15th longest running Broadway show in history with 3,388 performances, the production spawned many revivals around the world. *Grease* was adapted as a feature film in 1978. Set at fictional Rydell High School in 1959, it follows ten working-class teenagers as they navigate the complexities of peer pressure, politics, personal values, and love.

Chapter Five

*V*incent Wilde *arrives in the* newest of Carter Slade's fleet of Rolls-Royce vehicles. Every inch of the limousine's extended exterior glistens, including the front grill with its iconic Spirit of Ecstasy hood ornament. Mercedes points to the shiny double-winged decoration. "You missed a spot. Daddy may have to fire you."

Both girls laugh. Skylar puckers her lips and winks at Vinnie.

"Grease is the word, babes. Hop in."

"What? You're making us open our own doors, too?" Skylar crawls in first and slides seductively across the premium leather seat. "See anything you like Vinnie?" She flicks her long curls over her shoulder as his eyes follow her movements through the rearview mirror. "You always smell extra yummy. What's the name of your cologne?"

"Thanks for noticing. It's called Rising Star," Vinnie says.

Skylar growls like a tigress, "It certainly gets a rise out of me."

"Yeah, it's delightful," Mercedes gags, "but do you have to wear the whole bottle?" She shoves her shopping bags on top of Skylar. "Move it, lard-butt."

Vinnie's devilish snicker makes him even more attractive.

Skylar ignores Mercedes' comment and begins to play with the HD flat-panel TV. The surround sound suddenly blares. Mercedes steals the remote control from Skylar and flips it off.

"Isn't *Bachelor in Paradise* on?" Skylar asks.

"No! Neither is *The Real Housewives of Beverly Hills!*"

"Sorry, Miss Grumpy! What's gotten into you?" Skylar fiddles with the fiber optic lighting and checks to see if the bar is stocked.

"So, did you two get everything you need for your big dance competition?" Vinnie says.

Mercedes clutches her shopping bags and thinks of Danny.

"What Mercedes needs is a way to get rid of her biggest competitor," Skylar laughs.

"Is that so?" Vinnie says. "And who might that be? Let me guess. Is it you, Skylar?"

"Not in a trillion years," Mercedes scoffs.

"That's only because I'm such a good friend. You know I deliberately bowed out of the solo competition for your sake."

"So, you honestly believe you could have beaten not only me at regionals, but Daddy Warbucks' granddaughter, too?" Mercedes says.

"No, just you," Skylar snorts.

Mercedes wrinkles her face.

"Who's this other dancer?" Vinnie's radar pings. "And tell me about Granddad Money Bags."

Skylar bends forward. "She's none other than the tall and beautiful, Cynthia Cunningham. She's one of Chicago's top dancers from L'Esprit Dance Studios. Her nickname is C.C., and she placed third over Mercedes' dismal fourth-place finish at nationals last year."

Mercedes slouches, the disgusted look on her face growing larger by the second.

"But I thought chicks from the Midwest all look like dancing cows. I heard they balter more than dance," Vinnie says.

"What the heck is balter?" Skylar asks.

"I'm not just a pretty face. Check your Urban Dictionary."

Mercedes scrolls through her smart phone and announces, "I've got it right here. It means 'to dance artlessly, without particular grace or skill but usually with enjoyment.' Nice job, Vinnie. That's most of the Midwest dancers we've seen."

"Unfortunately, it doesn't apply to C.C.," Skylar says. "She's a gorgeous redhead that can do it all. Her forte is tap, but she's quite amazing at everything. She's undoubtedly the one to beat."

"What happened to the first and second ranked girls?" he asks.

"The lucky winner graduated and is dancing professionally. And Miss Connie told us the runner-up, Brooke Allen, won't be competing this year because she almost died."

"Did Mercedes hire a hitman?" Vinnie jokes.

"Good one, Vinnie. No! I did not," Mercedes says. "Guess she was in a coma for a while. She'll be in New York, but I heard through the grapevine that she's not cleared to compete."

"Yeah. Too bad for Miss Twinkle Toes, but it's great news for Mercedes," Skylar says.

"You're heartless," Vinnie says. "Tell me about the granddad?"

"He's Preston Bailey, and according to Wikipedia he's the founder and CEO of Bailey Spice Company. C.C. stands to inherit a major fortune someday. She'll make Mercedes and me look like the dreaded middle class. And you, Vinnie," she hesitates then giggles, "will look like the dirty, little street urchin you are."

Privately, Vinnie detests her comments and hates carting the two spoiled brats around Hollywood. He vividly remembers growing up poor on the sketchier side of L.A. Abandoned by his father as an infant, his mother overdosed on drugs. After years on the streets, his desperation for success drives him to stay in Carter Slade's good graces.

"Be nice, Skylar," Vinnie says.

"I'll be *real* nice if you let me," Skylar purrs.

Ignoring her, he says, "I recall reading an article that made it sound like money grows wherever Bailey walks."

"Not only incredibly sexy, you can read, too," Skylar says. "How adorable you are."

"You're home, Miss Wilkins. My pleasure as always."

"Thanks for the ride, Vinnie. Call me later, Mercedes." Skylar saunters from the limo and blows Vinnie an exaggerated kiss.

After she enters her family's massive, Mexican-styled hacienda, complete with lush, tropical gardens and lavish pools, the wheels in Mercedes's head spin faster than the limo's tires.

"Mercedes, you seem upset. Is it about Skylar?"

She gives him a probing glare. "What's it to you?"

"Just curious. Do you think you can beat her?"

"Skylar Wilkins? Without a doubt!"

"No. I mean the rich one from Chicago?"

"C.C.? No. Well, yeah, maybe."

"Which is it?"

"I don't know."

"Well, how badly do you want it?"

"How badly does anyone want anything?" Mercedes thinks hard about Vinnie's question then searches her cell phone for a saved video clip. "You're the one who mentioned a hitman. I could win if she vanished for a while."

"Excuse me?"

"You heard me."

"You know I wasn't serious."

"Well, I always knew witnessing your little romp with Avery in the pool house would pay off someday. You help me; I'll help you."

"Dammit, Mercedes! I told you before. Nothing happened with Avery. You're delusional."

"Who's delusional?"

"It's not like you have any proof," Vinnie says.

"Oh, don't I?"

Just then his cell phone pings. Mercedes feigns ignorance as she gazes out the window. When he hits play, he almost swerves off the road. Mercedes grabs the head rest in front of her and whispers in Vinnie's ear. "Too bad you'll never make it in Hollywood. X-rated movies might be more your style."

"You little bitch!" He hits the accelerator hard and sends Mercedes flying to the back of her seat.

"Careful, Vinnie. I wouldn't want to accidentally copy Carter in on your juicy secret."

BILLION DOLLAR BABY

Billion Dollar Baby is a musical with book by Betty Comden and Adolph Green, choreography by Jerome Robbins. It premiered on Broadway at the Alvin Theatre in December of 1945. The production was not well received although Robbins' choreography was widely praised. The show gained notoriety for an event that happened in rehearsals. Robbins, walking backward while ranting at the dancers, fell into the orchestra pit. The storyline follows the adventures of an ambitious young woman in her quest to have it all.

Chapter Six

Ten competition costumes rest on Mercedes' bedroom floor in a tangled heap of bedazzled lace, tulle, and chiffon. The glorious profusion of color creates a pretty mess when exposed to the sparkling California sunlight that explodes across her purple carpet. Another smaller pile holds her convention dancewear, L.A.'s best and trendiest fashions. Having spent hours carefully choosing each outfit, she's determined to create a memorable impression. The sequined booty-shorts and halter tops in every imaginable shade are all part of her calculated mission to attract maximum attention. Since her spending always goes unnoticed, the sky's the limit. Sometimes it's good to be Mercedes Slade.

Nestled among the two dozen pillows on her bed, she admires the cover of the latest edition of *Dance Star Magazine*.

This month, it features a hip-hop dancer. She's attractive but in Mercedes' opinion, not *that* special. Her cover will be spectacular; all she has to do is win the damn competition. Somehow her innocent desire for fame and the female DOTY crown became an unholy obsession. God help anyone or anything standing in her way. It didn't happen before, and no one knows better than Mercedes that this is her last chance. She's off to college in the fall and turning eighteen soon. It's now or never!

The door to her bedroom opens with a simultaneous soft knock.

"Miss Mercedes, take that silly tiara off your head and get moving. *¡Vámonos!* Your flight to New York departs at 6 a.m., and the Fed Ex driver will be here in an hour to pick up your costumes." Regina Lopez, the full-figured, middle-aged housekeeper is Mercedes' former nanny. Despite her tone and coal-black hair, severely pulled into a neat bun, Regina fails in her attempt to look stern; her brown eyes are much too kind.

"I don't know why I have to fly commercial when my dad could send me on the company jet at a decent hour."

"Your studio is flying together. I suppose he thought you'd want to be with Skylar and Danny."

"Danny's flying solo after his audition." Mercedes crosses her arms and pouts. "And Carter's not fooling me for a second. I know he's keeping the plane for a quick trip to Cabo with Avery. They'll probably be sipping mojitos before I even land in New York. Meanwhile, I'm stuck with TSA checks and Homeland Security crap. And *one* bag? Puh-leease!"

"I can see how that's going to be a problem for you," Regina chuckles. "Come on, let's get it over with. Aren't you excited? You love the city, and you'll be with your mother. It's been a while since you've seen her."

"Unless she shows up in a disguise, we'll be mobbed by her fans and . . ." Mercedes' voice fades.

"*Mi niña*, maybe it'll be different this time. Your mother's learning how to handle the public. You may not believe it, but she loves you very much."

"You don't leave the people you love."

"I know it broke your heart, but it broke hers, too. She didn't leave *you*; she left your father. I'm sure she'll do everything she can to make this a good time for the two of you."

"But, Regina, when your mom's a Broadway star, it's hard to keep a low profile. I tend to get lost in the shuffle."

The two pack Mercedes' costumes into an extra-large, opaque garment bag and organize the outfits and accessories into a loudly patterned suitcase. Regina's heart bleeds for the child she's watched grow up and loves dearly. She knows all of Mercedes's faults and cheerfully overlooks most of them. Having been a member of the Slade household since Mercedes' birth, she understands the devastation Mercedes suffered when her parents split, and the resentment she holds for Mr. Slade's current girlfriend, Avery. Regina dreads breaking the bad news.

"Honey, your father will be home tonight. He's planning dinner for seven o'clock."

"Just the two of us, right?"

Regina's slight hesitation speaks volumes.

"Oh no! She's not invited, is she? She wouldn't dare come. I don't want her here!"

"Mercedes, I've been told to ask the cook to plan dinner for three."

"Then I'll eat in my room like I usually do when she's here."

"You could make a quick meal of it, and that way everyone will be happy."

"Regina, what planet are you living on? Don't you see that everyone's not always happy, especially in the Slade house?"

As a gift to Regina, Mercedes forces herself to dine with her dad and Avery. Carter, acting on good behavior, only takes two calls during dinner. Mercedes pushes the food around her plate claiming to be too excited to eat. While Avery blah-blah-blahs on and on, Mercedes' blood boils. She's never known anyone who could talk so much and say so little. She honestly can't understand what her father sees in the woman. Oh, maybe she can, but that's disgusting, and she refuses to go there. Clenching her steak knife, she realizes she's having very evil thoughts. Luckily, Avery isn't a mind reader. In fact, in Mercedes' opinion, Avery's reading skills are limited to scripts she has zero chance of being offered. She is, however, extremely talented at multitasking. No one can balance a martini better in one hand while clinging to Carter with the other. Avery's only claim to fame is that she holds the title of singles and doubles tennis champion of Mercedes' school, Beverly Hills High, a fact which Mercedes finds absolutely humiliating. Graduating in the same decade as Avery is a nightmare that her friends find hilarious. She shouldn't be so sensitive. Admittedly, she's had plenty of laughs when some of their parents act like idiots. Even Skylar's family members often overachieve at putting the fun in dysfunctional. If Mercedes didn't fear getting in trouble and driving her dad further away, she would've used her damaging video to destroy Avery long ago. But Mercedes has bigger fish to fry, and keeping the video secret has proven to be the exact leverage she needs. When Regina quietly pries the knife from Mercedes' grasp while clearing the dinner plates, Mercedes dismisses Avery as nothing more than an annoying distraction.

"Carter, who's coming over tonight?" Avery asks. Her overly sweet voice gives Mercedes an instant headache.

"Just a few clients for a quick drink or two." Carter shoots his daughter a "sorry kid" look. "Hollywood's current favorite star, Johnny Shallows, has a friend he wants me to meet, a young actor he says would be ideal for his next movie."

Avery's eyes light up brighter than all the neon in Las Vegas.

"I'm sure you won't want to hang around for a boring business meeting, Mercedes," Avery says.

Mercedes doesn't, but Avery's patronizing tone stings nonetheless, and she's stubborn enough to stay for no other purpose than to ruin Avery's evening. *Why can't my dad hang out with me for one lousy night without using our home as an excuse to entertain guests? Welcome to party central.*

Mercedes retreats to the pool, determined to work off her anger by swimming laps. When she stops, she notices a shadow looming over her. Although the setting sun obscures her vision, she recognizes his famous voice immediately.

"Hey, Porsche," he teases. "How's my Billion-Dollar Baby?"

Mercedes blinks the water from her eyes. "Hey, Johnny, everything's great. By the way," she reminds him as she always does, "it's Mercedes. I almost didn't recognize you. What's with the scruffy beard?"

"Do you like it? I'm growing it for my next role. I think it makes me look dashing, dangerous, and . . . what's the word I'm searching for?"

"Deranged?" Mercedes laughs.

"That's cold! Just wanted to step out and say hi. I hear you're leaving for New York in the morning."

"Yeah. It's my last dance competition. I plan to make the most of it."

"I'm sure you will. Take care and good luck."

Mercedes wants to tell him that luck is vastly overrated. To get what you want, it's crucial to have a plan and leave nothing to chance. Instead, she observes him casually stroll into the house. She loves him for being her dad's only client who ever pays her any attention. He walks on water as far as she's concerned.

Mercedes floats at the edge of the infinity pool and thinks about sneaking a shot of vodka into her lemonade. It isn't as though she's never done that before. No one ever checks the stock. But with her masterplan in motion, she needs to stay clearheaded. As the disappearing sun sets, she reviews her scheme for flaws and finds none. It's pure genius. As long as Vinnie can be trusted to keep his end of the deal.

THE PRODUCERS

The Producers is a multiple Tony Award winning musical comedy with book by Mel Brooks and Thomas Meehan based on Brooks' 1967 film of the same name. The original Broadway production, choreographed by Susan Stroman, opened at the St. James Theatre in April of 2001. This highly acclaimed show won 12 Tonys, one in every category for which it was nominated. The story concerns two theatrical producers who scheme to get rich.

Chapter Seven

This Morning
Broadway Center Hotel, New York City

Still smarting from Danny's indifference last night in Times Square, C.C., Brooke, and I make our way into the grand ballroom where hundreds of dancers gather. I'm exhilarated by the multi-colored stage lights that pulsate to the beat of loud music. "This is it! My first nationals," I say. "Every part of my body and soul is ready for the challenge."

"You'll need your energy, Libby." Brooke says. "You're dancing for both of us this week."

We toss our bags beneath the chairs that line the perimeter of the vast space. Miss Aimée and the L'Esprit staff signal us forward. Jarrell leads the way, and we weave through the eager crowd. In spite of my hurt feelings, I search the packed and noisy area for Danny, but I can't find him anywhere.

Stop obsessing. I came here to dance. So what if the most special guy I'll ever meet spent a full day flirting only to forget about me? Could my dad be right? Maybe Danny's some sort of Casanova? Dang, I'm a mess.

I turn my attention to the raised stage. The enormous, midnight-blue backdrop, with an illuminated, faux staircase at its center, sparkles with a thousand twinkling lights. It's magnificent and reminds me of the marble staircase at the Grand Dalton House that leads to the studios of L'Esprit. *Dear God, please don't let me lose sight of why I'm here.*

Pushing Danny out of my head, I hop around with my friends. When the music stops, a hush falls. Howard and Clare Lexford, the legendary owners of Stairway to the Stars, step onto the stage. Both in their mid-sixties, the sharply dressed pair obviously enjoys the spotlight. Former dancers themselves, the elegant couple resembles Fred Astaire and Ginger Rogers. They eagerly wave, anxious to kick off the convention. Mr. Lexford, lean with long legs and a full head of silver hair, unbuttons his navy-blue sport coat. He taps the microphone. "Welcome dancers to our annual competition. We're thrilled to be here at this top-notch venue. How about you?" Everyone screams and applauds.

"My beautiful wife and I couldn't be happier to have so many wonderful studios with us today. There are dancers representing nearly every state in the U.S., from Florida to Maine to California." When he says California, I turn to see the Star Struck dancers celebrating. Sure enough, standing alongside my handsome Danny are those glamour girls, Skylar and Mercedes. I hide my frown.

"And let's not forget Canada and Mexico," Mr. Lexford continues, "they're here, too!"

Their dancers acknowledge the energetic welcome with bows and curtsies.

Clare Lexford takes the mic. She's coordinated from head to toe in a flowy, cream-colored outfit. Her platinum curls frame her delicate features and wispy bangs highlight her large eyes. She's gorgeous and was, no doubt, a rare beauty all of her life.

"We know you dancers are going to work with great enthusiasm this week and give us a show we'll never forget. You've already provided the best regionals we've ever seen." Once more, the audience erupts.

"Thank you for coming and making this magical event possible," Howard says. "Next, we'd like to introduce our host for the remainder of the convention, the multi-talented, Tony Award winner, Mr. Guy Fisher."

The famous Broadway sensation is a natural on stage. Portly and broad-shouldered, he's well into his late fifties with curly, salt and pepper hair and a face so animated it lights up the stage. His agility surprises me when he clicks up his heels and executes a double spin. C.C. tells me the man's comedic timing is nothing short of brilliant and that his agreeing to host the annual convention was a major stroke of luck. Attendance has soared ever since. But I'm sure the teaching staff, with the likes of Trent Michaels and a surprise guest teacher each year, is another major draw. The three of us can't wait to see who the unnamed headliner will be. Mr. Trent refused to give us the slightest clue, other than he knew we'd go nuts.

"Thank you, Clare and Howie. You may take your leave. Shuffle off to Buffalo!" Guy says.

He tells a few jokes about his life as an aging Broadway star. "Yes, it's true. I'm an exploding supernova dancing through the universe. Did you know there are only four stages of life? First, you believe in Santa Claus. Second, you don't believe in

Santa Claus. Third, you play Santa Claus, and fourth, you look like Santa Claus. Guess which stage I'm at?" he asks, rubbing his belly. We all laugh. Guy reminds us what a special treasure dance and theatre can be at every age. "So, this week try not to focus on titles and awards. Expressing yourselves through the mutual passion of performance, with its ability to connect on such an intimate level, is the true gift we share. What matters most is not the size of the trophy, but the size of the dancer's spirit and passion."

He motions backstage. "Remember, Clare and Howie, not that I care," he winks, "but my contract states you agreed to polish my Tony and keep it on display at all times." Everyone roars, especially when Howard, white-gloved and comically subservient, produces Guy's trophy. Guy snatches it with a devilish grin. "My goodness, how I love this thing." He plants an amplified smooch on the award.

When we laugh again, Guy acts startled as though he'd forgotten we were there. He fumbles and pretends to drop the Tony on the floor. "Now look what you've done," he sighs, deadpan. "Great, you broke it! Security, arrest these people."

"C.C., you're absolutely right. The man's hilarious." I say.

"Seriously dancers, are you going to spend this week stressing about being judged or worrying about winning some title or trophy?" Guy says. "Of course you are. That's what we performers do, but please promise you're going to learn something new and have fun in the process."

"Yes!" we shout.

"Well then, do your best and let the trophies fall where they may!"

"Eloquently stated, my friend," Howard says.

"Time to meet your executioners," Guy says, "I mean the panel of judges. This year's teaching staff and surprise guest instructor are sensational, so kindly hold your applause until the end. Oh, who am I kidding? Clap all you want. First to grace our national convention is one of my all-time favorite tap divas, the classic and timeless former Broadway star: Miss Myra Gold."

When Miss Gold appears and performs a fast series of running flaps high on the balls of her feet, Guy pats his chest in loving admiration. Her pewter-streaked hair is tucked in a messy bun, and she's radiant as she glides across the stage.

"Next, we have Canadian born, world famous danseur, one of today's renowned choreographers of the New York City Ballet, Mr. Baxter Banks." He's a man of average height with cropped, thinning hair. His demeanor reeks of arrogance.

"Ugh," Brooke says. "He's the toughest ballet instructor around. Now I'm glad I'm not taking class."

"Don't worry, Libby, he hates everyone," C.C. says. "He's the worst snob and meanest teacher I've ever had."

"Did you see him in that dance documentary on PBS? The man's evil," Jarrell says.

"I noticed Mr. Trent and Miss Aimée seated in the coffee shop with him earlier," I say.

"Yeah, that's because he was Mr. Hyde then. It's only at the ballet barre he transforms into Dr. Jekyll," Jarrell says.

Next is a woman who recently burst onto the dance scene. In her mid-twenties, she's sexily dressed in glam rock style. Her open and bedazzled leather vest partially hides her cropped T-shirt and diamond-pierced belly button. The highlighted streak of neon-pink in her choppy haircut matches her eyeshadow and lipstick. Guy introduces her as Miss Crystal LaMond. She snarls and claws like a lioness before breaking out with a jaw-dropping center split leap that hangs in the air longer than seems humanly possible.

"I love her," C.C. says. "She's a jazz performer and choreographer whose credits include dancing in several movies. Rumor has it she's quite the party girl."

When Miss LaMond throws kisses, the guys reach in the air trying to snag one. I'll bet Danny's into her, too. I'm shocked when I catch him looking at me. I give him a lopsided smile and turn away.

Although Mr. Trent isn't a judge, when he's introduced as a master teacher, Guy lists his extensive Broadway credentials and the audience goes wild. I'm in awe, often forgetting his many professional accomplishments. Because he's so unspoiled by fame, I guess I'm guilty of underestimating Mr. Trent's star power. Danny's gawking resembles hero worship. When his applause fades, C.C. punches my arm.

We're stunned into silence by the appearance of the much-anticipated surprise guest teacher. Dressed in ripped jeans and a T-shirt, his soft leather jacket fits his toned body like a glove. He effortlessly performs a moonwalk side-glide combination across the stage. When he reaches the spotlight, he taps the brim of his straw, Fedora and cocks it to one side. Tipping the hat to the audience, he exposes his chin-length, sandy-colored hair. His electrically charged moves, like bolts of lightning, enter one part of his body and smoothly exit another. The room spontaneously chants, "Zach, Zach, Zach Attack!" Danny is wide-eyed, and so are Mercedes and Skylar.

"That's right! He's none other than young teenage heartthrob, the up-and-coming actor and hip-hop virtuoso, Zach Dugan, or Z-Dug as we like to call him," Guy says.

"Libby, it's him! The hip-hop guru from our favorite movie, *Breakin' Down Walls*. He's perfection," C.C. sighs.

"We must have seen his film over a hundred times. You were totally gaga for that guy," Brooke says.

"Were? Always was and still am!" C.C. says. "I've been following him on Instagram forever. His social media said he was up to something special this week. Who knew it would be *our* convention! I post comments all the time, but with so many followers, I doubt he ever sees them."

"Man, can Mr. Trent keep a secret or what?" Jarrell says.

The females in the room shout, "We love you, Zach!"

"I love you more!" C.C. screams. Unbelievably, Zach hears her. I swear I see sparks shoot between them. My friend's face is so flush even her adorable freckles glow. In the full year since I've known C.C., I've never seen her act this way. Their instant chemistry is undeniable. While the excited mob shouts his name, Zach zeroes in on C.C.

I notice a sudden change of energy in the room, one that has nothing to do with the laws of attraction. None of us saw them earlier, but Whitney Ruthers and her overbearing mother, the producers of unending drama from our Chicago rival, B-Bop Studios, stand nearby. Like everyone else, Whitney, a Barbie doll look-a-like with a plastic personality to match, can't take her eyes off Zach. Carol Ruthers is a frustrated divorcee whose ex-husband cut her and Whitney out of his life, more preoccupied with his new family. Everyone knows Mrs. Ruthers lives vicariously through her daughter's dance achievements. She studies us with utter contempt. Ever since her darling Whitney was refused admittance to L'Esprit after several failed auditions, Mrs. Ruthers has considered us mortal enemies.

Although happy for C.C. and her current state of euphoria, there's no denying the Ruthers' presence is unnerving and doesn't bode well.

DANCIN'

Dancin' is a Tony Award winning musical revue with no storyline that's billed as a tribute to the art of dance. The dance vignettes, using a wide variety of styles, were directed and choreographed by Bob Fosse with additional choreography by Christopher Chadman. It premiered at the Broadhurst Theatre in March of 1978. According to Richard Eder of the *New York Times*, Ann Reinking (American actress, dancer, and choreographer) is clearly the star and at her best in the show-stopping number, "Sing, Sing, Sing." Revivals were difficult due to the demanding choreography.

Chapter Eight

*O*nce *staff and parents clear* the grand ballroom, the convention begins with the most intense warm-up I've ever endured. Led by a teaching assistant, we're soon sweating and dancin' to the oldies. After nearly an hour of working on our strength and flexibility, she starts the cool-down. When finished, the DOTY contestants are instructed to pick up their audition numbers. They're to be worn at every class throughout the week so instructors can take note of each dancer's individual ability, attitude, and work ethic. Although Miss Aimée explained my regional solo score was high enough to participate, my parents thought I should wait since this is my first nationals. Next year, I'm determined to be a member of the elite group. C.C. and

Jarrell return looking nervous. Jarrell is number 122, and C.C. wears number 141.

"Don't look so glum. You guys are gonna be great!" I say.

Together we search the schedule board that rests on an ornate easel in the main hall. It directs us to Ballroom A for our first class.

"C'mon everybody. It looks like we have senior level hip-hop from 9:30 a.m. to 11:15 a.m.," Jarrell says.

Brooke gives him two thumbs up before dashing to Ballroom C to run Mr. Trent's jazz music for the intermediate level. The rest of us plow through the hundreds of dancers scurrying every which way.

"Why so quiet, C.C.?" I ask.

"I'm in silent prayer at the moment."

"You really want to win the title of female Dancer of the Year, don't you?"

"No, it's more than that. I'm actually praying to the dance gods that Zach's our hip-hop teacher today."

I laugh, and then suddenly a warm hand touches my shoulder. I turn to see number 107 and above it, Danny's gorgeous face. "Hey, Libby, aren't you going to say good morning?"

Why should I? You didn't say goodnight to me once your Star Struck girlfriends arrived in Times Square. "Hi, Danny," my voice cracks.

"Sorry about last night. I feel bad that we were separated," he says.

"I understand. Your studio friends were happy to see you." *Especially Mercedes.*

"Can you believe Zach Dugan is the guest instructor this year? I took a few of his classes in L.A. I hope he remembers me," Danny says.

"You've met him before?" C.C.'s head snaps.

"Uh huh. At Hollywood's Millennium Dance Complex. They offer hip-hop workshops several times a year. I signed up for Zach's classes. He's not much older than we are, but for his age, he's a surprisingly great teacher and super cool guy," Danny says.

"Well judging by C.C.s expression, all she wants to know is if he's a super great kisser," Jarrell says.

C.C. pinches his ear.

"Ouch, sorry. Don't want to rile Grandpa Bailey's red-hot chili pepper," he laughs.

"She's here to dance. Not chase boys!" I say.

"Stop, Libby," C.C. says. "Jarrell speaks the truth."

This time we all laugh.

In Ballroom A, Whitney Ruthers, minus her favorite B-Bop sidekick, Tia Murphy, who mysteriously vanished from high school and the dance scene several months ago, charges ahead to share front and center with kindred spirits, Skylar and Mercedes.

"Why isn't Whitney standing with B-Bop?" I say.

"I don't know," C.C. says. "But figures she'd glom onto those two."

"I bet the other B-Bop dancers are glad to be rid of her," Jarrell says.

We take the middle of the floor along with the other L'Esprit senior level dancers. Danny acts obliged to join his Star Struck friends who hold a spot for him. When he leaves our group, Mercedes' smirk makes my stomach turn.

Lacing up our sneakers, we stretch for a few minutes. Soon dancers rowdily cheer. C.C. physically melts when Zach enters the room.

In one quick leap, he hops onto the raised stage and introduces his lucky assistant.

"Are you ready to jam?" he yells. The dancers' shrieks rattle the crystal chandeliers. "Again, I'm Zach and this is Miss Lorna. This hour we're going to teach you the first section of a hip-hop duet I helped choreograph with Sammie Keets for the Grammys."

"She's one of my favorites," I tell C.C. Danny smiles when I jump up and down like a toddler on a trampoline.

"First, Miss Lorna and I will perform the routine for you," Zach says, "then we'll begin breaking it down."

He hits the play button, and every dancer watches in awe. We're enthralled by their moves and the beat of the music's pounding base. As they perform, C.C.'s expression is priceless. Cupid's arrow strikes deep.

Zach and Lorna make the fast and intricate routine look easy. Z-Dug's the finest hip-hop dancer we've ever seen. His body's pure, fluid motion.

When they finish, Zach catches his breath. "Now this routine is obviously choreographed for a guy and a gal. Let's split into two groups. Boys are ones, girls are twos. But in life, I get it ladies, you're always number one. Isn't that right, fellas?" The girls high-five each other. "And let's face it," Zach continues, "the females easily outnumber the males in the room four-to-one. We'll need some of you lovelies to volunteer to learn the boy's part today. Take some time to pair off on your own."

I desperately want to partner with Danny, but Mercedes has already claimed him.

"Hey, Libby, since Brooke can't dance with me, will you?" Jarrell asks.

"Sure, that'd be great." I tell him.

C.C. immediately decides to learn the guy's role and

partners with Jenna, one of the sweetest dancers from our studio. I swear Walt Disney designed princesses with her in mind.

Puzzled, I ask, "C.C., you want to do the boy's steps?"

"Sure. I'm used to playing a guy anyway. Miss Aimée always has me help teach the dads for the father/daughter dance in the recital," she says.

She's no fool. When the dancers learning the female role are asked to work with Lorna, C.C. can't hold back a conniving grin. "Everyone else, you can join me over here," Zach says.

C.C. lights up like a Christmas tree. "Jackpot!" She skips away with Jarrell in tow.

Unfortunately, Danny's headed to the boy's side of the floor, too. Maybe I should have been smarter. I wish I hadn't been so quick to say yes to Jarrell. Even Whitney, the beast of B-Bop, was intelligent enough to team up with Skylar and will dance near Danny and Zach.

Jenna and I head to the other side of the room. Mercedes and Skylar look less than pleased, but Miss Lorna welcomes me with a friendly nod. Although she's no Z-Dug, Lorna does a great job instructing us, and I find her bubbly personality delightful. She takes a multitude of questions without frustration and remains polite while being hounded by dancers looking to make a good impression. I like her. The challenging choreography moves like rapid fire. But some portions, Lorna explains, need to be a bit more stylized and smoother, especially the sexy hip rolls and opposing rib cage isolations. "No pretend touches here, ladies. Let those hands caress your bodies."

In my opinion, Mercedes and Skylar are over-selling the sensual part. I have to admit, I'm envious of how strikingly Mercedes' shiny hair whips in the air when she flicks her head from one shoulder to the other while rolling her narrow hips. She proudly wears the number 116 on the side of her gray-camouflage, baggy pants with the words 'nothing butt attitude' stamped on her backside. Her defined abs, long torso, and tiny waist suddenly make me feel insecure and chubby. *I hate her.*

I must be doing something right because Miss Lorna picks me to demonstrate. From across the room, Whitney's looks could kill, but Mercedes' icy glare could obliterate an entire city. I ignore the pack of she-wolves and dance full-out, determined to accentuate every detail. Jarrell and Danny stop and stare, too. Afterward, everyone showers me with praise, except Mercedes and Skylar who don't bother to hide their contempt. Danny's eyes register a mix of shock and total turn-on. Now that's a rush I can't begin to describe.

During a quick water break, I see Zach and C.C. talking. I swear he's as interested in her as she is in him. When I overhear Whitney telling Skylar that apparently Zach likes flirting with ugly, freckle-faced redheads, I'm certain. The two give C.C. their typically rude scowls. I'm relieved when they take a full pitcher of ice water and join Mercedes by their dance bags.

Out of nowhere, I feel a breathy voice in my ear. "Libby, that was *magnifique.*" My spine tingles, and I burn with excitement.

Danny's beautiful face glistens with perspiration. He swipes his wet locks of Dr. McDreamy hair. "I figured you were a good dancer, but I had no idea you were *that* good."

"Um," fixated on his muscular arms and sexy mouth, I stutter, "that was nothing. I, well, thanks. It's great choreography, and I think great choreography makes every dancer better."

"No, an awesome dancer makes any choreography better. And you made that exceptional."

"Well, I can't wait to see you perform either," I say.

With a glint in his eyes, he throws his empty cup into a

nearby trash can. "Well then, I should get back to work, because I have some major impressing to do." As he jogs away, I sip my water, suddenly aware of my profound reaction to his slightest attention. *What's happening to me?*

I must have been gazing too long, because Jarrell's on me in seconds. "Oh, Libby! You've got it *baaad* for that guy, and C.C. for Zach, too. Where's my Brooke when I need her? I'm suddenly Charlie minus two angels."

"Jarrell, you'll always hold a special spot in *my* heart."

"Actions speak louder than words. Those dance moves of yours and round pieces of dark chocolate you call eyes just told me everything I need to know." With a sweaty hug, he kisses my forehead and joins the others.

After giving us time to practice with our partners, Zach and Lorna ask us to come together and perform—four or five couples at a time. I want to physically throw up when Mercedes takes front and center with Danny. They're amazing, and I can't help wondering if it's the choreography or if he's more into her than he realizes. While others in their group do a great job, Mercedes holds nothing back, and her booty-pop section trumps everyone's. Whitney and Skylar perform full throttle, and I can tell Whitney's upped her game since regionals, but it's mostly Danny and the bewitching Mercedes that command my full attention.

Jarrell and I take our places next. We knock it out of the park. It seems our close friendship pays off when Z-Dug applauds. "You two are phenomenal together."

"Let's keep his comment between us," Jarrell says tongue-in-cheek.

"Don't worry," I say. "Brooke will never hear it from me."

As transfixed as I was on Danny's performance, when C.C. and Jenna dance, I notice Zach only has eyes for my friend which spurs her performance into overdrive. And for the first time, Mercedes looks nervous.

The rest of our day zips by uneventfully until the unfortunate incident in Mr. Bank's ballet class. His miserable lesson takes a torturous turn, when switching into our pointe shoes, a dancer slices her foot on a piece of broken glass inexplicably found inside her slipper. With our bags open next to hers, we shudder to think it might easily have been one of us. And why does Mercedes appear disappointed that it wasn't?

42ND STREET

42nd Street is an iconic Tony Award winning musical based on a novel by Bradford Ropes and subsequent 1933 Hollywood film adaptation with book by Michael Stewart and Mark Bramble. It originally premiered on Broadway at the Winter Garden Theatre in August of 1980. Director and choreographer, Gower Champion, who created a series of tap-infused extravaganzas, died on opening night from a rare blood disease. He was posthumously awarded a Tony for his choreography. The show is considered a celebration of Broadway, Times Square, and all those who make the magic of the musical.

Chapter Nine

☆

It's late afternoon, and we're ready to cut loose after surviving our first full day of classes.

"You girls clean up nicely," Jarrell says. Danny whistles as the hotel's revolving door spits C.C., Brooke, and me onto the sizzling New York City sidewalk.

"Glad you approve," C.C. strikes a fashion model pose.

"You guys don't look too bad yourselves," I say. Brooke nods in agreement.

Platform shoes complete our outfits of summery, fit and flare dresses. Since our feet will be killing us anyway after a steady week of classes, we figure—why not? We'd rather look good than feel good. We slide on our sunglasses, hook arms, and head for the canyons of Manhattan. The streets are a sea of taxis, and I feel as if I'm standing in the center of the universe. I can't shake the nutty delusion that this city is mine for the taking.

With our parents not far behind, we set off in search of Benji's Deli. In spite of my sad realization that my funky, orange shoes are clearly not made for walking, I pretend there's no pinching pain creeping up my legs. Looking like a tourist, I stretch upward at block after block of towering skyscrapers knowing that my aching neck will soon form a partnership with my blistering toes.

The deli is a blast filled with a mix of New Yorkers and visitors like us. Everything we order comes out of the kitchen unexpectedly huge. We laugh like lunatics when Jarrell is served a matzo ball in his chicken soup the size of a grapefruit. Our heads spin at every plate that goes by, each looking more delicious than the last.

"How are we supposed to eat all this?" Brooke says.

"Beats me," says Jarrell. "I've always been able to finish a bowl of soup before. Maybe it's a plot to sabotage us so we can't dance."

"Sure. That's it. And, all of New York is in on it," C.C. laughs.

Suddenly, Danny stands, knocking over his chair. He narrowly misses a waiter carrying a tray laden with desserts.

"What is it?" I ask. "What's wrong?"

"There's Trent," Danny says.

Miss Aimée enters the deli with her fiancé, Trent Michaels. Spying us, they approach our table.

"Hey everybody, are you ready for a dazzling night at the theatre?" Mr. Trent asks.

"Ready," we chorus. "If only we can find the strength to waddle there." C.C. says.

"Please don't tell me anyone ordered the matzo balls. Those things will stay on your hips for a year," Mr. Trent teases.

"Great," Jarrell moans, "I'm screwed."

"Mr. Trent," I say, "this is Danny Landry, the dancer from L.A. He's a big fan of yours."

"Thanks, Danny. I've seen you dance. Very impressive! I'm glad you could join us tonight."

My smooth Danny barely manages to squeak out a polite thank you.

Waiting a beat, Mr. Trent lets Danny off the hook. "Well then, it's all arranged. You can pick the tickets up at the will call window. I'm glad Libby found someone to fill the extra seat. My friend couldn't make it, so I'm happy you can take his place. I hate to see a ticket go unused," Mr. Trent says.

When he and Miss Aimée take a table near my parents, Danny rights his chair and takes a seat. "That was awkward! Why can't I form a full sentence in that man's presence? I'm such a fool!"

We comfort Danny. "Don't feel bad. I don't think Mr. Trent has any idea the effect he has on people," I say. "I reacted the same when I first met him. You'll get over it. You'll see. He's a nice guy, albeit good-looking and supremely talented, but an all-around great person."

"Yeah, but that was *so* not cool," Danny says.

"Don't beat yourself up. I'm telling you, he won't give it a second thought. We're all awed by his talent, aren't we?" I say.

"Absolutely," C.C., Brooke, and Jarrell agree. "You're only human, and it's not every day you meet a mega-star." I say.

"Good thing you're getting to know me before I become famous," Jarrell says, slurping his soup. "I wouldn't want to freak you out."

"Yeah, thanks dude. I'll keep that in mind when you're my

understudy on Broadway waiting for your first break," Danny says.

"I think it will be the other way around, but I understand. You're a tad shook up right now, so I'll let it slide," Jarrell says.

After finishing our meals, the server clears our dishes. "Okay, wannabes. Time to limp off to the theatre," C.C. says.

Brooke and I reach for Jarrell and Danny, but realizing C.C.'s alone, we take her arms instead. *Too bad there isn't an extra ticket for Zach.* "Please tell me the theatre's nearby," I say.

"A mere eight blocks," says Jarrell. "You can do it!

"Let's go, fashionistas. Here we come, 42nd Street!" C.C. announces.

Danny steers us on a shortcut through Schubert Alley, a narrow pedestrian passageway originally used by stage actors of the past going to and from the nearby theatres. I get chills and swear I can feel their unearthly presence. We girls want to visit some of the shops, but it'll have to wait for another day if we want to make it to the show before the curtain rises.

Aimée and our parents wait underneath the sprawling marquee, having wisely hailed a cab from the deli. I edge close to Mom and Dad, wanting to share my first Broadway musical with them. I've dreamt about this my entire life. We parade down the center aisle behind Mr. Trent and Miss Aimée to the third row. Except for Danny, we've grown comfortable with Mr. Trent's celebrity status and feel special when heads turn and fingers point. He tells us the tickets are compliments of the show's choreographer, Steven Chen, his friend and former Juilliard roommate.

"Trust me. Being so close to the stage and performers will be an intimate and magical experience," he says. "I hope you love your first Broadway show, Libby, and may it be the first of many."

I hold hands with my parents as the lights dim and catch

a wink from Danny, who's elated to be seated alongside Mr. Trent. For the next hour and twenty minutes, I'm in heaven. The dancers are superb, the choreography original and bold. Try as I might, I can't seem to take it all in. It's too much, too everything. Steadily, my conviction grows. This is where I want to be someday. I can do this. Every number dazzles, every line and song lyric delivered with perfection. We applaud the most and laugh the loudest. I'm simply blown away scene after scene. Intermission comes too soon.

Gathered in a little alcove in the crowded lobby, Mr. Trent asks, "Libby, why do you look sad?"

"I don't think I can possibly explain what I'm feeling. I never want it to end."

"This is what Broadway is all about," Miss Aimée says. "They're supposed to knock your socks off!"

"Yeah, hit a home run every time," Dad says.

I laugh. "Thanks, Dad, for comparing the most brilliant night of my life to sports."

"Let's buy a T-shirt and poster," Dad says. "That'll cheer you up."

"I want one, too," Mom says.

The lobby lights flicker three times, signaling the end of intermission. We make our selections and hurry to our places just as the heavily draped curtains slowly open. My usually overprotective father offers Danny his seat this time. When our hands touch, Act Two flashes by in a daze. I couldn't wipe the smile off my face if I tried.

After the final bow, we stay and soak in the energy of the performance. When most patrons head for the exits, we're drawn forward toward the orchestra pit where we offer a ceremonial tip of the hat to the musicians. They wave in return, seeming to appreciate our unexpected gesture.

C.C., Brooke, Jarrell, Danny, and I can't stop talking about the show. C.C. is absolutely sure it's the best she's ever seen and deems it Tony-worthy in every category. She should know. She flies to New York with her parents or grandfather, Preston Bailey, every year. She's seen all the top Broadway hits.

"Let's find the stage door. Maybe we can meet the show's leads and dancers," Brooke says.

"Do people actually do that?" I ask. "I thought that only happened in the movies."

"Sure, they do," C.C. says. "But you can't dawdle. Sometimes the actors leave in a hurry."

We skirt the rim of the lobby to avoid the slowly exiting audience. Outside in the warmth of the summer night, we make a beeline for the corner of the building. Feeling smug, we're the first to arrive. C.C. was right. Two gleaming black town cars sit curbside with passenger doors wide open awaiting the stars. We position ourselves near a wooden barricade, set up to keep fans and crazies such as ourselves a healthy distance away, and prepare to capture the encounter with our smartphones. Soon, Mr. Trent, Miss Aimée, and our parents are behind us. Before I can ponder why someone like Trent Michaels is standing with the adoring public at a stage door, it bursts open. An amiable, middle-aged man emerges.

"Mr. Michaels, you and your party can come in."

"What? What did he say?" we scream.

"I have a little surprise for you," Mr. Trent says. "I didn't want to make a promise that I couldn't keep but tonight my dancing divas, the stars have aligned in your favor. My friend, Steven Chen, is in the house. He's invited us to come back and meet the cast."

"For real?" we squeal.

"For real!" he says.

We follow him around the barricade and step inside the theatre. The fully lit wings buzz with activity. The crew resets the stage for the next performance, and the stage manager, clipboard in hand, reviews the night's production with a lighting technician. I want to tell him that nothing could possibly be improved upon. But Mr. Trent once explained that after every performance, the show gets evaluated to guard against a slip in quality.

"Great job, everyone!" yells the manager. "Matinee tomorrow. See you at twelve sharp. Dancers at eleven."

We hear a few grumbles and groans in the shadows, probably from the dancers.

"Hey, Buddy, long time no see." A striking Asian man dressed in straight-legged jeans and an untucked shirt greets Mr. Trent. He has the long, lean body of a dancer. When Mr. Trent extends his hand, the man pulls him in for a bear hug. They're almost equal in height, about six feet tall. His silky hair reaches his collar and frames his high cheekbones, full mouth, and brown eyes.

"Steven, great to see you. Looking good, my friend. Congrats on your choreography. I particularly enjoyed the parts I saw after Aimée woke me up," Mr. Trent laughs.

"You're too kind, but I know you need your beauty sleep."

"Touché. You know I saw every second of your marvelous work."

"Thanks, Trent, but nothing compares to *this* stunning angel. Hi Aimée," Steven says, giving her a soft peck on the cheek.

Mr. Trent turns to us. "Everybody, meet Steven Chen."

We surround Mr. Chen and profusely express our congratulations.

"Please, call me Steven," he says. "What are your names?"

We introduce ourselves one by one.

"I hear you're all dancing at the Stairway to the Stars convention," he says. "Anybody competing for the Dancer of the Year title?"

"We are," C.C., Jarrell, and Danny say.

"Great. I'll see you there. I've choreographed the production routine with Trent's assistance. Dance well and work hard. You never know what can happen," he says. "That's where I got my first break. I was the male titleholder in . . ." he mumbles the year.

"Excuse me. What year was that?" Trent says.

"Never mind," Steven jokes. "Sorry I brought it up. Take a look around. Check out the stage. After a few more years of training with Miss Aimée and college degrees under your belts, it'll be waiting for you."

I step onto the stage. The immensity of the opulent theatre with three levels of velvet-cushioned seats overwhelms me. I wonder about its history and the performers that once stood on this very spot. I swear their impassioned spirits roam the catwalks just beyond the upper lights. Having had the frightening, yet mind-expanding experience of traveling through time at L'Esprit last year, I wish this stage could come alive and reveal its past. Uplifted by the energy in the house, I'm tempted to break into dance but stop when the lead actors appear and say hello. Although they look totally ordinary in street clothes, we freeze in place, imitating Danny's earlier state of idol-worship, multiplied by four.

"Kids, meet Greg Carver and Felicia Wheaton," Steven says.

We blubber incoherently. I silently pray that one of us will be able to finish a thought, but I didn't think it would be me. "You were wonderful tonight," I gush. "This was my first Broadway show, and I'll never, ever forget it." My words break the ice, and talking all at once, we shower them with praise.

"Wow!" they laugh. "You guys can keep this up all night." They take a few minutes to autograph our playbills and pose for photographs. In each, our faces are flushed with excitement.

As we step outside, we thank Mr. Chen.

"So nice to meet you. Have a great time in New York. Try and stay out of trouble, at least until I see you in class," he laughs.

At the hotel, Danny and Jarrell walk us along the angled corridor. C.C. lags behind while texting with Zach. When a man dressed in dark clothing and a Mets baseball cap suddenly pops out of the stairwell, she startles and screams. When the stranger sees the four of us, he quickly retreats. "Sorry, miss, wrong floor."

C.C. laughs it off, but the hair on the back of my neck stands tall. "I'm fine, Libby. Don't worry so much." C.C. returns to her text but scoots between Brooke and Jarrell.

"Didn't Mr. Chen warn you to stay out of trouble?" Jarrell teases.

Danny holds me in his arms and calms my nerves.

"I have a bad feeling that I can't shake," I say.

"Since that guy on the plane, you've been uptight. But I'm here, and I promise I won't let anything happen to you." His eyes search mine. *I wish I knew what he's thinking. Does he feel the same as I do whenever we're together?*

"You're right, I won't let anything spoil this amazing night."

"The evening was great and so are you. Thanks for inviting me."

I want Danny to kiss me, but with our friends nearby, he doesn't.

At our room, C.C., Brooke, and I say goodnight to the boys and bravely hold our smiles until the door shuts. With our shoes instantly forming an evil pile of pain in the middle of the room, we limp to our beds and throw ourselves onto the fluffy coverlets. Each of us grabs an aching foot to massage. "I couldn't walk one more step," C.C. moans.

"I agree. But what a night! Could anything have been more charmed?"

"Trust me, Libby," C.C. says. "You'll always remember your first Broadway show. I'm happy that Brooke and I were here to share it with you."

"Yeah," Brooke teases. "It's more than special. Kind of like your first love, Mr. Landry."

"C'mon you guys. It's too soon to say that."

"Well, if the shoe fits," they chorus.

"Oh, please," I beg, "don't say shoe."

We slip into comfy T-shirts, and as much as I want to revisit every second of the evening, my sleepy eyes insist on closing.

"We have a huge day ahead. I guess we should get some rest." I bury my face in the softest pillow I've ever met. The sound of my friends' steady breathing tells me they're already asleep.

"Sweet dreams. Love you guys," I whisper. I let my last thoughts hang on Brooke's words. *Has she stumbled onto something? Is this what it feels like? Am I falling in love for the first time?*

KISMET

Kismet is a multiple Tony Award winning musical with book by Charles Lederer and Luther Davis. It's based on the 1911 play by Edward Knoblock. The show, choreographed by Jack Cole, premiered at the Ziegfeld Theatre in December of 1953. Although it featured a great score, sumptuous sets and costumes, it was both panned and praised by critics. Fortunately, a lack of reviews due to the show's opening during a newspaper strike may have inadvertently bolstered sales. The story, set in Baghdad, concerns a wily poet and his beautiful daughter and follows the love interest of the girl and a young Caliph.

Chapter Ten

"**W**akey, wakey, sleepyheads. We have class in an hour. Up and at 'em," C.C. says.

I lie with my eyes closed and marvel at the fact that I can hear traffic on the street thirty floors below. "Does it ever stop?" I say.

"What? The noise?" C.C. asks. "Nope. You snooze, you lose. Let's go my pretties."

"You sound like the Wicked Witch of the West this morning. What has you up at the crack of dawn?" Brooke says.

"Did you forget? I have the DOTY audition class today with

Mr. Trent and the judges during my lunch break. I plan to earn a front row spot in the Gala Night production routine."

"Of course! You'll be great. Just take a deep breath and relax," I say.

"My family thought having breakfast together would settle my nerves. But it didn't work. By the way, care to guess who I saw leaving the hotel in a taxi a few minutes ago?"

"Oh, I don't know," I say, "perhaps your flying monkeys?"

"Nice try. But no."

"Well then, have a heart. It's too early for guessing games. We give up," Brooke says, rubbing the sleep from her eyes.

"You're going to have to do something about that attitude, missy," C.C. teases.

"Good grief," I say. "How much coffee did you drink this morning?"

"Actually, none. But that's beside the point. Miss Aimée and Mr. Trent hailed a cab, and I overheard him tell the driver to take them to The Cloisters."

"That would be immensely interesting if I knew what The Cloisters were," Brooke laughs.

"Same here," I say, rolling out of bed and stretching.

"The Cloisters Museum and Gardens, my dear, sweet, uneducated primas is a branch of the Metropolitan Museum of Art overlooking the Hudson River."

"And this is important to us, why?" I say.

"Because the number one thing people do there is get married," C.C. announces.

Suddenly, we're wide awake, convinced she's discovered the secret of the century.

"C.C.," I say, "do you honestly think they're going to tie the knot here in New York?"

"I don't know anything for certain except they were behaving like a couple of giddy teenagers. Kind of like you and Danny," C.C. says.

"You mean they were all googly-eyed and lovey-dovey?" Brooke teases.

"I make no apologies," I say. "However, in my defense, I am a giddy teenager."

"You better get ready, too, Libby," Brooke says. "I'll google The Cloisters while you two are at your morning classes. And don't forget to eat something. I've seen dancers drop like flies by the second day of convention."

Trent and Aimée's twenty-minute ride to Upper Manhattan reassures her. "I've worried since we reserved The Cloisters for our wedding that our guests would have a hard time finding it. But it's not too far, is it, Trent?"

"I know three girls who would walk over hot coals to get here," Trent laughs.

"You're right. I can't wait to see their faces when they witness our special day. But the girls can't find out yet. They need to stay focused until the convention is over, especially C.C."

"I trust their parents to keep our secret, Aimée. They won't let us down. Let's stroll through the garden to the reception area. We have plenty of time before our meeting with the event manager to review the wedding arrangements."

"Never in my wildest imagination did I think I would be getting married in a setting like this." Aimée gazes past the medieval sculptures and architecture that's set against the gentle flow of the Hudson River. "This place offers a mesmerizing backdrop. Thank goodness for Preston Bailey and his association with the museum. He's like our fairy godfather providing this exclusive venue. And thank you, Trent, for making all my dreams come true."

"Well, that's what I'm here for, honey, and don't you dare say you're not worthy. There's no one on earth more deserving of happiness than you. It's kismet; we're meant to be together," he whispers and gently kisses her lips.

"How did I get so lucky? Can you possibly know how much I love you?"

"I know it every minute of every day. Always have and always will."

Together they admire the exquisite works of art dating from the ninth to the sixteenth century.

Mason Evers, the Cloisters' event manager, is a studious man of medium build. His vibrant, blue eyes are magnified by his round, tortoise shell glasses. Observing the pair from his second-floor office window, he blinks hard. He puzzles over the four orbs that dance above their heads and whether or not he should mention their spiritual presence. Being an amateur psychic, it's not the first time he's witnessed a supernatural phenomenon on the grounds, but sometimes things are better left unsaid.

When he joins the happy pair, he leads them to the Langon Chapel where they'll soon wed. Standing before the altar where they intend to repeat their vows, Trent places his arm around Aimée and their circle of love fills with peace. Silently, he praises God for blessing them with the gift of each other. Aimée fails at her attempt to hide the single tear that slides down her face, knowing how it pains Trent to see her cry.

"What's wrong, Aimée?"

"Nothing," she says. "I'm just thinking of my parents and Daniella and A.J. Dalton. I wish they were here."

"You never know. They may be closer than you think," Mr. Evers says.

"We pray you're right," Aimée says, comforted by his comment.

Aimée, orphaned at a young age when her mother and father were killed in a car accident, regrets that they will never see her marry the man she loves or hold her babies in their arms.

Trent wipes her tear. "I only cry when I'm happy. And I've never been happier in my whole life," Aimée says.

"This is just the beginning," Trent says. "The best is yet to come, my love."

Trent, Aimée, and Mason Evers share parting handshakes confident that The Cloisters' staff has expertly tended to the wedding reception's every detail, large and small. The couple discusses their afternoon schedules on the return trip to the hotel. "I've agreed to lead auditions," Trent says. "I'll soon have the top fifty DOTY contestants tapping their way into my heart."

When Trent asks Aimée about her plans, she hopes he'll forgive her slight deceit. "I'll be catching up on convention paperwork in my room . . ." *At least until the courier arrives with a very special delivery: my wedding gown.*

A CHORUS LINE

A Chorus Line is a multiple Tony Award winning musical with book by James Kirkwood, Jr. and Nicholas Dante. It was an unprecedented box office and critical hit with music by Marvin Hamlisch and choreography by Michael Bennett. In addition to being a nine-category Tony Award winner, it won a Pulitzer Prize for drama in 1976 and ultimately became the sixth longest-running Broadway show ever. It premiered at the Shubert Theatre in July of 1975. The musical is set on the bare stage of a Broadway theatre and centers on seventeen Broadway dancers auditioning for spots on a chorus line. The performers provide a glimpse into their personalities and the life events that led them to become dancers.

Chapter Eleven

I *forgo my lunch break* when Mr. Trent offers me the chance to assist Brooke with his audition class music. I'm happy to be inside the closed ballroom with the dancers vying for special parts in Steven Chen's Dancer of the Year production. It showcases the top contestants in contention for the title and will be performed Saturday evening during the annual Gala Night to celebrate the close of the convention.

Parents and friends linger in the hall shouting encouragement.

"Break a leg, Mercedes and Danny!" Skylar says. Before a staff member closes the door in her face, Brooke and I hear her mumble, "Break an ankle, C.C."

Only Brooke and I hear, and since C.C.'s stressed enough, we agree to keep Skylar's nasty comment to ourselves.

The dancers heap their bags around the edges of the room and nervously adjust their numbers and ponytails. Some bounce in place, attempting to shake away their jitters. Brooke and I move to the stereo equipment where Mr. Trent gives us a quick review of what he wants. When certain we understand, he confers with the judges for several minutes. He instructs them to take a notecard and respond to a question written on it. "I'll be collecting them in a few minutes," he says.

I'm tempted to wish Danny luck, but I back off because of Mercedes' icy glare from behind his shoulder. I suspect that when Whitney and Mercedes whisper, it's about me. They might both be beautiful, but the evil stepsisters are a toxic duo. I'm no fool. Mercedes' desire for Danny is as obvious as Whitney's eagerness to befriend her and annihilate anyone from L'Esprit. Suddenly, my insecurities take over. Maybe Danny's only interested in me to make Mercedes jealous. Maybe it's her that he wants. I don't know if I should be rooting for him or Jarrell, but one thing's certain: Brooke and I will be supporting C.C. all the way.

After Myra Gold, Baxter Banks, and Crystal LaMond take their places at the front of the room, Mr. Trent introduces a guest assistant. All heads turn as Zach Dugan runs across the floor. C.C. freezes, but her sudden change in body language doesn't escape our notice.

"C.C.'s gonna die," Brooke says, jabbing her elbow into my side.

Zach scans the crowd and locks eyes with C.C. For a split second, it seems C.C. is the only person in the room. Their intense awareness of each other is unmistakable. When his tunnel vision returns to normal, he greets the judges and dancers and thanks Mr. Trent for the opportunity to work with him.

"It's my pleasure, Zach." Mr. Trent says. "The kids are pumped; let's get started. Dancers, please form five lines and stagger into windows as quickly as possible."

Mercedes pulls Danny to the middle of the first line. Whitney takes his other side. Jarrell and C.C. stand off to the right in the fourth row.

"Welcome to audition class," Mr. Trent says. "Our next several days are going to be tough and fast paced. I'm trusting you'll still love me when we're done." He puts his hands together in prayer with a comical expression. Everyone laughs.

"Congratulations to each of you for making it into this elite group," Miss Myra says. "You've worked hard to get here. We understand that being critiqued by a panel of judges is a high-pressure situation, but regardless of your ranking in your quest for the title, you should be proud of yourselves for making it this far."

Miss Crystal nods her head.

True to his reputation, Mr. Banks scowls. "I've judged thousands of dancers and competitions. If you want us to judge you properly, don't make it difficult. Have your audition numbers clearly visible."

Every dancer frantically checks the placement of their number.

"As Guy Fisher says, it's not the size of the trophy that matters." Mr. Trent continues. "Making the most of this opportunity will be its own reward. We understand each of you aspires to win, but it's the chance to dance that matters most."

"Look at me," Zach says. "I've never won a title, and I'm fairly successful. So never give up." I swear that C.C., who can usually remain levelheaded, swoons as the group applauds and whistles. Baxter rolls his eyes.

"Well said, Z-Dug!" Miss Crystal says. "As you know, twenty-five percent of your score for the national title is based on how well you perform during this week's audition classes. We're fortunate to have Trent Michaels assisting with Steven Chen's original choreography. As previously explained, the scores you receive on your solos this week will also account for another quarter of your ranking. Classroom participation and observations made by the STTS teachers make up another fourth, and the dreaded personal interviews will determine the remainder of your total score. Don't let the process rattle you. Be yourself, and you'll do fine. Also, before you leave class today, pick up your scheduled appointment times and read the guidelines for tomorrow's interview sessions. Baxter, have you anything to add?"

"Today we're primarily looking at your technique and presentation as well as your ability to pick up choreography quickly. You must work well with others, meaning *us*!" Baxter barks. "We'll also note your ability to make corrections in your body once a directive is given. I simply cannot tolerate repeating myself. If I tell you I want to see longer extensions, a tighter core, better spot, or higher leap, I will not ask you twice. If I say it to one, I'm saying it to all. Apply every critique to yourself! If you want the title, get your body to figure out what's being asked of it."

Everyone becomes noticeably uncomfortable with Mr. Banks' tone. Being greatly disciplined in the art of ballet is one thing, but I'll always believe kindness outranks talent any day of the week. "That man should step away from the barre long enough to acquire some social graces," I whisper to Brooke.

"Libby, hush. You better hope he didn't hear you or we'll both be permanently banished from his sight."

I gulp. *I should learn to keep some thoughts to myself.*

Counteracting Banks' gloom and doom, Mr. Trent lightens the mood. "Yes, the dance world can be mighty tough, even downright cruel at times, but it can also bring joy beyond compare. There's nothing greater than losing yourself in music and choreography. Dance is a constantly shifting work of art. And with every choreographer's creation, you have the opportunity to be a part of something larger and more spectacular than you could ever achieve on your own. It doesn't matter your role, front line or back; your contribution is vital. So, try your hardest. That's all we ask, and trust us on what we're about to teach you regarding auditions. We're not going to lie to you. They can be intense and leave you confused and doubting your abilities. If you want to be successful, don't let any talent agent or casting director convince you that you're not good enough. If I had listened to naysayers, I wouldn't have a career today."

I'm blown away by his words of wisdom. He and Miss Aimée never fail to inspire.

After collecting the notecards, Mr. Trent shuffles and randomly redistributes them to the judges. "Let's get to work," he says. "I'm going to teach you a thirty-two-count combination. Pay close attention. This choreography will be in the DOTY production. After you perform, you'll stand quietly in place as we select a male and female dancer for a special part to open the number. If a judge taps you on the shoulder, please sit down."

Mr. Trent and Zach demonstrate the routine while calling out the various steps and explaining particular nuances they'd like emphasized. It's awesome choreography, like the Charleston on steroids. Brooke and I agree the moves are super cool. Every dancer does an excellent job as they work to pick up the combination and figure out the details.

"Now, once again with music!" Mr. Trent says. Brooke pushes play and the dancers bust it out. We're captivated by their showmanship and technique. Watching the elite competitors makes me wish I could be on the floor, too. *They're amazing!*

Mr. Trent lets the class run through the choreography again on their own for a minute or two. He then asks them to perform line by line. "No second chances. This is it!" he says.

"I'm glad I'm not a judge. They're all so good. How will they pick just one boy and one girl?" Brooke says.

"I have no idea."

"I can't believe it. Even Whitney looks great!" Brooke whispers.

I bob my head. But then, I realize I hadn't even noticed her. I never took my eyes off Danny; he's the real deal. When the fourth row takes their turn, C.C. and Jarrell are equally impressive.

After the individual lines perform, the judges walk around carefully studying the faces and bodies of each contestant. Some dancers fidget and look downward while others nervously focus straight ahead. Each judge examines their notecard. When several hopefuls are tapped to sit, their disappointment is apparent. Brooke and I are shocked when Jarrell, C.C., and Danny eventually join them on the floor. Even Whitney stands longer!

No way! How could Zach tap out C.C. before Whitney, and why were Danny and Jarrell tapped? This doesn't make any sense.

"What's going on?" Brooke says. "C.C. looks like she's about to cry."

In the end, only Mercedes Slade and a surfer-type dude with shaggy hair stand. Mercedes wears a wicked grin and wiggles her eyebrows.

"Someone poke my eyes out with a stick," I say in my best ventriloquist impersonation.

"I hear ya, Sista," Brooke whispers.

"Let's clap for these two," Mr. Trent says. Whitney cheers the loudest. She must be upset that she didn't get the part, but she's absolutely thrilled that C.C. didn't either.

"Now, why were they given the spot and not you?" he asks the class.

"They did a better job than we did," one dancer remarks.

"Yes, in some instances that's true," he says. "Why else?"

"Better technique or stage presence," another says.

"Maybe, but you're all the best of the best, right? What other reasons?"

The dancers sit quietly.

"C'mon, I know dancers are intelligent. Think outside the box."

"Because we didn't fit the idea of what the choreographer or casting director has in mind," Danny says.

"Now we're getting somewhere." Mr. Trent says. "Sometimes you'll be judged before you even get the chance to prove yourself. You may be asked to do a single pirouette and told to leave. It sounds harsh, but someone casting a commercial or a choreographer with a major company will have an image of exactly what they want and for whatever reason, you don't fit the bill. Casting calls may feel like cattle being led to slaughter. You could be waiting in a chorus line all day going through countless callbacks only to be cut in the end. Or, you might get axed immediately because you're too tall, not strong enough to partner with a dancer already hired, or they need an ethnic look and you're too all-American. Maybe your talent outshines the lead, or you don't look chorus enough, or you're missing the illusive 'it' factor."

Mercedes, in her lime-green shorts and midriff top, plays with her pony tail and acts deserving. I wanna gag.

Mr. Trent continues. "Before class, the judges wrote specific requirements they'd like the two dancers to possess for the opening of the routine. Remember, all of you are here because you have strong technical abilities. I asked them to note any random attribute they wanted in addition to talent. Then, based on those ideas, we'd select the one male and female who came closest to meeting all the criteria. I tapped dancers from each line that didn't have accurate timing or an understanding of the details of the choreography. Keep in mind, ultimately, everyone needs to know these steps for the gala. Next, let's have the judges share what's on each of their cards."

"I only kept females five-feet-five-inches or under and tapped out guys five-feet-nine-inches or over." Crystal says. "Think of it this way," she continues, "if any ladies in the room want to be a Rockette, you have to meet certain height requirements. Often, men face the same scrutiny."

"I tapped male dancers wearing socks instead of dance shoes and females who didn't have their hair neatly pulled back. If you can't dress the part, you won't get the part," Baxter says.

"I tapped dancers who lacked personality or didn't change their expression enough during the routine. This is a Broadway production number. The audience in the mezzanine wants to share the energy of the performance with you," Myra says.

Little by little, the picture becomes clear.

"Unfortunately, I could only choose females with dark hair and males with long hair. Otherwise our selections would be different," Zach says, looking at C.C. When the lightbulb turns on in Mercedes' head, her brain explodes.

Mr. Trent drives home the point that it not only takes tons of talent to succeed but sometimes tons of luck, too.

"Your technique will take you far, but if you don't get the spot you wanted, don't be crushed," he says. "It may be a unique quality or trait the choreographer needs to complete his or her vision."

"Grow thick skins because auditions and rejections are simply part of the business," Zach adds.

"Everyone, stand up," Mr. Trent says. "You're all winners today because this exercise was held to teach you what it's like in the real world. For our convention, however, we won't be using the random criteria on these index cards to determine who dances in special roles. Formations, placements, and groupings of dancers will strictly be based on talent, and final decisions won't be made for a few more days."

Except for Mercedes, the whole class celebrates. "I can't believe they did that to us," she quietly hisses. Her surfer dude partner wraps an arm around her shoulder and says, "You gotta go with the flow," he shrugs, "no worries—just part of the lesson. We'll get the next one." Mercedes fakes a smile for the judges' sake, but when they're not watching, she roughly brushes his hand away.

"Now let's learn some more of this awesome routine," Zach says. He glances at C.C. and she beams.

Later in Mercedes' room, Skylar consoles her friend.

"Stop pacing! It's not so bad. You know you're going to get what you want. You always do!"

"No, you don't understand! First, Danny ditches me last night to see a stupid show with that loser, Libby. Then today, when I think I'm getting the lead in the DOTY production, I end up with nothing but humiliation. If you'd have seen the look on C.C.'s face, you'd know what I'm talking about. I'm telling you, Sky. It sucks! Danny and his new L'Esprit pals are probably still laughing."

"Get real! You know how much Danny cares about you. I'm sure you made a great impression in class. There's no way they can overlook you for a special role, and you have your interview tomorrow. If anyone can razzle-dazzle the judges, it's you."

Rolling over, Skylar turns off the light. Still fuming, Mercedes pounds out an angry text. *Go ahead. Do it now!*

ON YOUR TOES

On Your Toes is a musical comedy with book, music, and lyrics by Richard Rodgers, Lorenz Hart, and George Abbott. The show was choreographed by newcomer, George Balanchine, who for the first time in Broadway history, incorporated the dramatic use of classical ballet and jazz as part of a direct proponent of the plot. Fred Astaire, a dancer/movie actor, refused the lead because he thought the role clashed with his debonair image due to the mix of highbrow ballet with lowbrow humor. The show opened at the Imperial Theatre in April of 1936. Reportedly, in one of the funniest set pieces ever devised, the male lead, played by Ray Bolger, dances while being shot at from the audience by thugs in a case of mistaken identity.

Chapter Twelve

*T*he doors of ballroom C are clearly marked: "Quiet Please! Interviews in Progress." DOTY competitors arrive dressed to impress. Guys wear neatly pressed slacks and shirts while the ladies don their favorite summer fashions. Each proudly displays their audition number and holds a black and white headshot, the kind every performer dreams of seeing in a Broadway Playbill. They also carry sealed envelopes that contain personally written essays outlining what dance means to them, along with a list of their achievements in community service and academics.

When one girl's picture accidentally flutters to the floor, I flashback to the creep on the plane who dropped a small photograph of someone and spent the rest of the flight eyeballing the back of C.C.'s head. And what about that guy with the camera in Times Square? I swear it was him, but no one believed me. Fortunately, the unwelcome thoughts recede when I see C.C. turning a series of perfectly executed chaînés.

Brooke and I helped select her emerald-green dress accented with a skinny, wheat-toned belt. Her earrings, bracelet, and strappy sandals complete the outfit. C.C.'s lightly applied makeup allows her natural beauty to radiate, especially when she smiles. And let's face it: ever since locking eyes with Mr. Zach Dugan, she's doing a lot more of that lately. If ever a fresh summer morning resembled a person, it would look like C.C. She twirls in her skirt, and when she throws her head back with laughter, her coppery curls bounce. Her vibrant personality lights up the darkest sky. Brooke and I pray the judges recognize her authenticity and passion. We're positive she'd be the finest ambassador for the Stairway to the Stars program.

Outside the ballroom, a low-ranking staff member sits on a folding chair. He has a friendly, familiar face, almost like a younger version of Mr. Stan, L'Esprit's beloved doorman and caretaker. Atop his blue STTS baseball cap, he wears headphones and a small, wired mic awaiting instruction to send in the first group of dancers. He nearly spits his coffee when Mercedes steps onto the scene. She surveys the hall and appears angry when she spots C.C. She poses confidently in a revealing, black dress. Her thigh peeks through the parted slit in her skirt as if ready for Oscar night or another Instagram photo shoot.

"Mary, Mother of Saints, does she think she's a Kardashian? We were told to dress for a professional interview." Jarrell says.

"She can't be serious," Brooke says. "Why is she wearing those ankle-busting four-inch heels?"

"Because she can," I say. "Danny can quit staring anytime. If that's the type of girl he likes, he can have her."

Skylar hoots when she sees Mercedes. "Work it girlfriend! You're sure to get the judges' attention in that outfit."

The door attendant makes an announcement. "On your toes! The judges are ready!" After the first two groups exit, he studies the list of names. "Next up: Cynthia Cunningham, Jarrell Jordan, Daniel Landry, Whitney Ruthers, and Mercedes Slade." But where's Whitney? No one has a clue.

"Whitney Ruthers! Number 136," the man shouts.

"She must be running late," C.C. says.

"You four go ahead and line up without her," he says.

As other groups await their turn, the girls fiddle nervously, except Mercedes who seems laser-focused on C.C. Many of the boys continue gawking at Mercedes.

"Didn't I tell you that you'd stand out?" I overhear Skylar say.

"I always do! But the only one I want to notice me is Danny. Is he looking?"

"He can't tear his eyes from you, and neither can any other guy."

I'm fully irritated but shrug them off. "Just be yourself in there, C.C.," I say. "You'll be awesome!"

"What do you suppose happened to Whitney?" C.C. asks.

"Her mom's probably coaching her somewhere. Don't worry about her. Just think about the task in front of you."

Mercedes double-checks her hair and lip gloss. Jarrell practices his introduction line with Brooke while Danny jumps up and down. *Is he still drooling over Mercedes?* I don't know how to act. "Break a leg, Danny," I say.

He stops hopping and gives me a quick peck on the cheek. "Thanks, Libby," he says. "That means a lot."

Mercedes swoops in like a hawk and pulls him away. "C'mon," she says. "I'll be sure to break a leg, too, Libby."

In those heels, it'll be a miracle if you don't.

They enter the ballroom, and everyone but Mercedes acknowledges the man in the cap who politely wishes each dancer well. Leave it to C.C. to respond with a bright smile and a cheerful, "Thanks!"

"You're welcome, Miss," he smiles, "there's hope for the youth of the world after all."

The dancers greet the panel of interviewers which includes Clare and Howard Lexford, Baxter Banks, Myra Gold, Crystal LaMond, and Guy Fisher. Next to them sits a perky, young lady who says her name is Elena and describes herself as the Lexfords' Assistant and Convention Manager. Her features strongly resemble Clare's and gauging the Lexfords' doting expressions, everyone assumes they're related.

Jarrell's first impression dazzles, his handshake firm. C.C. executes an impromptu turning-cramp roll. "Call me C.C. It's my lifelong goal to be here." Daniel lets his boyish charm and confidence shine while Mercedes carries herself as if she's already won.

The contestants sit in a row of chairs several feet away from the panel of judges. Elena begins the interview process. "Because you represent our organization, we're not only looking for talent and commitment to the art form, but also your community volunteerism and academics. We like our titlists well-rounded."

She gives each dancer a sheet of paper with a list of questions. "Have no fear," Elena says, "there are no right or wrong answers.

Although you've written essays, your verbal responses will give us an idea as to how you think on your feet and a little more insight into your personalities and character."

INTERVIEW QUESTIONS

+ **Why do you dance?**
+ **What is your favorite dance memory?**
+ **Which dancers inspire you?**
+ **Outside of dance, who are you?**
+ **What is your favorite and least favorite part of dance?**
+ **Do you prefer performing as a soloist or in a group?**
+ **Which is your favorite style of dance and why?**
+ **What has dance taught you about yourself?**
+ **What is the best routine you've ever performed?**
+ **How have you used your talent to benefit others?**
+ **Do you plan to pursue dance professionally? What are your goals?**

"This is how it will work," Elena continues. She motions to a gold, sequined hat on the judge's table. "When called, each of you will step forward, turn in your photo and essay, and draw a question from the hat. Please read it aloud, give it to me, and then answer the question for the panel. You may return to your seat when finished. This process will be repeated twice so that everyone receives a fair opportunity to respond. Finally, the judges will have one last request for each of you. Describe yourself in a few short words."

The contestants scramble to think of a clever description.

Mercedes purses her lips. *A gifted dancer—or should I say passionate, powerful, determined to win? Or perhaps I'll name-drop. I am, after all, Olivia Hampton-Slade's daughter. Oh wait,*

I've got it! I'll say Stairway to the Stars' next female Dancer of the Year.

Jarrell thinks fast. *Charismatic, humorous, strong. Or maybe just the best male dancer ever.*

C.C. struggles. *Oh no, nothing's coming to mind. I'll have to make something up on the spot. I'll have to be spontaneous. That's it! Spontaneous and, and . . . adventurous and friendly . . . or feisty or, or what? Grandpa's red-hot chili pepper . . . ahh, I don't know.*

Daniel furrows his brow. *Hmm. How would Libby describe me?*

Elena checks her notes, "Let's have contestant number 136, Whitney Ruthers." The room goes silent.

"Whitney, B-Bop Studios. Don't be shy," Elena says. Clare and Howard grimace at the sight of her empty chair.

WICKED

Wicked is a Tony Award winning musical with music and lyrics by Stephen Schwartz, book by Winnie Holzman, and choreography by Wayne Cilento. Based on the 1995 Gregory Maguire novel, *Wicked: The Life and Times of the Wicked Witch of the West*, the production is an alternative telling of the 1939 film, *The Wizard of Oz*. Since its premiere at the Gershwin Theatre in October of 2003, the show has broken box office records around the world and is the ninth-longest-running Broadway show of all time.

Chapter Thirteen

An Hour Earlier

Determined to avoid her mother, who's certain to have one of her famous conniptions, Whitney Ruthers inspects her hair and makeup in a luxurious restroom far from the hustle of the hotel's main lobby. Primping her bangs, she puckers her lips into a sexy pout and styles her recently colored, cascading locks. She pins on audition number 136 and basks in her bold, new look.

"So, Mr. Zach, how do you like me now?" She engages in a full-blown conversation with her reflection. "I'm prettier than your little heartthrob, aren't I? This L'Oreal Long Lasting Copper Red is exactly what I need to spice up my appearance for the interview session. Won't mommy dearest be surprised? Heck, Carol probably won't even recognize me. And with any luck, you, my dear Zach, might fall for me over that tease, C.C. I'm positive Mercedes, Skylar, and the judges will love it as much as I do."

Outside the same ladies' lounge, convinced he's alone, a graying bellhop tucks a wallet-size photo into his breast pocket. He smoothly strokes his thick, gray mustache and eyebrows. Out of the security camera's range, he unzips a large, opaque garment bag. He places it over his arm and leaves the stacked luggage cart unattended. Quietly, he slips inside the ladies' room.

"Hey, Mister, you can't be in here!" Whitney says.

"Sorry. My mistake."

"What a moron," Whitney mumbles into the mirror.

The man pretends to leave but in one swift motion pounces on his target. He covers Whitney's mouth and nose with a chloroform-soaked rag. Within seconds, he shoves her limp body inside the empty garment bag and zips it nearly shut. He hoists her, like a rag doll, over his shoulder, carries her into the hall, and plops her onto the cart. He then carefully positions the suitcases around her in an attempt to conceal the body. Casually, he strolls toward the nearest open elevator, whistling a carefree tune and greeting passing guests. Before the door closes, one other passenger boards.

"Floor fifteen please," a mature woman says.

The bellhop begrudgingly obliges. The ditzy, sixty-ish Miss Bea, owner and director of B-Bop Studios, is clueless to the fact that her prized student, Whitney Ruthers, lies barely breathing on the bottom of the luggage cart. Observing the handsome man and his cargo, she says, "I see you come with tons of baggage."

"Excuse me?"

"Suitcases, silly."

"Oh, yes, you're right. I do. You know how these teenagers are," he says with a smirk.

"I sure do," Miss Bea bats her eyelashes.

When a low rumbling moan emanates from the cart, he makes a show of patting his stomach. "I should have eaten breakfast this morning."

Miss Bea bobs her head and chuckles.

"You look like a dance mom," he says.

"Heavens, no. I'm old enough to be a dancing granny. But I am one of the studio owners and a former Rockette."

"I thought so," he says. "You certainly have a special grace and flare. I knew a classy lady like you must have been on stage."

Miss Bea, overly excited by the attention, giggles. "Looks like this bag's a little lumpy." When she reaches to touch it, the bellhop abruptly stops her. Her eyes register shock.

"Sorry ma'am. I don't want anything tumbling off the cart. Wouldn't want to harm those fancy feet."

"Oh, you wicked man. How did you know I just had a pedicure at the spa? They do look nice, don't they?" She wiggles her toes.

"Lovely," he says.

Miss Bea blushes as the door opens. "I look forward to riding you, I mean your elevator, again soon." She laughs at her own foolish remark before saucily walking away swinging her hips side-to-side.

"Goodbye and good riddance, you dumb broad," the man mutters. "You could use a dose of chloroform yourself."

He continues to his room without further interruption. Once inside, the man plops the heavy garment bag onto the bed and rolls Whitney out. When she opens her eyes and groans, he flashes a .45 caliber Smith & Wesson in her face and swiftly restrains her wrists and ankles with zip ties.

"Shut up you spoiled diva, or I swear you'll never dance in the spotlight again."

Whitney's eyes dart in terror. She desperately tugs at her restraints. Each frantic movement binds them tighter.

"Relax, babe. You're not going anywhere," her kidnapper jeers.

The man points the barrel of his gun dangerously close to her head and roughly yanks her hair. Whitney moans when the attacker chloroforms her a second time; her fear fades into unconsciousness. The man slaps her cheek to make sure she's out cold. He then presses his lips to her ear. "That's it, Sleeping Beauty. Sweet dreams."

He removes his disguise and carefully places each piece along with the stolen hotel uniform inside the empty garment bag. Satisfied with his work, he sends a single word text on his recently purchased burner phone. *Done.*

A short time later, he steps into a pair of well-worn jeans and answers a knock at the door. Bare-chested, he checks the peephole, unhitches the lock, and pulls the summoned visitor inside. "Get in here!" the man hisses.

"You got her?"

"She never saw me coming," he lies.

His partner flinches upon witnessing the motionless body on the rumpled bed. "Is she dead?"

"I didn't think you wanted me to go that far."

Approaching the bed with caution, the stranger swipes a strand of red hair from Whitney's face. Mercedes' eyes flare. "Vinnie, you idiot! You've got the wrong girl!"

RUTHLESS! THE MUSICAL

Ruthless! The Musical is an off-Broadway, all female musical with book, lyrics, and direction by Joel Paley and music by Marvin Laird. The show opened at the Players Theatre in March of 1992 where it won the 1993 New York Outer Critics Circle Award for Best Off-Broadway Musical. The production spoofs shows like *Gypsy* and *Mame*, and movies such as *The Bad Seed* and *All About Eve*. Featured understudies for the lead role were Natalie Portman and Britney Spears. According to Paley, "In this staging, we've done away with the intermission and have streamlined it into 90 minutes that is rollercoaster sharp and fast."

Chapter Fourteen

*I*n *the silent ballroom, Elena* glances at Howard who shrugs his shoulders and looks to his wife. In the history of their convention, no contender for the title, especially one as driven as Whitney Ruthers, has ever missed an interview. "Well, Howard and distinguished judges," Clare says, "we all know the show must go on. Elena, please call the next dancer."

Elena asks Jarrell to draw a question. He nervously rubs the tops of his thighs before standing. "You've got this," C.C. whispers.

He approaches the table, gives Elena his photo and essay, and then reaches into the sequined hat. "What is the best routine you've ever performed?" He pauses to think of his answer. A happy memory lights up his face as he recalls the pas de deux he once performed with Brooke. "For anyone who knows me, you know my favorite style of dance is jazz, but to be great at it you need strong ballet technique."

Mr. Banks nods in complete agreement as if to say the discipline he teaches is most important.

Jarrell continues without hesitation. "In my best routine, I, more of an athletic dude than a graceful ballet dancer, was paired with the strongest little ballerina in our studio, Brooke Allen. Talk about intimidating! Who would think some tiny, five-foot-nothin' prima could scare me? Well, she did! And that's no lie." He laughs, and so does everyone else. "But partnering with her taught me a lot. You see, until I worked with her on this routine, I never truly believed in myself. I was afraid to be the real me. I played sports throughout middle school and hid the truth from my teammates that it wasn't just my sister taking dance lessons. I lost most of my friends who misjudged me when I eventually dropped out of sports to dance. But it was my dance teacher and Brooke who taught me being true to who you are and what you love is more important than anything. And I love dance!" The judges reward him with understanding smiles, and he relaxes.

"Miss Aimée and Brooke were ruthless, spending countless hours at the barre preparing me for the role I never thought I could do. I wasn't good enough, let alone worthy to partner with Brooke. But their faith never wavered. They taught me about never giving up and committing to my passion, just like Misty Copeland did, despite her many critics. I guess, because I almost lost Brooke to a terrible illness last year, that pas de deux will forever remain my best routine. I danced it to near perfection, and for the first time in my life I was true to myself. I'll never forget the pride in my teacher's eyes or the reflection in my own after we performed." Jarrell returns his question to Elena and takes his seat.

C.C.'s name is called next. She excitedly springs upward and passes her headshot and essay to Elena. Although her stomach is twisted in knots, she doesn't show it. Instead, she holds her chin up and silently prays. *Thank you, Lord, for giving me this chance. Please send your dancing angels to guide me.*

If her grandfather's and Libby's examples of the power of prayer and faith have taught her anything, it's how to show the world you can handle pressure with dignity. And of course, when your nerves start getting to you, by all means, keep a sense of humor.

C.C. tap rolls her fingers on the judges' table. "Drum roll please!" Reaching into the hat, she pulls out a piece of paper. "Today's million-dollar question is . . . Why do you dance?" She exhales a sigh of relief unshaken by the judges' intimidating faces.

"Why does one breathe?" she asks. "In order to live, I suppose. Dancing is what sustains me. When I'm happy, I smile." She pauses long enough to make eye contact with each judge and receives their encouragement. Sensing Mercedes' negativity, she refuses to allow it to influence her.

Like an intricate tap step, C.C. speaks at a rhythmic pace. "When you're sad, you cry. If angry, you shout. Or at least want to. When I'm frightened, I tremble, and when I'm in love, I want to tell the world. Because I live, I dance. To me, dance is freeing. It gives me the ability to express myself in a way nothing else can. It's the only way to release my joy, my pain, my fears, hopes, and dreams." She pauses. "Dancing is like air. I can't survive without it."

When C.C.'s reminded of L'Esprit's adored ballerina, she's engulfed with calming peace. "To paraphrase Daniella

Devereaux, whose everlasting spirit continues to inspire, 'Dance is a universal language, and I want to communicate beyond the limitation of words. Somehow, I'm more connected to life when I dance. Every color under the sun shines brighter, music echoes lovelier, and every emotion is felt more deeply. Why would you walk through life when you can dance?'" And with that, C.C. pirouettes into a saute' arabesque and returns to her seat.

Jarrell overhears Mercedes' disgusted harrumph. *Let's see you try that, Miss Snarky Slade, especially in those fancy shoes.*

"Thank you, C.C." Elena refers to her notes and asks Mercedes to step forward. Never one to shy from the spotlight, she confidently saunters to the judges' table. Reaching into the hat with her French-manicured fingers, she slowly shuffles through the folded pieces of paper. With dramatic flair, she extracts a question and reads it aloud. "Do you prefer performing as a soloist or in a group?"

With no attempt to conceal her true nature, she addresses the judges. "That's easy. A solo! I bet most would say a group routine because it sounds politically correct, right? It's true. In groups, we can achieve more when we work together. Who doesn't want to be part of a great team or company of dancers? I, too, love my studio, teachers, and fellow dancers." She glances at Danny. "But let's be honest. One can easily hide in the background. Some dancers blend into a performance like added scenery and depend on the strengths of others to carry them through. When you're a solo artist, you stand on your own merit. You command the stage and audience with your power, technique, and passion. You must stretch yourself more than ever before and grow in ways you never thought possible. It's a challenge I embrace. When there's nowhere to hide, you're the star! You create your destiny on stage and in life."

She flings the paper on the table and takes her seat.

"She's a bold one, but there's a lot of truth in her answer," Jarrell tells C.C.

Danny's called last. He draws a question from the hat and unfolds it. All eyes are on him as, for several long seconds, he stands perfectly still, his expression blank. Then he reads aloud, "How have you used your talent to benefit others?"

Danny sweeps his fingers through his hair. *Hello brother.* He closes his eyes and lifts his brow. Rubbing the shooting star tattoo on his forearm, and trusting his favorite mantra to always have faith, he whispers, *"Ayez la foi."* He inhales deeply and begins. "Yes, I guess I have used my talents for a greater good, but not because I was born philanthropic, a do-gooder kind of guy. And it's not to improve my resume for a scholarship or college application. The plain truth is, I made a promise to someone."

He stops to keep his emotions in check. "For the last four years, I've organized a local talent show called Dancing Courage for Kids with Cancer. It's in honor of my brother." His voice trembles slightly. "My apologies, this is never easy for me to talk about." He clears his throat. "The annual performance helps raise awareness and funding for St. Jude Children's Research Hospital. Several years ago, I lost my closest friend, my brother. His name was Jacob Alexander Landry. He liked to call himself Snakey Jakey when his hair fell out during treatment. If you think I have nice hair, you should have seen his." Danny looks up. "Jake was an awesome guy, athlete, honor student, and friend to many. One ordinary, sunny day, he collapsed on the soccer field, and our world was forever changed. My brother was diagnosed with a rare form of blood cancer."

Danny shakes his head as though trying to force the painful memory away. "It was a long, hard-fought battle, but Jake remained inspiring to the end and never lost faith. Days when he was too weak to get out of his hospital bed, he'd insist I dance for him and the other sick kids. They loved it when I'd breakdance or perform hip-hop routines. Before Jake died, I promised to volunteer as a St. Jude Hero and find a way to raise money and awareness for the foundation. He knew dance always lifted my soul. He was remarkable that way and told me to never give up. He wanted me to live a life full enough for both of us. Dancing Courage is my mission to keep my brother's memory alive, and my greatest desire is that my actions honor him every day. Although Jake wasn't lucky enough to survive, the truth is, he's the one who taught me how to live."

More than a few judges dry an eye when Danny returns to his seat. Jarrell and C.C., deeply affected by his story, wonder how he'll share his grief with Libby. The friends understand Danny and Libby have much to discover about one another.

When the second round of questioning begins, each dancer answers like a pro. Even Mercedes softens her response, but she reverts to her old self when Elena throws the group a curve ball. "I know we said our final inquiry would be to briefly describe yourself, but what we actually want is for you to describe your top competitor in this room."

Everyone appears comfortable except for C.C. whose eyes reveal panic.

Jarrell speaks of Danny without pausing. "Daniel Landry is a genuine person, hard-working, and probably the most talented dancer here. And I hate him because he does have great hair." He laughs. "Seriously, if I don't win the title, I hope this guy does." He reaches over and pats Danny on the back.

"I believe Jarrell is one of the strongest, most powerful leading male dancers at the high school level I've ever met," Danny says. "His technique and performance quality are undeniable. Jarrell's past, present, and future are all about dance. He's got a great sense of humor, a true heart of gold, and I believe he'd represent STTS with the utmost integrity."

Mercedes goes next. "I don't know C.C. very well. Rumor has it she's the best tap dancer here. I think Z-Dug has a major crush on her because she's so quick-footed, or should I say fast?"

Several judges shoot curious glances at each other. C.C. wishes a trap door would open beneath her, even Danny and Jarrell fidget in their chairs. The silence is awkward.

"Why the long face, C.C.? I'm only kidding. You're talented enough, but not to be rude, I don't consider you my top competitor." Like a true Broadway whiz, Mercedes performs. "I'm my strongest competitor. I challenge myself to excel every time I step onto a stage. Winning the title would be great, but I don't dance for titles. I'm committed to my passion and want to inspire greatness in others. I don't want to win the title, I want to earn it!"

When the judges scribble their notes, C.C. wonders if they bought her act and senses herself wanting to throw up. *Mercedes isn't committed, she should BE committed!*

C.C. keeps her comments short and sweet. "I, on the other hand, believe Mercedes is the one to beat."

Beat up is more like it! Jarrell thinks.

"In my humble opinion, she's every female dancer's biggest threat. Triple threat really. She can dance, and if she's anything like her mom, she can probably sing, too. And, let's face it, her acting abilities are clearly exceptional." The judge's heads drop but their eyebrows lift. "I can honestly say Mercedes is like no one else I've ever met. I truly wish her all the luck in the world. She deserves everything she gets in life and inspires me in ways I can't begin to explain."

Everyone sighs with relief when Elena announces the end of the interview session.

SOMETHING ROTTEN!

Something Rotten! is an original Tony Award winning musical comedy about musical comedies with book by John O'Farrell and Karey Kirkpatrick. The shameless, silly parody—an outrageous spoof of all things Shakespeare—premiered at the St. James Theatre in April of 2015. The *New York Post* proclaimed *Something Rotten* "Broadway's big, fat hit!" The show has a killer opening production number choreographed by Casey Nicholaw mocking everything from Bob Fosse jazz hands to the synchronized line dancing of the Rockettes. The combined clever and wacky humor make the show irresistible.

Chapter Fifteen

Rooftop of the Broadway Center Hotel

*C*arol Ruthers' head of professionally-styled hair looms over her daughter, eclipsing the blinding sunlight from Whitney's eyes. "Whitney Calista Ruthers! Thank goodness I've found you. Are you all right? What are you doing up here? What's happened to you? You look like a billboard for Red Lobster. Is that an empty liquor bottle you're holding?"

Whitney stirs, troubled by her waking thoughts. *Where am I? How did I get here? Will my head explode from the sound of my mother's high-pitched screech and this excruciating headache?*

All good questions, Whitney thinks to herself. Unfortunately, she doesn't have a single answer or even the slightest idea what her mother's talking about. The only thing making sense is the empty liquor bottle because she certainly feels as though she's consumed a whole lot of something rotten. Although miserable, she chuckles. *Too bad I don't remember the party. It must have been a doozy.* She struggles to gather her wits and form a reasonable response.

"This isn't funny, young lady. Are those bruises on your wrists and ankles? Baby, are you hurt?" Finally, dissolving into a fit of tears, her mother asks, "What have you done to your hair?"

"Good grief, Carol. I'm half-dead from something unexplainable, and it's the color of my hair that sends you over the top? Really, Mom?"

"I'm sorry, but I hardly recognize you. I have hotel security searching high and low for a blonde."

"Searching? What do you mean? How long have I been gone?"

"Most of the day, honey. When you didn't show up for your interview this morning, I was convinced the absolute worst happened. I couldn't reach you on your cell, and you didn't answer any of my texts. I was frantic!"

"I missed my interview? Oh, Mom. I would never screw this up. You know how much I want to win," Whitney rubs her throbbing head and cries.

"None of that matters. You don't look well. I'm notifying the authorities, and you're going to the hospital!"

Hotel security descends like a swarm of angry hornets. They immediately close the rooftop pool, treating it like a crime scene. Whitney's confusion is met with skepticism, and she's sure they think she's lying or covering for somebody. They probably see kids in trouble all the time. With the incriminating alcohol bottle at her side, she can hardly blame them. Mystified, Whitney only remembers being in the ladies' room admiring her hair and stressing about the upcoming interview. After that . . . nothing.

Too dazed and pained to be embarrassed, Whitney's placed on a stretcher and wheeled through the busy hotel lobby to a waiting ambulance. That's when she unexpectedly spots her friend, Tia Murphy, from B-BOP. She's plain and lithe with mousy brown hair, the kind of girl you wouldn't look at twice. Yet, with the right hair and a little help from Maybelline, her delicate features pop, and heads turn.

"Tia! It's me. What are you doing here?"

"I came with my mom to surprise you and support B-BOP. What's wrong? Where are they taking you?"

"To a hospital. Please come with me. I'm frightened. Something bad happened, and I need you. Tia can come; can't she, Mom?"

"If it'll help, of course. Text your mother and tell her you'll be with us, Tia. I don't want her to worry about you. One missing girl a day is enough."

"Missing? Whitney? What have you been up to?"

"That's a good question, Tia. I wish I knew."

The extensive medical examination reveals that, thankfully, Whitney's injuries are minor, and there is no indication of alcohol in her system. Except for a slight, almost undetectable trace of chloroform, a monster headache, darkening bruises, and her blistering sunburn, she's well enough to leave. However, because the emergency room personnel have an obligation to report unexplained injuries, New York Police Department detectives, Gary Grabowski and Nina Rizzo, arrive to interview Whitney.

"Mrs. Ruthers, if you don't mind, I'm going to ask you to

step away while we speak to your daughter alone. You too, Miss." The attractive, middle-aged man, the type that wears a suit well, motions to Tia. After exchanging hugs, Carol and Tia reluctantly leave Whitney with the detectives who promise not to take too long.

"We'll be right outside. We love you," Carol says.

When the door closes, Detective Grabowski hovers discreetly in the background. Ms. Rizzo, an olive-skinned woman with intelligent, wide-set eyes pulls up a chair. She crosses her legs and takes a moment to collect her thoughts. "Miss Ruthers, I have a job to do, and I am truly sorry to bother you. Is your head clearing?"

"It is, thank you," Whitney says. She nervously touches her wrists. "What happened to me?"

"You must have gotten a powerful whiff of chloroform for it to have knocked you out so heavily. The good news is you were not sexually abused." Whitney exhales deeply and wipes her eyes. "However, the marks on your wrists and ankles indicate you were probably bound with zip ties while unconscious. Do you know of anyone who would want to harm you, Whitney?"

"No. I mean the competition is intense, but it doesn't reach that level of crazy. At least I don't think it does."

"It appears that some person or persons took extreme measures to get you out of the way. Was anything special happening today?"

"Yes. The personal interviews for the Dancer of the Year contest, which count for a quarter of our final score. I don't even know if they'll give me a chance now. I might be done. If that was someone's plan, they've succeeded."

"The Stairway to the Stars convention has been taking place in this city for many years, Whitney. It has a great reputation for fairness. My own daughter participated in it when she was your age. I'm sure they'll understand that missing the interview wasn't your fault," Grabowski says.

"I hope you're right. This means everything to me."

"Can you think really hard, Whitney?" Rizzo says. "What's the absolute last thing you recall before you woke up at the pool? Even the smallest detail is vitally important."

"I was looking in the mirror in the ladies' room." Whitney trembles.

"Then what? Don't be afraid," Rizzo consoles. "Tell me what you saw."

"My hair."

"Do you remember what you were thinking?"

"Yeah. That I loved it, but my mother was going to kill me when she found out that I dyed it without her permission."

"Well, she may kill you, but I don't think she tried today." The corners of the detective's mouth turn upward. "I want you to dig deep. Did you see anything else? Anything at all?"

Whitney hesitates for a long time. "Wait a minute. There was a guy in the restroom!"

Rizzo leans forward in her chair. "This is news. What guy? What did he want? Can you describe him?"

"He wore a uniform, like a hotel bellman. He stepped inside, and I told him to get out. I thought he left me alone."

"Tell me what he looked like."

"It happened so fast. I'm pretty sure he was medium height and older with a gray mustache. I remember thinking his tan seemed bogus, but I only saw his reflection for a split second. Actually, his smell lingered longer than his image. I'll never forget his strongly scented cologne."

"That's great, Whitney. Good job. Remember, you didn't do anything wrong. You're the victim here," Detective Grabowski says, stepping closer to her bed.

Whitney's body shakes and tears flow. Detective Grabowski's seen it often when the shock of the day's events wears off and reality sets in. He summons Mrs. Ruthers and Tia to comfort Whitney during her emotional meltdown.

As the detectives leave, they offer a warning. "Stay alert and never roam the hotel alone. Call us if anything else comes to mind. We'll stay in touch and keep you informed as our investigation unfolds."

"Tia, will you stay with Whitney while I talk to the detective for a minute?"

Carol Ruthers follows Detective Grabowski out the door. Tia flies to Whitney's bedside. "Don't cry, Whitney," she says. "Everything will be all right. Somehow even the worst things tend to work out in the end. I know you've been through a nasty ordeal, and I'm here for you."

Tia's kindness makes Whitney cry harder. "I know I've been a rotten friend, especially during these past months when you were away having your baby."

"I'm fine, now," Tia says. "I'm more worried about you."

"I'm a complete mess. I can't even wrap my brain around this. I need something else to think about. Tell me about your baby."

Tia recognizes Whitney's desperation. "Well, my grandparents in Florida taught me that everything happens for a reason, even a bad one-time hookup. They took me to church services, and the people there were wonderful. Believe it or not, I even joined the choir. They unconditionally accepted me and my baby."

"That's great, Tia," Whitney sniffles. "I'm truly happy for you. Do you have any pictures?"

"Of course! What mother doesn't bore her friends or guilt them into saying her baby's the cutest thing ever?" Tia laughs.

Fishing in her bag, Tia proudly produces a dozen darling shots of her adorable little girl. "I named her Madeline after my favorite character in my childhood books. I can't wait for you to meet her. You can be her Auntie Whitney!"

"Tia," Whitney cries, "you'll always be my best friend."

"And you, mine. After all, we share a lot of secrets."

When Whitney recalls how Mercedes and Skylar pried the secret of Tia and her baby out of her during a recent gossip-digging conversation, she's overcome with guilt. Wishing it had never taken place, she masks her shame. "I've missed you, and I'm so happy you're back."

"Can we change the subject? What's with the red hair?" Tia says.

"It's part of my winning strategy."

"Of course, it is," Tia laughs. "Pray tell, what are you up to now?"

Just then, Carol returns, flush-faced. Whitney, familiar with her mother's fanciful daze, shakes her head. *Poor Detective Grabowski, he must be the unlucky new love interest on Mom's radar.*

DON'T BOTHER ME, I CAN'T COPE

Don't Bother Me, I Can't Cope is an award-winning, all-singing, all-dancing musical revue with book by Micki Grant and choreography by George Faison. This mixture of gospel, jazz, funk, soul, calypso, and soft rock opened at the Playhouse Theatre in April of 1972. It was the first Broadway play to be directed by an African-American woman, Vinnette Carroll. One critic praised the production, "This is the kind of show at which you want to blow kisses."

Chapter Sixteen

*C**ell phones buzz with the* announcement that all scheduled convention classes and activities are cancelled until further notice. Misinformation and half-truths circulate, including the unconfirmed report that the dead body of a dancer was found at the rooftop pool. Speculation regarding the identity of the victim runs rampant.

The Lexford's lavish penthouse suite quickly becomes damage control central. The opulent furnishings and magnificent panoramic view of New York City cannot settle Clare's rattled nerves. After a complete briefing regarding Whitney's condition and the rooftop drama, their door closes behind Elena and the NYPD detectives.

"Poor Whitney! Howard, how could something like this happen?" Clare's trademark Southern belle composure crumbles in the face of certain ruin. She rants while pacing the length of their luxurious tower suite. "Our empire! Everything we've worked so hard to achieve. I can't believe this. Why would someone want to hurt one of our dancers? Nothing like this has ever occurred in our thirty-plus years in the convention business. It makes me livid! I don't know what the world is coming to, Howard. What are we going to do? And don't you dare tell me to calm down."

Of his many talents, Howard, a lifelong hoofer, takes pride in his ability to assess and solve problems. He believes that tap dancers are not only quick-stepping but quick-thinking. There are no stupid dancers, he loves to proclaim.

"Clare, the detectives appear competent. Let's allow the police to handle the matter, and I'll have the hotel beef up security. We'll demand they add extra personnel to patrol the building. Unfortunately, bad news travels fast. To diffuse the rumor mill, I'll instruct Elena to schedule an immediate, mandatory meeting with the staff and studio heads to apprise them of the situation. She'll follow up the cancellation text with one that urges every dancer to maintain the buddy system at all times. We'll offer assurances that we have everything under control and promise that our convention will keep the students safe."

"Thank goodness for Elena and her technical skills. She's a godsend," Clare says. "She's worth her weight in gold. Only, I fear it's going to take more than a few texts to make this mess go away. And unfortunately, we have no idea what kind of perverted maniac is out there. And what if there's more than one?"

"Don't let your imagination run amok, dear. Reality is bad enough. Grabowski and Rizzo don't seem to suspect a band of terrorists. There's no reason to overreact. Whitney Ruthers is recovering from her scare, and soon we can put this unpleasantness behind us. In a day or two, as the excitement of the competition builds, it'll all be forgotten. Or it might be if it were anyone else. Why is it always the Ruthers family that's involved when any controversy arises?" Howard laments.

"We can't blame her this time, Howard. The child is a true victim of some sort of foul play. Even though it's not our fault, I feel like I'm walking on eggshells waiting for the storm fueled by Carol Ruthers' fury to hit. She's a force to be reckoned with—possibly the most mean-spirited woman I've ever met."

"We'll be ready for her, Clare. There's no way I'm going to let her spin this out of control and soil our impeccable reputation."

As lifelong partners in marriage and business who consult on everything and agree on most, Clare knows that Howard's sensible, unemotional approach to a problem is usually best. Admittedly, the Ruthers girl is a known troublemaker from past conventions.

"Howard, remember the time she was accused of having boys in her room?"

"Yes, a matter the silly girl vehemently denied, even though the hallway camera proved otherwise," he says.

"But this is clearly more than one of her usual pranks."

"Yes, dear. But Whitney never takes responsibility for her actions nor shows the slightest remorse for her willful behavior. Making matters worse, her mother fiercely defends her, right or wrong."

Deep down, Howard's lack of compassion stings. Clare fears that the importance of the almighty "bottom line" has replaced his concern for the well-being of the dancers—even one as repugnant as Whitney Ruthers. If Howard's talent is tap dancing, Clare's is an uncanny ability to rationalize everything to her benefit. "You're right, Howard. We've done nothing wrong. Surely, we can't be held accountable."

Under the adoring gaze of her loving husband, Clare buries her emotions and puts on a happy face. Collapsing into one of the overstuffed armchairs that flank the ultramodern, Italian-tiled fireplace, she reaches for her vodka-infused Cosmo. As it slides smoothly down her throat, she realizes it's a little early, but her deflated morale needs the boost.

The distasteful discussion far from over, Clare pleads with Howard. "Can we drop it for now? Give me five minutes of peace. I promise to pull myself together before tonight's meeting, but right now don't bother me, I can't cope."

Clare expertly swirls the glass, spilling not a drop. Her courage builds. She's confident her husband, already on the phone consulting Elena and issuing orders to the hotel staff, can charm the socks off anyone, even the ill-tempered Carol Ruthers.

HELLZAPOPPIN

Hellzapoppin is a musical revue written by the comedy team of John "Ole" Olsen and Harold "Chic" Johnson. The show opened on Broadway at the original 46th Street Theatre in September of 1938. Filled with sight gags, risqué humor, and audience involvement, it created a fast-paced, circus-like, anything-can-happen atmosphere. The show was continually rewritten throughout its run to remain topical. Some seats were even wired with electric buzzers that were triggered during the performance. Chorus girls often left the stage to dance with audience members or sit on their laps. When this started to overwhelm, an actor began loudly selling tickets to the competing Broadway show down the street.

Chapter Seventeen

W*ord of a private meeting* for convention staff and studio directors spreads. C.C., Brooke, and I gather outside the closed doors of the fourth-floor conference room. We probably shouldn't be here, but, technically, no one told us to stay away. A handful of dancers mill about looking perplexed. The gossip flies fast and furious, each version more farfetched than the last. An L.A. girl says that a dancer has been murdered. Another says someone was drugged and kidnapped while another is sure a dancer was missing but found poolside, drunk and naked.

"Geez," I say. "Murdered! Kidnapped! What are they talking about?"

C.C. shrugs. "Don't listen to them, Libby. They don't know any more than we do."

Inside the conference room, Howard offers kudos to Elena for putting the impromptu meeting together on such short notice. The Lexfords gather their thoughts and scan the anxious faces of the staff, studio owners, and Carol Ruthers, the only parent included. If there's a woman more high-strung, Howard's certain he never wants to meet her.

Mrs. Ruthers sits straight-backed, in a front row seat alongside Miss Bea. While Carol sports a Botox-defying frown, Miss Bea, relieved that her missing student has been found safe and sound, chats with Miss Aimée as though she's attending the social event of the year.

With a nod to his wife, Howard takes a sip of water and stands to address the crowd. A hush falls over the room. "Most of us have met, but for any newcomers, I'm Howard Lexford, and this is my wife, Clare. We're the STTS convention's founders and owners. As you may or may not have heard, one of our young dancers was abducted from a public restroom in the hotel this morning." The attendees collectively gasp.

"Clare and I appreciate your attendance at this unscheduled meeting and apologize for the late hour. As a safety precaution, the authorities have advised us to postpone student classes until further notice. We anticipate having the all-clear as early as tomorrow afternoon, so we suggest you keep your cell phones handy to receive the notification. Although an unfortunate incident, the dancer was later found poolside. Other than apparently being chloroformed into unconsciousness and a few small bruises, she was not, I repeat, *not* seriously harmed. She was taken to Lenox Hill Hospital for observation. She is, of course, welcome to rejoin the competition as soon as she feels ready to resume her schedule. Clare and I offer our sincerest apology and deepest regret that this unprecedented event took place during our convention. We pride ourselves in our long history of providing a safe environment, and we are as befuddled and shocked as you are. The main thing to consider is that we've been assured the dancer in question has been released from the hospital and is eager to return. On behalf of all of us connected with STTS, I ask you to take this matter to heart. Please remind your dancers to stay alert and travel in groups at all times. Now, I'd like to introduce the members of the panel who will speak in turn and take your questions afterward. Robert Wright, the hotel manager, Chief Ray Watts, head of hotel security, and NYPD Detectives, Gary Grabowski and Nina Rizzo, in charge of the investigation." Each acknowledges the group with a small nod.

The hotel manager and security chief outline measures implemented for the dancers' safety, then turn the floor over to the detectives. Because the investigation is ongoing, Grabowski and Rizzo can offer little except to express their belief that this isolated incident is unlikely to recur.

"Our motto since 9/11 remains, 'If you see something, say something,'" Detective Grabowski says. "We ask you to be extra vigilant. Pay attention to your natural intuition and take note of any characters or activities that appear suspicious. Report anything unusual to hotel security."

In the shadows, with his back to the room, a member of the kitchen crew listens intently. He stalls for time by performing his tasks slowly. When the water pitchers are filled and the ice buckets replenished, he maneuvers his service cart toward the exit. With his head lowered and eyes averted to conceal his cocky demeanor, he mutters, "Idiots. Good luck with that."

"Thank you, detectives," Howard says. "Are there any questions?"

Carol Ruthers leaps to her feet. "What exactly are you doing to catch whoever did this to my daughter?"

"Well, so much for anonymity," Clare whispers.

The room erupts, everyone speaking at once.

"Quiet! Quiet, please," Howard demands. "Mrs. Ruthers," he says, "the police are investigating. The hotel is on heightened alert."

"As we discussed at the hospital, ma'am," Detective Rizzo interrupts, "we have reason to believe that a hotel employee may be involved, and individual interviews are being conducted as we speak."

All eyes turn as the kitchen employee wheels his noisy cart toward the nearest door.

In the hall, curiosity gets the best of us. Brooke presses her ear against the crack between the ballroom's entrance.

"Do you hear anything?" I ask.

"Someone's shouting," Brooke says. "It sounds like Mrs. Ruthers."

"That's interesting. Has anyone seen Whitney?" I ask.

"Maybe this is why she missed her interview," C.C. says.

"What can Whitney be involved in that's enough to stop the whole convention and cancel our classes?" I ask. "Is everybody from our studio okay?"

"I think so," says Brooke. "There's usually tons of drama at nationals, but never anything like this. No one's ever disappeared before."

"Brooke's right, Libby," C.C. says. "If Whitney's involved, she'll have a hard time talking her way out of this mess."

The conference doors burst open. The hotel employee pushing a loaded service cart zips past, leaving one of the doors slightly ajar.

C.C. and Brooke deftly jump out of his way. "Excuse me!" C.C. says. "You nearly ran over my foot."

"You shouldn't be blocking an exit." He steers the cart down the hall then stops. He focuses on C.C., and his intense look gives me chills. We observe him closely until he rounds the corner.

"Is it me, or is there something odd about that guy?" C.C. says. We shrug our shoulders and hold our noses. "Phew, he reeks," Brooke says.

The man ducks into the nearest restroom. He tears off the white jacket bearing the hotel's gold, embroidered *BCH* insignia and dumps it into the trash bin. He takes care to stash it deeply where it won't be discovered by a nosy, *real* hotel employee. He slicks his hair, dons his stylish Ray Bans, and inspects his image, taking note of his similarity to Ryan Gosling. Pleased with his transformation, he exits the men's room and blends with the guests that mingle in the hotel's massive lobby.

From inside the conference room, we hear more shouting. Carol Ruthers' shrill words make our blood boil.

"While interviewing the employees, I strongly suggest you interrogate each L'Esprit dancer as well," she says. "They've always been jealous of my Whitney."

The meeting is a train wreck, and we can't help but sneak a peek.

Miss Aimée shoots out of her chair and faces Whitney's mother. "You can't be serious," she says. "I understand that you have every right to be upset, but please do not accuse my dancers. I promise you they would never get involved in a scheme to hurt your daughter or any other competitor for that matter." Although Carol's sour expression tempts Aimée to say more, she refrains from uttering another word.

"If anyone harbors resentment and jealousy, it's Whitney for her failed auditions into L'Esprit. How dare Mrs. Ruthers implicate our studio!" I say.

"If we wanted to do Whitney in, we had plenty of chances to throw her down the elevator shaft at L'Esprit during her debacle at Mr. Trent's dance intensive last summer," C.C. says.

"Geez, C.C.! Don't let Dance-mom-zilla hear you. Not that it's an entirely bad idea," Brooke says.

"Nationals can be insane, but this hellzapoppin drama is extreme," C.C. says.

"Thank goodness Miss Aimée has our backs," I say.

"Shhh! One of the detectives is talking," Brooke says.

"Mrs. Ruthers, Detective Rizzo and I assure you that we will not rest until the culprit is apprehended and brought to justice."

"If I have *your* word, Gary, I'll try to be patient," she purrs.

"Oh, Howard," Clare mumbles. "Is she flirting with the detective?"

"Heaven help him if she is," Howard says.

Seething, Carol Ruthers further unleashes her wrath. Pointing at the Lexfords, she voices her final decree. "Clare and

Howard, you have my word. Should anything else happen to my daughter, I will not hesitate to shut this convention down permanently!"

We scurry when the conference doors swing open with a bang. Whitney's mother exits, eyes blazing. She plows through the smattering of dancers and doesn't seem to notice that she nearly knocks one over. Without a word of apology, she heads for the nearest bank of elevators. We pity any poor soul confined in the small space with her fiery temper. Our curiosity mounts as the teachers file by, tight-lipped and frowning. We decide to scram before we're caught by Miss Aimée. We pass the cart of empty pitchers that sits abandoned in a side alcove. "That guy's a lousy employee," C.C. says, "I don't like him."

"Then he'd be wise to stay out of your way," Brooke says.

"I still want to know what's going on," I say.

"I'm sure Miss Aimée will fill us in." Hooking arms, Brooke leads us to the elevator.

Later in the penthouse, Clare and Howard, still shaken from the lethal tone of Ruthers' tirade, console each other.

"That went well!"

"Hilarious, Howard. I think my head's going to split in two. Maybe it's time to retire."

"Nonsense. You have to take the good with the bad. Just another day in paradise! We love this convention. What else would we do? We can't let the bullies of the world get to us."

"I swear I saw steam shooting out of her ears. Do you suppose I should talk to Whitney's mother one-on-one?"

"She's worried for her child and angry at the world. Give her a chance to cool down. As they say in the South, we can think about it tomorrow."

"Thanks, Rhett."

Howard chuckles. "You're welcome, Scarlett."

"Get some sleep," Clare advises. "It's your favorite day tomorrow, and you'll want to be your best. The only class not cancelled until further notice is your 9 a.m. tap session with the teachers, and they line up early in anticipation every year."

"I do love it. It'll be a nice reprieve from today's mayhem." Howard yawns. "I better dream up some new moves," he says, laughing as he scrambles across the width of the humungous bed to kiss his cherished wife of thirty-five years goodnight.

Clare marvels over Howard's ability to instantly fall asleep. Tonight, his soft snoring annoys rather than soothes. A wailing alarm inside her brain keeps her wide awake. There's more trouble brewing, it warns, the kind that will make dealing with Carol Ruthers feel like a walk in Central Park, the kind that a well-intentioned informational meeting won't fix.

On the thirtieth floor, we're tucked into our beds. "Girls, what do you think happened to Whitney today?" I ask.

"God only knows. With her, anything's possible," Brooke says.

"Whether she's guilty of something or completely innocent, I kinda feel sorry for her," I say.

"I don't. She's probably guilty as sin," C.C. says. "Knowing Whitney, this whole fiasco's most likely a ploy for attention."

"I don't know, guys. It sounds pretty serious," Brooke says.

When we shut off the lights, I pray Whitney's simply involved in another one of her ridiculous pranks, because the alternative seems like a far worse nightmare.

INTO THE WOODS

Into the Woods is a Tony Award winning musical with music and lyrics by Stephen Sondheim, book by James Lapine and choreography by Lar Lubovitch. The show opened on Broadway at the Martin Beck Theatre in November of 1987. Numerous productions have been staged around the world, and a Disney film adaptation was released in 2014. The musical intertwines the plots of several fairy tales, exploring the consequences of the characters' wishes and quests. Its fascinating setting is haunting and mysterious.

Chapter Eighteen

The cancellation of morning classes brings an unexpected opportunity to flee the hotel and explore the city. Except for a small cloud of fear that hangs over us due to Whitney's baffling disappearance, the day is picture perfect—nothing but blue skies and sunshine. C.C. doesn't hesitate when she reads Z-Dug's text inviting her for a stroll through Central Park. She's dressed and out the door in five minutes flat.

"Cover for me," she says. "I have my phone, and I'll be careful."

"Are you sure this is a good idea?" I ask.

"No, it's a great idea," C.C. laughs. "Don't worry!" she shouts from the end of the hall. "I've already sent a message to my parents, and they're fine with it. See you later. Don't have too much fun without me! Bye."

"I hope she knows what she's doing," says Brooke.

When Miss Aimée calls and tells us to pack our dance bags and meet her in the lobby, we spring into action. We're always ready in the hopes that our fantasy of filling in for an ailing Broadway dancer might come true. We hustle to the elevator and consider it a stroke of luck that it's open and empty.

"I have a feeling this is going to be a great day," I say.

Brooke pushes the lobby button. "Where could Miss Aimée be taking us?"

"I don't have any idea. I only know she said to wear walking shoes, so I think we're in for a bit of a hike."

When we reach our floor, the elevator doors part. Miss Aimée waves us over. "Hi, you two. That was quick. Where's C.C.? I'd hate for her to miss this."

"Um, she said something about texting her parents and going to Central Park, I think." I hide behind Brooke who reluctantly nods, and I doubt if covering for C.C. and Zach is the right thing to do because it definitely doesn't feel good.

"Shoot," Miss Aimée says. "That's disappointing! As long as she's in good hands."

"Oh, she's definitely in good hands," I mumble to my co-conspirator.

"Then off we go. Do you need anything? Water? Juice? I trust you're both ready for an adventure."

At a remote side door, C.C. and Zach meet. She's dressed in faded jean shorts that reveal her trim legs and an off-the-shoulder crop top. Though excited, she plays it cool. Zach looks yummy in his chino shorts and V-neck T-shirt. The heaviness of his gaze gives her a sudden rush.

C.C. gulps before speaking. "Hi, Zach. Sorry if I kept you waiting."

"From what I know of you so far, you're well worth my time. You look great by the way." He hails a cab and tells the driver to take them to Central Park. Holding hands in the backseat, he warmly smiles. "Thanks for agreeing to hang out. You don't mind that I asked you to meet me at a side door, do you?"

"I understand. I know we're practically the same age, but you're an employee of the convention, and I'm a dance competitor. I wouldn't want to jeopardize your working relationship with STTS."

"And I don't want to distract you from your pursuit of being named their female Dancer of the Year," Zach says.

"Don't worry. I don't think my interview went that well yesterday."

"What do you mean?"

"Another dancer may have sabotaged my chances by mentioning our mutual attraction."

"Let me guess. Whitney from B-Bop? But I heard she was taken to the hospital."

"Apparently she was attacked. It's all anyone's talking about, but it wasn't her."

Zach shrugs. "Rumor among the staff is that she and her mother are quite the attention-seekers. Maybe they staged it."

"It's possible, but would they really do something *that* bizarre? What if there actually *is* a psycho loose in the hotel?"

"It's scary, but it sounds like she'll be all right. And if some guy's causing trouble, I'll protect you."

"Good to know. Thanks, Zach," C.C. smiles.

"So, if it wasn't Whitney talking about us during your interview, then who?"

"I don't want to name names, but this other dancer hinted to the judges how much you liked me and my dancing."

"Well that's true," he laughs. "Did she say anything else?"

"I don't remember. My mind sorta went blank after she said it."

"Don't worry. It's not an issue. I'm sure I can handle it. I'm paid to watch dancers and critique them, and I'm allowed to have friends."

"But friends that you're judging?"

"I wasn't hired to judge the interviews, auditions, or solo performances. I only observe and score abilities in class and assist when needed. I'm one of a dozen faculty members evaluating you. Trust me. I can't control the final outcome of who wins the national title. I know it, they know it, don't you?"

"I'm so relieved to hear you say that."

"Thank goodness. For a second, I thought my influence was the only reason you agreed to see me today," he says.

"Darn it," she teases. "You know me too well. I'm all about taking advantage of people. I'll even hang out with homely guys like you if I can get what I want."

He leans closer. "Ha! Ha! Ha! And what is it you want, Miss C.C.?"

His mouth and fresh minty breath are less than an inch from C.C.'s lips. *He's completely gorgeous. Thank God we've arrived, or I'm afraid I'd tell him exactly what I want.*

Zach pays the cab driver, and the two step onto the crowded sidewalk. "C'mon, I want to show you Central Park in style." He leads her to the fanciest horse carriage on the street.

The driver is a muscular man. He wears a black top hat over his long-braided dreadlocks that are neatly pulled back into a thick ponytail. His teeth are blindingly white, and his massive biceps threaten to burst through the sleeves of his shirt. His tailcoat hangs from a hook on the carriage, and his cobalt-blue suspenders and plumed hat create quite the regal impression.

He speaks with a charismatic, Jamaican accent. "Hello beautiful couple! I am Kymani and dis hansum creature is Prince Navaro." The gallant horse wears head gear consisting of black leather straps with silver medallions and a long, blue feather that matches Kymani's.

"Hello sir. We're Zach and C.C. Would you be willing to take us for an extended ride through the park?"

"Shur ting, man. A glorious day to be alive, no?" Kymani offers his assistance to C.C. "Come wit me, pritty lady." He escorts her onto the waiting carriage with its plush upholstery and leather canopy. While C.C. takes pictures with her cell, Zach whispers to the driver and slips him extra money. When Zach joins C.C. on the velvety seat, he casually rests his hand on her knee.

I love this carriage ride already, C.C. thinks.

Kymani swings onto the driver's perch. A vase of fresh roses sits next to him. He picks the loveliest bloom and gives it to Zach. "You know watt to do, man. Tell di girl di truth."

C.C. looks at Kymani quizzically.

"Nutt'n beat a trial but a failure." Kymani winks at Zach and gives a hardy belly-laugh before the snap of his reigns sets Prince Navaro into a slow trot.

"What did he say?" C.C. says over the rhythmic clip-clop of the horse's hooves.

Zach inhales the fragrance of the rose. "I think he said I should tell you the truth."

"Truth about what?"

Encouraged by C.C.'s beguiling eyes, Zach continues. "Although we haven't known each other very long, I'm . . ." he hesitates.

"You're what, Zach?"

"I'm really glad I met you. I can't say what the future will bring, but let's make the most of today and enjoy the ride."

"You're so sweet. I know I will."

"I'm not sure you understand."

"What aren't I getting?"

"I'm not usually this forward. But I think you're special. You're the one I want to spend as much time with as possible," he says. His words possess such conviction, C.C.'s body tingles from head to toe. She accepts the long-stem rose and hides her face behind the softness of its petals.

Zach no longer speaks. He gently pushes the flower aside and studies her every freckle and delicate feature before softly brushing a loosely coiled lock of hair from her cheek.

Her green eyes shine. "I like you, too." *Is this a fairy tale? Will Kymani's horse turn into a mouse and his carriage a pumpkin?* She looks away before he can kiss her, which makes him want her even more. He likes the chase. Zach sits back and puts his arm around her. He trusts his gut. She wants to kiss him, too. And in time, she will.

"Ya man. Nutt'n better den dis ting called love." Kymani nods to a passing fellow carriage driver.

C.C. relaxes into Zach and soaks in the lush landscape. She drinks in the scent of the freshly cut blossom and thinks of Daniella and A.J.'s epic romance. *Is this that indescribable feeling Daniella wrote about in her diary when they first fell in love?*

Central Park's Cherry Hill teems with life. Leaves from towering trees lace the sky while streaks of golden sunlight flood the grassy hillsides. Joggers and bikers race. Couples on blankets study the shapes of billowing clouds. A young woman under an old, knotted tree reads a book while children frolic after butterflies or play with frisbees. C.C. observes the festive activity from her own glorious bubble, oblivious to the danger lurking in the shadows.

Unbeknown to Kymani, a young skateboarder has hitched a ride on the side of their carriage. He wears loose athletic shorts and a sleeveless, muscle shirt. His mop of stringy-hair blows in the wind. When C.C. spots him, she can't see his face. Sunglasses and a bandana cover most of it. Like an urban outlaw, he rides a Tony Hawk skateboard decorated with orange and yellow flames and an evil-eyed skull. With his free hand, he holds a cell phone.

"Zach, what's he doing? Is he taking a selfie or videotaping us?" C.C. turns her face from the camera.

When her body tenses, Zach reacts. Unsure if they're about to be mugged, Zach reaches for the punk. "Hey jerk, what the hell do you want?"

"Your woman, fool!" Having succeeded in what he came for, the kid laughs and lets go.

Kymani looks over his shoulder and sees the young skateboarder showing his phone to an older man who's slightly hidden behind the cover of a nearby oak tree. "Chicken merry, hawk deh near."

"What's that mean, Kymani?" Zach asks.

"Bad tings happen when ders too much merriment. You fine, Miss?"

"Just caught off guard maybe."

"No worries. Every boy spots pritty girl stare too much."

Not wanting to alarm the couple, Kymani keeps his thoughts to himself. He's seen plenty in the park over the years and senses the stranger wearing a Mets cap hiding in the shadows is trouble.

Zach rubs C.C.'s arm. "I'm sorry. I didn't realize you had a stalker. Was he there long?"

"I don't know. I was too busy daydreaming. Besides, the only stalker I want is you! I'm sure he's just an idiotic kid. He probably did it on a dare."

"Good call, C.C. You're amazing."

They talk effortlessly as the ride continues. Soon the event is forgotten. Kymani points out the park's fascinating landmarks. He explains how the Strawberry Fields memorial is an area dedicated to honor former singer, songwriter, and peace activist, John Lennon of the Beatles. Its focal point, a circular mosaic of inlaid stones, surrounds the single word, "Imagine." Kymani points to the historic Dakota Apartments on the corner of 72nd Street and Central Park West, where Lennon lived until he was murdered in front of the building in 1980.

Kymani explains Strawberry Fields was actually the name of an orphanage in Liverpool near the home of John Lennon's aunt. She disapproved of him playing with the children there and his response was always, 'It's nothing to get hung about.'

When the carriage approaches Bethesda Terrace, Kymani pulls Prince Navaro to a stop. Located in Mid-Park, it's considered one of the highlights of Central Park with a sweeping promenade called the Mall that leads to a grand terrace overlooking the lake.

C.C. snaps a series of photos. "It's a gorgeous sight, isn't it?" The sun-splashed water rivals the sparkle in her eyes.

"Yes, it is!" he says, never looking at the lake.

"Not me, silly! The water."

"No. Not the water. You! Let's get out and walk."

Zach offers Kymani a generous tip to wait and jumps to the pavement to assist C.C. "Have a nice stroll," Kymani says.

Zach holds C.C.'s hand and likes how comfortably they fit together. In the distance, they catch a glimpse of a man wearing a Mets baseball cap. He seems fixated on C.C., yet in Zach's presence, she's unconcerned by the stranger's sudden appearance. Zach pulls C.C. closer to let the intruder know she's with him. Both keep moving along, unaware that the man follows.

They stop to admire the famous Angel of the Waters statue rising from the terrace of Bethesda Fountain. The statue references the *Bible's* Gospel of John, which describes an angel blessing the Pool of Bethesda, giving its water healing powers. The angel carries a lily in her left hand, a symbol of the water's purity. C.C. thinks of L'Esprit's Whispering Statue and wonders if Zach would believe her if she told him about her studio's dramatic events of several months ago. *Will he believe the missing statue of Daniella Devereaux mystically reappeared and inspired me and my friends to solve the century-old mystery of the great prima's untimely death?* Uneasiness envelops her.

"You look like you've seen a ghost."

C.C. pushes the vivid memories from her mind. "I'm fine," she says. Although she's at peace with the hauntings of the past, the present suddenly feels menacing. As they stroll near the tree line, Zach leads C.C. on a well-worn path into the woods. The crack of branches behind them startles her.

"Why are you so jumpy?"

"I'm sorry. I don't know why. I can't explain this weird vibe."

"From me?"

"No, no. You're great, Zach. It's me."

C.C.'s relieved when two squirrels dart from the trees chasing one another. She forces herself to focus on Zach and his soothing voice. He holds her in his arms until he feels the tension in her body melt.

"I'm here for you, C.C. You're becoming a part of me." His words speak to her soul, and she slowly exhales. With her back against a tree, he presses his lips to hers. They kiss long and hard, and this time she doesn't shy away, his passionate caress seared in her heart for all time.

The man in the baseball cap quietly steps out of the woods, cell phone in hand. He angrily whispers, "Chill, Mercedes. They can't stay lip-locked forever. I said I'll take care of her, and I will."

SUGAR BABIES

Sugar Babies is a musical revue with book by Ralph G. Allen and Harry Rigby and choreography by Ernest Flatt. It opened on Broadway at the Mark Hellinger Theatre in October of 1979 to warm reviews. The show, a tribute to the old burlesque era, features swing numbers, a sister act, fan dance, and vaudeville dog act. Fast and funny, it ended with a patriotic number performed by the entire cast. The production included the hit song, "Let Me Be Your Sugar Baby," which inspired not only the Broadway musical itself but also the popular candy, *Sugar Babies*.

Chapter Nineteen

*B*rooke and I, adrenaline surging, walk through the hotel lobby keeping pace with Miss Aimée. "We're ready for anything. Where are we going?"

"When I'm in the city, I always try to fit in a dance class or two at the Broadway Dance Center. The training's top notch. I cleared it with your parents, Brooke. You can try a tap class. I trust you brought your shoes. However, you must promise to rest if you feel the need. Sound like a plan?"

"Oh, Miss Aimée, thank you!" Brookes cries. She stops our trio and draws us close for one of her ferocious hugs. "You're the best! How did you ever get permission for me to dance?"

"I have my ways," Aimée says. "Let's just say we all agree it's time for you to put on your dancing shoes again. Just remember, *don't* overdo it!"

"I won't. I give my word," Brooke says.

My friend has never been happier. She doesn't know that behind her back, Jarrell and his parents are half-hidden behind a potted palm. When they each wipe away a tear for Brooke's joy, I get misty-eyed, too. Wishing I had a potted palm of my own, I drop to the floor and pretend to tie my comfy, walking shoes. As long as I'm down on one knee, I whisper a heartfelt prayer of gratitude. Brooke's illness brought her so close to death that the arrival of this long-awaited moment is truly miraculous.

"Let's get going," Miss Aimée says.

When we step outside, we wilt. The sizzling heat momentarily sucks the air from our lungs.

"Welcome to New York City in July," Miss Aimée says. "The Broadway Dance Center is located between 8th and 9th on West 45th in an area that used to be known as Hell's Kitchen. Now it's an upscale part of town called Clinton or Midtown West. It's not too far away," she explains as we hustle along the busy sidewalk.

I'm excited when we take the shortcut through Shubert Alley again. The grand, old theatres give me chills. "I doubt that they do it today, but the performers of the past would often dash through this alley during intermission for a quick drink at Sardi's," Miss Aimée says.

"What's Sardi's?" I ask.

She points to a fancy restaurant at the end of the alley on the opposite side of the street. "It's a famous Broadway eatery and celebrity hangout. Look, there it is." We gawk like tourists and get a kick out of Miss Aimée's enthusiasm. "Trent thinks I'm silly, but there's something extraordinary about the energy here that I love."

"I feel it, too," I say.

"By the way," Miss Aimée says, "if you're hungry, we can always grab something along the way. That's the great thing about this city and Trent's favorite part of New York. The bodegas and food carts are plentiful and delicious!"

We arrive at The Broadway Dance Center and enter beneath its red canopy. Grateful for the comfort of the air-conditioned lobby, we're awe-struck by the renowned studio that, according to the inscription on its marquee, 'inspires the world to dance.' I'm intimidated by the photos posted of master dancers, teachers, and stars of the stage who studied in this legendary place. *Can I do this?* I'm suddenly terrified. I sense that Brooke feels the same. *What are we doing here?* Miss Aimée doesn't appear to notice our tumbling self-confidence. She's busy chatting with dancers and fellow teachers coming and going from the many cavernous studios.

We study the photographs of the illustrious staff and are awed by their impressive bios. According to the glossy Broadway Dance Center brochure, lessons are offered for every level of dancer, from beginner to professional. When we pass a group of women waiting for a class to begin, Miss Aimée asks, "Libby and Brooke, do these ladies look familiar?"

Brooke and I exchange glances and our eyes light up. "I can't believe it," I squeal, "you're the dancers from the Broadway show we saw two nights ago."

"Your performance was flawless, and you're so beautiful," Brooke gushes.

"We could never forget you! And that finale production number was the most spectacular routine we've ever seen! You looked like you were having the greatest time," I say.

Aware that we might continue babbling forever, Miss Aimée makes introductions. We blush when she calls us L'Esprit's gifted, prized pupils.

The dancers insist that they remember us, too! One tall, hazel-eyed, brunette proves it. "Aren't you two the cutest sugar babies? You were in the third row, center aisle seats." Another, with raven hair and a dazzling smile, thanks us for the lively applause we gave every dance number. "You made us feel extra special," she says. "Dancers often go unappreciated. You guys were the best audience *ever*! And we were super excited to have you and Trent Michaels in the house," she tells Miss Aimée. "Have fun today, girls."

"Thanks! You, too!" I say.

When the door swings open, we filter into an enormous practice hall. The walls are solid-brick, and its high-arched windows remind me of L'Esprit. Wooden floors appear heavily scuffed from years of dance classes. The room fills with at least a hundred extremely fit bodies, only a few younger than me. Based on how everyone moves and stretches, I'm certain they're all accomplished dancers.

Aware of my growing discomfort, Brooke touches my shoulder. "It'll be okay," she says.

"I'm sure I belong anywhere else on the planet," I say. "I hope I'm good enough."

We take our places with Miss Aimée in the middle section. I appreciate that she trusts us to handle whatever we're about to experience today.

For the next hour, Brooke and I suffer through another grueling warm-up routine. I'm mildly grossed out by the puddles of sweat on the floor from the overheated bodies that attack each stretch, contraction, and isolation with intense energy. I worry that if I can barely make it through this pre-workout, how will I survive the class? I feel the pressure and wish that I didn't. When the warm-up assistant leaves the studio, the master teacher enters, closely followed by a middle-aged woman carrying a bundle of sheet music. She takes a seat at an upright piano in the corner of the room. The teacher, a slender brunette with pink-rimmed glasses perched on the tip of her upturned nose, scans the dancers who greet her with a huge round of applause. She pretends to be overwhelmed by their display of affection and recognition. Brooke and I join in although we have no idea who she is. However, now that we're practically dead, she apparently deems us ready for her instruction.

"Who is she, Miss Aimée?" I whisper.

"Today's your lucky day," Miss Aimée says. "That's Marla Cross, a well-known Broadway choreographer. She only stops in to teach class once in a blue moon. She may be looking for some new talent for her next show. I hear it's going to feature some fabulous tap numbers. Darn it, C.C. should be here."

"If I pass out from the fear that's creeping up and down my spine, just dance around me," I tell Brooke who's rosy-cheeked and pumped.

"Don't worry," she says, "if you hit the wet floor, I won't let you drown."

"Z-Dug better be worth it," I mumble. "C.C. could ace this class, and she would love it," I say, slipping into my tap shoes.

"No kidding," Brooke says. "She's missing a golden opportunity. Let's show 'em what we've got and make Miss Aimée proud."

"I'd like to see your pullbacks, please." Miss Cross says.

Yikes! I hate those! We practice a few as a group and then one by one the professionals fly across the floor never missing a single sound. *Buh bump, buh bump, buh bump.* I swear I've never seen feet move so fast. Miss Aimée's are exceptional. I could watch her do hundreds and never get bored. From across the room, she waves. We're the last to go. Brooke's next, and I'm sad because she's been off her feet for so long. This isn't fair. But like a trooper, she gets up over her taps and begins to travel backward. Her first few pull backs are rusty but then they smoothly transition into clean snaps across the floor. I'm so proud of her. She actually gets a smattering of applause. I bravely step forward, turn my back to the opposite side of the studio, and rise over the balls of my feet. From somewhere deep inside, I hear Danny's voice remind me to "always have faith."

Miss Cross counts me down, "five-six-seven-eight," and off I go. Giving it all I have, I make it across the studio which has suddenly grown to the length of an entire football field. Miss Aimée and Brooke catch me, and I remember it might be a good idea to exhale. One of the show's dancers pats me on the back and I get a few thumbs up from others, but when Miss Cross tells me that I have excellent sounding taps, my knees go weak.

Brooke and I stick together through the rest of the class. It's mostly syncopated work and a lot of turns, all performed in hyper-speed. Miss Aimée and I keep a close eye on Brooke, but she never misses a step. All we're missing is C.C.

After class, we notice Miss Aimée and Miss Cross engaged in a lively conversation. Brooke and I linger in the background until Miss Aimée suggests we visit the dance store that we passed near the main entrance when we arrived. Feeling entitled to a reward for having survived Miss Cross's master class, we head for the gift boutique to put a small dent in our dads' credit cards.

"What do you think they're talking about?" I ask while sifting through a selection of Broadway Dance Center dance bags.

"No idea."

"It seems like an awfully high-powered discussion."

"I don't think Miss Cross has any other speed."

"Maybe she's asking Miss Aimée to give us both up for her next Tony Award winning Broadway show."

"Yes. I'm sure that's it, Libby. And Miss Aimée's explaining how L'Esprit will simply go out of business without us," Brooke giggles.

"Wait a minute," I say, snapping my fingers. "I've got it. I'll bet she wants Mr. Trent."

"Of course! You may be onto something. After all," Brooke says, "if she can't have us, I guess she could settle for Trent Michaels." We pay for three matching T-shirts, certain that C.C. will love hers.

"There you are, my pullback queens," Miss Aimée says. "Time to get back to the hotel. I've received a text that the convention will resume this afternoon. I'm very proud of both of you. I've always seen your potential, but today you proved it. Not every student your age could keep up with a room full of professionals."

"Thanks, Miss Aimée. This is a day we'll remember forever," I say.

On the way back to the hotel, we stop for lunch at the Brooklyn Diner. Miss Aimée warns that every portion on the menu is huge. Brooke and I play it safe and order bowls of chicken soup, having forgotten that Jarrell's was served with a matzo ball the size of his head. When the waiter places our bowls on the table, we howl with laughter. "Instead of calling NYC the Big Apple, they should rename it the Big Matzo Ball." I scoop the last tasty spoonful into my mouth, amazed that even a simple lunch of chicken soup is now a cherished New York memory.

Brooke and I bust into our hotel room anxious to tell C.C. about our morning at the Broadway Dance Center only to find it empty.

"Where is she? Should we text her?"

"She still has forty-five minutes. Let's give her a little more time."

"Do you think she even knows that classes are resuming?"

"Yes, Libby. I just checked my phone. I'm sure we all got the same notice. Don't worry. She'll be here. Right now, I need a shower. I feel like I've spent the morning in a swamp!"

"Yeah. Me, too! You go first. I'll listen for C.C."

Fifteen minutes later, a subtle bump on the door is followed by C.C.'s unmistakable giggle. I shush Brooke who steps out of the bathroom looking like a cute marshmallow wrapped in a fluffy, white *BCH* monogrammed bathrobe.

"Come here," I whisper, motioning to Brooke.

We both stand on our tiptoes taking turns peering out the peephole.

"Is that C.C.? What's she doing out there? Is she all right?"

"Oh yeah. She's fine," Brooke says.

"What! How fine?"

"Shut up. They're kissing."

"Move over." I shove her aside.

I take a peek and sure enough—they're making out. "Holy crap!"

Brooke drags me away from the door just as C.C. slides her keycard into the lock. We leap onto the bed striking an obviously fake pose.

"Hey," C.C. says. "I'm back." She throws herself on the bed not even attempting to wipe the giddy expression from her face.

"We missed you. Where did you go? You were never alone, were you?" I quiz.

"No dear, sweet, mother hen. I most definitely was not. I think I had the most romantic morning of my life. Zach took me on a carriage ride through Central Park. I've been there a million times, but it's never felt like this before."

"Like what, C.C.?" Brooke says.

"Like a fairy tale."

"That's exciting. Anything else?" I ask.

She changes the subject. "Did you know, Zach actually asked my parents' permission to let me go with him before he invited me? Everything's cool."

C.C.'s on cloud nine. We wait for her to spill the beans. *What was the kiss like?* But no such luck. I guess she wants to keep that part to herself.

"Wait a minute," I say. "Zach's super cute, but how old is he, anyway?" And should a judge be hanging out with a competitor, especially one who's up for Dancer of the Year?"

"Put your mind at ease, Libby. He's nineteen, and since he has nothing to do with the judging for the title, there's no conflict of interest. What about you guys? How did you spend your morning?"

We show C.C. her T-shirt and tell her about going to the Broadway Dance Center with Miss Aimée. When we get to the part about meeting the Broadway dancers and taking class from Marla Cross, her happy-meter dips. But when her cell buzzes with the name Zach Dugan, it rebounds sky high. Seeing my friend so happy is frosting-on the cake to an already perfect morning.

GOOD NEWS

Good News is a musical with book by Laurence Schwab and B.G. DeSylva. The original Broadway production was choreographed by Bobby Connolly. It opened at the 46th Street Theatre in September of 1927. Set in the roaring twenties, the show reflected the decade's jazzy sound and assertive, explosive beat. To emphasize the collegiate atmosphere, ushers wore jerseys, and the band reached the orchestra pit by running down the aisles as they shouted college cheers. "Varsity Drag" was its energetic, show-stopping hit number.

Chapter Twenty

As another day goes by, our dance schedules intensify.
"Hurry C.C.! You have DOTY rehearsals in thirty minutes."

"I know. I've got my special invitation right here," C.C. says. She shakes the letter in our faces. "Allow me to read it to you one more time."

We roll our eyes. "Do we have a choice?"

"Of course not." She laughs.

"Dear Dancer,

Good News! As an elite dancer competing for the national title of Male or Female Dancer of the Year, you will be participating in the highly anticipated Gala Night production routine. We are pleased to announce that this year's guest choreographer is

*Broadway's Tony Award winner, Steven Chen. We look forward
to seeing your performance.*

   Break a leg and Happy Dancing!

                              Clare & Howard Lexford"

   "So which title are you after? Male or female?" I say.

   "No reason to get snarky! I'll be happy with either one," C.C.
laughs.

   "Well then, I suggest you get your elite butt to class!"
Brooke says.

   The highest-ranked fifty regional soloists from across the
country have the honor of dancing in the production that's
showcased during the most festive evening of the competition,
Gala Night. I'm told it's a black-tie event that has the makings
of an extravagant, red carpet affair. In addition, the national
top scorers will perform their numbers along with last year's
titleholders. It's every dancer's dream to appear in the show and
rub elbows with the guest celebrity. Rumors range from Neil
Patrick Harris to Justin Timberlake.

   It's the climax of the season, a hot ticket attended by many
New York dignitaries and Broadway performers. Of course,
every dancer cheers for their own studios' competitors. Talk
about a nail-biting event; we can hardly wait to find out if any of
our routines will qualify, and especially if C.C., Jarrell, or Danny
will be named one of the new champions. I can only hope it isn't
Mercedes Slade or Whitney Ruthers.

   We say goodbye to C.C. at the rehearsal ballroom where
we find out that the DOTY contestants have exactly two hours
to learn the routine. Everyone appears ready for the challenge.
Brooke and I wait for Jarrell and Danny.

"Geez, Brooke. Is that Whitney coming our way? What happened to her hair? It's almost the same color as C.C.'s."

"Well, that's a shocker! And is that the long-lost Tia Murphy with her?" Brooke says.

When they see us, they stop.

"Tia, you're back! Whitney! We almost didn't recognize you," I say.

"Yeah. I wanted to change things up," she says, scrunching her hair.

"We're so sorry. We heard you were in the hospital," Brooke says.

"You've probably heard a lot of things, some of which are true. I have the bruised wrists and scorching sunburn to prove it. Thank goodness for body makeup and a high tolerance for pain. But I survived, and I'm fortunate to still be competing."

"How awful! Do you have any idea why or who did this to you?" Brooke asks.

"No, I don't, and I really don't want to talk about it anymore."

"We get it. We're just glad you're okay," I say.

"I know none of us have been the best of friends, but it's nice that you care."

Brooke and I exchange glances. We wonder if this kinder version of Whitney can be trusted.

"So, how are you, Tia? It's been a while," Brooke says.

"Doesn't she look great?" Whitney says.

"I haven't danced in ages, but I signed up to take Mr. Trent's performance class today. I'm a little nervous," Tia says.

"Don't worry, Tia, you'll be terrific," Whitney says. "I'll meet you after class. I want to hurry and find a good spot on the floor for the DOTY rehearsal. Have fun everybody, and take my advice: stick together and be careful."

Tia says bye, waves to Whitney, and leaves for Mr. Trent's class with another B-Bop dancer.

Just then, Danny and Jarrell appear. "A kiss for luck, ladies?" they ask.

Brooke rewards Jarrell with a sweet peck on his cheek.

I reach for Danny to do the same, but the moment's ruined when Mercedes and Skylar show up. "Hey, Danny boy," Mercedes smiles.

"I love you, Brooke," Jarrell says.

"Wait! What?" Brooke sputters.

While she's distracted by Jarrell's sudden admission, I overhear Mercedes whisper to Skylar before she walks away, "Remember to get chummy with Tia. I'm counting on you," and I wonder what she's scheming.

Mercedes links arms with Danny and takes him away. He frowns at me over his shoulder. Joined by Jarrell, the three enter the rehearsal hall. "Sorry, Bro, timing's everything." Jarrell says, rubbing his lip-glossed cheek.

"Sorry you missed your chance, Libby," Brooke says.

"Yeah. I guess kissing Danny will have to wait. We better get moving. We don't want Mr. Trent to start without us."

The soloists pack the rehearsal hall and are surprised when Steven announces the production number will be "Varsity Drag" from the 1920s show, *Good News*. When he explains they'll be playing co-eds in campy, collegiate-style costumes, he senses their lack of enthusiasm.

"I know what you're thinking. It's an out-of-date piece, but I promise you that it's a revamped, modernized version. Before this rehearsal's over, we'll make it new, and you'll love it! Trent's already taught you some of the combinations during his audition class. And, if you can't have fun doing the Charleston, then there's no hope for you," he teases.

Mercedes angles next to Whitney, desperate for information. "Weren't you a blonde? Red hair can get a girl into trouble. I heard you had a bad accident."

Whitney gives Mercedes a peculiar look. "It was no accident. And I don't know if my hair color had anything to do with it."

"Were you able to get a good description of whoever tried to hurt you?"

"I told the police what little I could remember, only it feels like there's more swimming in the back of my brain. I just wish it would float to the surface."

"That's terrible. I'm sure everyone's happy you're back. If I were you, I'd try and forget the whole ugly incident."

C.C. and Jarrell watch from across the room. "Danny, what do you suppose Mercedes and Whitney are gabbing about?" Jarrell asks.

"That's a head-scratcher. Mercedes usually doesn't bond with her competitors," Danny says.

"Don't I know it," C.C. winces.

When Steven turns the music on and demonstrates some of the roaring '20s-styled steps, the dancers' jaws drop. "Maybe this will be fun after all," Jarrell says.

While the DOTY's work on their piece, Trent Michaels' special performance class is attended by nearly every other senior level dancer. His allure as a Broadway choreographer automatically fills the ballroom. His dark, good looks don't hurt either. Even studio owners and other master teachers who have open schedules take a spot on the floor, eager to learn from the handsome legend.

Brooke and I join Mr. Trent on the raised platform situated in front of a large wall of mirrors. After briefly instructing Brooke about his music cues, he tells us to relax and follow his lead.

"Well, that's a little vague."

"No worries," Brooke says. "Mr. Trent likes to keep things loose. We'll be fine."

I trust that her confidence is well placed, and we won't end up looking like a couple of clowns.

Then Mr. Trent turns on the charm. "Welcome! It's humbling that so many of you want to take my class today. Thanks for the great turnout. I've been looking forward to dancing with you all week." Eventually, the hoots and cheers die down. "Let's hear it for my capable assistants, Miss Brooke and Miss Libby," he says. Along with the polite smattering of applause, he chants our names then comically twirls us each in a circle. He stops with a cavalier bow, and I respond with a curtsy that I immediately regret. It didn't take long for me to feel like a fool.

Mr. Trent directs the dancers into groups, and soon everyone is cast with roles to play. On his motion, Brooke hits the first song selection. He's masterful as he produces a mini musical comedy out of absolute chaos. We get a kick out of his goofy staging of a particularly athletic dance sequence until I notice Whitney's friend, Tia, limp off the dance floor assisted by Mercedes' sidekick, Skylar. When he calls a five-minute water break, everyone scatters, chatting and laughing. I overhear conversations singing Mr. Trent's praises and how this is the best class of the week, worth the price of the competition alone. Curious about Skylar and Tia's unlikely pairing, Brooke and I edge closer to our dance bags in order to catch some of their conversation.

"You're Whitney's friend, aren't you? How's she doing? I see she made it to rehearsals today, red hair and all."

"Yeah, I'm Tia. I'm her best friend, but she wasn't always a redhead. That's something new. And yes, she's had a heck of a week, but she won't let it stop her."

"Did she tell you about it, or who she thinks might have tried to hurt her?"

"She doesn't remember much, and I don't think she likes to talk about it."

"That's too bad," Skylar says, eager for details. "Everyone wants to know."

"Sorry to disappoint you. If you're looking for a scoop, there isn't one," Tia says.

Sensing Tia's irritation, Skylar switches gears. "By the way, I'm Skylar Wilkins. What's wrong with your ankle? Do you need some water or an ice pack?"

"Thanks, but no. I'll be fine. I haven't danced in nearly a year, and I'm sure I'm out of shape. But I miss it so much, and more than anything, I want to take this class."

"I hear you. Trent Michaels is something special, isn't he?"

"He really is! I studied at his Intensive in Chicago last year. Actually, I'd prefer he not notice me. Long story."

"I like long stories, Tia. What happened?"

"Whitney and I created quite the scene at L'Esprit. Let's just say it wasn't our finest hour."

"Isn't L'Esprit C.C.'s studio?"

"Yup. We're all from Chicago. But I attend classes with Whitney at B-Bop Studios, or at least I did."

"It couldn't have been *that* bad. I doubt that Mr. Trent would remember. He seems like a forgive-and-forget sort of guy."

"Yeah, but Whitney's fairly unforgettable."

"What kept you out of dance last year?" Skylar privately snickers. "Were you injured?"

"Not exactly, but that's an even longer story."

Skylar's phone buzzes. "Sorry, Tia. Gotta get this. It's Mercedes. They must be taking a break, too. I'm dying to know about their rehearsal. Take care of that ankle."

I listen to Skylar's side of the conversation. "What?" I hear her say. "Yes. I've been talking to Tia. I did ask if she knew anything more about Whitney, and she doesn't. She's sweet. Sounds like Whitney didn't tell her much. Why do you even care, and why don't you hound her yourself? How's it going in the elite room?"

When Skylar steps in our direction, we lower our heads and fumble through our dance bags. She continues her conversation with Mercedes. "That's ridiculous!" she says. "Why would they put C.C. front and center instead of you? You'd better step it up before you find yourself in the back row." Brooke and I stifle our laughs. Apparently, Mercedes doesn't appreciate Skylar's catty tone because the next thing we hear is, "Mercedes, no, *you* shut up!" Skylar clicks off her cell and flings it into her dance bag.

I can't stop myself. "Everything okay?" I ask.

"What do you want?" Skylar snarls.

"Nothing," I say. I count the imaginary daggers sticking in our backs as we walk away.

"I'm certain something's up," Brooke says, "but then what would a dance convention be without drama?"

We high-five our clever snooping skills but put our curiosity on hold when Mr. Trent calls the class to order. All is forgotten as we again become entranced by his creative mind and ingenious instruction. Inspirational writer, William Arthur Ward, once said, "The mediocre teacher tells, the good teacher explains, the superior teacher demonstrates, and the great teacher inspires." Trent Michaels obviously fits into the *great* category. What's not obvious is Mercedes' sudden interest in Whitney.

FOOTLOOSE

Footloose is a musical based on the 1984 film of the same name with book by Dean Pitchford and Walter Bobbie. It opened at the Richard Rodgers Theatre in October of 1998 with mixed, critical reception. A.C. Ciulla received a Tony nomination for outstanding choreography. In the storyline, dance is forbidden. A rebellious teenager defies the local pastor and calls for a rock-and-roll prom.

Chapter Twenty-One

*T*he next afternoon, C.C. *and* I walk to our room after a brutal ballet class with Baxter Banks. "Can you believe how he spotted out that poor dancer from B-Bop?" C.C. asks. "He told her he couldn't stand the sight of her flapping arms. What a jerk! Who says stuff like that?"

"Honestly, I'd die of embarrassment. She fought tears the rest of the session. I felt so bad for her."

"Me, too, Libby. Let's find Brooke and get outta here if even for a few minutes."

"Great idea!" I say.

In our hotel room, we convince Brooke to put down her favorite book and join us. C.C. and I quickly change into shorts, T-shirts, and flip-flops. "We have a few hours before the solo competition begins," I say, "but I'm glad everyone agrees that even a quick whiff of New York's stifling air will feel welcome."

C.C. breaks into a jog along the lengthy, winding hall toward the elevator. We race to keep up with her bobbing curls. When I lose a flip-flop, I stumble. "Way to go, klutz," Brooke says, nearly tripping over me.

We're more than a little slaphappy from being cooped up inside, and when the elevator takes forever to arrive, we start to giggle. By the time we reach the lobby, after stopping at practically every floor, we've dissolved into uncontrollable fits of laughter. Mr. Trent spots us falling out of the elevator and we attempt to control ourselves. He shakes his head. "I'm not even going to ask."

Of course, we find his comment beyond hilarious. Footloose and fancy-free, we skip onto the sidewalk with tears streaming down our faces. Amid the hustle of the Big Apple, we hold our stomachs and beg each other to stop.

"Thanks, guys," C.C. says. "I needed that, especially with my solo tonight."

"You're welcome, girlfriend," says Brooke.

I exhale realizing how uptight we've been. "Nationals is a lot more serious than I ever imagined," I say.

"It's true. For many, this competition is a lifelong goal that can make or break a dancer's dream. It's not hard to get your shorts in a knot," Brooke says.

"Your tinsel in a tangle," I add.

"Your . . . oh, I can't top that," C.C. says. "You two are demented. Besides, if I start to crack-up again, I won't have any energy left for my performance. Let's walk."

We wander around the historic Theatre District, stopping to admire each show's promotional poster. We imagine our names and headshots enclosed in the glass cases of the box office windows.

The temperature hovers at nearly one-hundred degrees, and soon we're ready to return to the comfort of our air-conditioned room. Just as we approach the Broadway Center Hotel, Mercedes exits the building, cell phone pressed to her ear.

"Let's hang back," says C.C. "This might get interesting." We shrink against the exterior of the skyscraper and are made invisible by the throngs of passing pedestrians.

"Where are you?" We hear her say. "No, I don't see a limo. Are you sure you've got the right hotel? I'm in hot pink shorts. You can't miss me!"

Just then, a shiny limousine drives up to the curb. The doorman rushes to assist while the driver, dressed in a dark suit, lunges for the trunk. A luggage rack miraculously appears pulled by an alert bellman. Mercedes flies into the arms of a stylish, middle-aged man who hugs her affectionately.

"Daddy! You made it. I was afraid you wouldn't be here for my solo."

"Honey, I know how important winning this title is to you. I would never miss your senior solo," Carter Slade says.

"I knew you wouldn't let me down."

We view the spectacle from the shadows. Mercedes' father has arrived, but he isn't alone.

"Excuse me! Can I get a little help?" The woman emerging from the rear of the limo is gorgeous. Blonde and super thin, she's dressed in a bare-shouldered, skintight dress that compliments her knee-high stiletto boots of soft, tan leather. Mercedes' happiness morphs into pure anger.

"What are *you* doing here?" Mercedes spits the words with all the venom she can muster.

"Mercedes, of course Avery came with me. She wants to be here for your solo and see you win as much as I do."

The plot thickens when an attractive brunette rounds the corner, nearly bumping into the threesome.

"Mom!" Mercedes shouts.

"I feel like I'm watching a bad movie," C.C. mumbles.

"Guys!" Brooke says. "That's Broadway star, Olivia Hampton-Slade." Although a seasoned performer, she's ingénue fresh. Her delicate features hide behind an oversized, floppy hat that compliments her buttery-yellow sundress and matching espadrilles.

We freeze like statues, afraid that if we move one tiny muscle we'll be spotted and somehow drawn into the Slade family soap opera. From the corner of my eye, I notice a man walk out of the hotel wearing a Mets cap. He looks at us before glancing at the Slades. But when Mercedes motions him away with an almost imperceptible nod of her head, he quickly retreats into the hotel.

"That was odd," I say.

"What?" C.C. asks.

"That guy. I'm sure Mercedes signaled him."

"I didn't see any guy." C.C. says.

"He probably just forgot something. Let's stick to one drama at a time," Brooke says.

Still in statue-mode, we hear Mercedes' mother say, "Hello, Carter. How have you been? Since the divorce, we hardly ever speak."

"Olivia, great to see you again," Carter says, seizing the opportunity to plant a polite, Hollywood kiss on her cheek.

"Oh, and this must be your little playmate, Avery. Mercedes described you to a T. You're striking in that outfit, but no one wears boots in New York in the summertime. You might want to peel those puppies off before you overheat."

"Not to worry," Avery says with a wink. "I'm never overdressed long when I'm with Carter. But thanks so much for your concern. It's truly heartwarming."

"Please," Olivia says, "don't let me hold you two up. Mercedes, let's go grab something to eat before your performance." She steers Mercedes away from the hotel, leaving Mr. Slade and the woman alone.

"Carter, I told you this was a bad idea. Your daughter resents me. And I don't need any snide remarks from your ex-wife either. Can't I just take the plane to Cabo and wait for you there?"

"Certainly not. We're here to support Mercedes. Try to get along. Be a good sport."

"I'll be good, but it will cost you." Avery warns, licking his ear.

"I'm sure it will. It always does."

"Ewwww! Gross!" I say. "How will I ever unsee that?"

"Wow. I'll admit it," C.C. laughs. "They're an interesting bunch."

"They say there are a million stories in the Naked City," Brooke says. "This one's a beaut!"

When the rear door of a second limo springs open, C.C. breaks away. She screams and embraces the distinguished, elderly gentleman who emerges.

"Grandfather! I can't believe you're here. I thought you were tied up with board meetings this week and couldn't get away."

"I know, Cynthia, but I decided that The Bailey Spice Company could carry on without me for a few days. You mean the world to me, my spicy Paprika."

C.C.'s face glows at the sound of his baritone voice, and we chuckle because her darling grandpa's constant spice-related nicknames always make her blush.

When he notices Brooke and me, we step forward. He gently pats the tops of our heads. "I'm happy to see you three are looking after each other. C'mon, ladies. Let's get out of this sweltering heat."

Together, we enter the coolness of the Broadway Center Hotel lobby. C.C.'s parents, undoubtedly aware of Preston Bailey's pending arrival, greet and escort him to his suite. With her family's support, C.C. beams like a newly named prom queen ready to rock-and-roll the night away.

FLASHDANCE THE MUSICAL

Flashdance The Musical is a stage adaptation of the 1983 film of the same name. The show, with book by Tom Hedley and Robert Cary, was choreographed by Arlene Phillips. It premiered in July of 2008 at the Theatre Royal, Plymouth, England. The musical toured the U.S. between 2013 and 2015, but an expected Broadway run was postponed due to the lack of available theatres and too many subplots. In it, the main character pursues her passion for dance and must perform the perfect solo.

Chapter Twenty-Two

☆

The darkening ballroom signals the start of the first round of senior solos. This all-important performance could seal the deal for C.C. The nervous energy is palpable. Everyone's excited: parents, teachers, and dancers alike. Even the judges chat more than usual, knowing that every number could potentially earn a solid ten. Scoring will be a difficult challenge, surpassed only by the task of ranking each dancer, a decision, I imagine, the judges dread. Except, of course, Baxter Banks.

According to our program, the boys will dance first. Guy Fisher emcees the event with his typical good humor. When he announces Danny's name, I get butterflies. The loud, thundering drumbeat of his music adds to my thrill. A slowly expanding spotlight casts shadows over Danny's chiseled form, enhancing every inch of his upper body. I admire his exposed, bronze chest and count his six-pack abs. My dad sits straighter in his chair and sucks in his stomach. My parents study my reaction, and I fight to hide my attraction. When you're built like Daniel Landry, the best shirt is no shirt. I'm sure that guilty pleasure is written all over my face.

He dances to war music from *Game of Thrones* and looks like a knight ready to battle dragons and conquer whatever he desires. My thoughts scream, *Let it be me!* I imagine every girl in the ballroom feels the same, especially Mercedes Slade. I want to gag when I notice her bewitching grin. *Why must she be so flawless?*

Like all dancers, Danny looks taller on stage. And right now, he owns it. His piece is captivating, not because of his undeniable good looks and intensity, but because of the complete power he exudes. Sometimes a dancer can hold a room hostage, and in my opinion, this is one of those times. The music and lighting, along with Danny's passionate choreography and artistry, command the audience to become active participants. His extraordinary moves equal the dynamic music, making it impossible to be a casual observer. Sometimes understanding a choreographer's or dancer's interpretation of music can be confusing, awkward, or even uncomfortable for the untrained eye, but Danny's performance resonates with everyone.

The audience responds with enthusiasm over his acrobatic pass across the stage. I count an incredible sequence of ten precise fouettés into several passes, followed by three barrel turns en lair. The judges appear spellbound. During other solos, some jot notes or share whispered comments. Not when Danny performs. He's as strong and convincing in the stillness of his routine as in its fullest crescendos. I can't believe he created this piece himself, and I'm so proud of him. Everything works!

C.C. and Brooke might think I'm partial, but he's brilliant in the spotlight. It's as if gravity pulls him down one second and then shoots him into space the next. He attacks each move with the cunning craftsmanship of a skilled crusader storming the castle gate.

Certainly, this is what such pioneers of contemporary dance like Isadora Duncan or Martha Graham had in mind. They believed dancers should have as much freedom of movement as possible, allowing for full expression. Danny fights tonight, not only to win the title but also to dance his finest. By everyone's reaction, he slayed the dragon, reached the tower, and saved the fair maiden—who incidentally will be played by me in the movie. I'm on cloud nine thinking that someone as good-looking and talented as Danny could be interested in me.

As the audience continues cheering, Danny exits the spotlight. Jarrell confidently enters stage right and strikes his opening pose. In the dark, he waits for his name to be announced. Danny may have won a battle, but if Brooke and I know anything about Jarrell, the war's far from over. He's more than ready to leave everything on the dance floor while performing his jazz solo or he'll die trying.

When the melodious beat of Michael Bublé's "Feeling Good" begins, the girls swoon. Jarrell slowly rolls his hips while rhythmically tapping his fingers against his sleek, black-brimmed hat. He's blindingly handsome, and I can tell Brooke is excited for him.

A complete change from Danny's attack-mode piece, Jarrell's solo is smooth, intricate, and stylized with long, fluid arm and leg movements. His extended hands and feet combine to accentuate the length of his masculine body lines and silky technique. When the saxophone plays, his turn and leap combinations astonish. No doubt his provocative smirk captures more hearts than we can count. He plays with his hat throughout the opening of the routine and then whips it toward the panel of judges. Brooke screams the loudest. Jarrell works his movements across the width of the stage, and hundreds of adoring eyes follow. He dances in a platinum-gray, fitted suit and skinny, black tie. Brooke chose the costume, insisting it made him look like a young James Bond, a man of mystery. Jarrell's dance gives me quite a rush, too. As he struts his steps, Brooke sings along with Mr. Bublé. "Oh yes, you know how I feel."

Someday audiences will pay to see him perform. I'm proud that Jarrell represents L'Esprit. With Miss Aimée's choreography and Mr. Trent's expert advice, his piece is sensual yet tasteful. His routine closes with a slow, swaggering exit. Brooke releases a myriad of emotions while stretching her fingers that were firmly crossed throughout his performance.

Attraction, whether to a person or an art form, is individual and subjective. Everyone responds differently to the qualities they see. Jarrell, just like Danny, appeals to all. Each of the twenty-five males that perform their solos are spectacular. The routines range from tap to musical theatre. The judges are clearly wowed by one dancer after another. Brooke and I agree we love watching the boys dance. But to be honest, none compare to Danny and Jarrell. Regardless of who wins the title, they all left their hearts on the stage.

When the guys' portion of the solo competition is over, Brooke and I use the short break to find seats closer to the judges' table. We hope to hear their comments and gauge their reactions while they critique the girls' performances. I can only imagine the drama taking place backstage. Whitney's scheduled first, followed by Mercedes. We search among the dozens listed for C.C.'s name and find it midway through the program. "Thankfully, she's not dead last," I say.

With the announcement of the next contestant, Whitney takes the stage. The flash of her newly colored, cascading curls still catches me by surprise. For an instant, I think C.C. has accidently taken Whitney's place. Seductive and spectacular, she wears the slinkiest costume I've ever seen. We reluctantly agree she looks fantastic in her dark-green velvet and mesh halter top with French, high-cut bundies that leave nothing to the imagination. Completing the outfit are her bedazzled character shoes and fishnet stockings with rhinestone embellished seams.

"She's bold! Appearing in front of thousands of people in your underwear takes guts," I say.

"Not so loud, Libby." Brooke pokes my shoulder, noting Mrs. Ruthers' presence a few seats away.

Whitney's nuanced, Fosse-styled, jazz number to a remix of the song, "Whatever Lola Wants," captivates. Except for the tiniest wobble on a set of turns that only the most trained eye would catch, her performance is spot-on, and she knows it. Casting charms across the ballroom with every refined detail and facial expression, her routine is fetching and unbelievably entertaining. Her confidence and comedic level are off the charts. I can't believe that I'm suddenly thinking she might actually be in contention for the crown. Mrs. Ruthers glows with obvious delight, and the judges look pleasantly pleased as well. B-Bop hoots and hollers as Miss Bea wipes away a tear, sensing the elusive Dancer of the Year title in her studio's future.

"Whitney sure brought her A-game," I say.

"Absolutely," Brooke agrees. "I've never seen her turn it on like that before. Red hair aside, she looks like a completely different dancer."

"She's got that same wow factor from the solo scene in *Flashdance*." I say. "It's like whatever happened to her earlier this week inspired her to dance without fear."

When the B-Bop dancers make a noisy, mass exit to congratulate her, Jarrell and Danny take seats alongside us.

"Whoa," Jarrell says. "I think I'm in love. Did my eyes and heart deceive me, or did Whitney just ace that number?"

Jarrell ducks Brooke's playful punch but isn't fooled by her exaggerated pout. "She's the ideal woman for you," Brooke teases. "We all know how warm and fuzzy she can be."

"I don't know her as well as you guys do," Danny laughs, "but man, oh man, she must have studied every Fosse move ever created. I'd love to meet her choreographer. That was totally impressive!"

"As far as I'm concerned, she gets points for not only wearing that costume, but also for her gutsy performance after her terrifying episode," I say.

Suddenly, there's a flutter of activity in the back of the ballroom. We turn to see the cause of the commotion. Danny clutches my arm. "It's Olivia Hampton-Slade!" he says.

The dark-haired beauty with big eyes and full lips is dressed in a chic, linen pantsuit. "Yeah, she's gorgeous." We saw her arrive this afternoon."

"I remember when she used to visit Star Struck before she hit the big-time in New York," Danny says. "She was nice to me, but I always felt intimidated around her."

Broadway's current gift to musical theatre takes a seat in the last row. Before we can process the importance of her presence, Mercedes' name is announced. Anybody who thinks girls can't do hip-hop as well as guys is undeniably mistaken. When Mercedes takes the stage, she steals the spotlight from every other competitor. Since the street-styles of popping and locking originated in her hometown of L.A., I bet her routine will be unforgettable.

As the lights catch Mercedes' silhouette, her opening pose and costume demand attention. She's fierce in a deep torso-twisting plié, an unmistakable predator's stance. Her strong and slender arms reach above her head as she extends long, clawed fingers that search for her next victim. When I witness the hypnotized expression on Danny's face, I fear she's found one.

Dressed in a one-of-a-kind, black, leather costume that fits like a second skin, her thigh-high, laced boot sneakers complete the racy ensemble. She puts Cat Woman to shame, and I'm uncomfortably jealous. Three, large, red diamond shapes run down the back of her bodysuit. Its open front reveals shimmering material that resembles a dew-dropped spider web. It's probably one of the hottest costumes I've ever seen. *Maybe after I kill her, I can wear it to C.C.'s Halloween party this year.* The design enhances her pushed up bustline while accentuating her tiny waist. Her ripped abs and sparkling studded belly button serve as the web's eye-catching center. To say I'm envious of how she looks and the effect she has on Danny would be a serious understatement.

The music and lighting ideally match her solo, and the crowd erupts when Rita Ora and Iggy Azalea's version of "Black Widow" begins. *Well I guess this song is ruined for me for the rest of my life!* For the sake of appearance, I clap along with everyone else, but who am I fooling? I could take a lap around the ballroom naked and Danny wouldn't notice me.

Mercedes' piece starts with slow breaking movements, followed by small disjointed pops and brief freezes. It's as if little electrical impulses gradually awaken the creature within. She has the judges fully entranced. Against my will, I'm pulled into her web of sheer talent. I can't believe how she's able to glide creepily across the stage in those specially made boots while keeping completely in character. Her routine involves fancy footwork and come-hither radial hip movements.

"Her body's sensitive to every beat," Danny whispers to Jarrell.

"That's 'cuz you don't *count* hip-hop, Bro." Jarrell slides his hands down his thighs. "You *feeeel* it."

"We get it. You're both *feeeeling* her," Brooke says.

As the music builds, so does Mercedes' choreography. She nails each step with precision, combining dynamic flexibility and isolations. She has the outrageous capacity to move any specific part of her body independently from the rest. Her feet firmly grounded with her chest down, she alternates between hitting the beat hard and moving smoothly through the music. She attacks the intricate steps as if her life depends on it. Her look says she's willing to do anything to make the judges her prey. She literally flies through the air during a tumbling sequence which seems to weave her web tighter. Danny's glazed eyes tell me she's bound him in her snug cocoon, and I wonder if he'll ever escape.

Sexy and aggressive, Mercedes is ready to bite off her victim's head. She whips her long neck and wild hair then suddenly drops to her knees and crawls toward the judges as if to say *I've got you now.* Jumping off the stage in a dramatic spider-like motion, Mercedes disappears into the dark amid screams and a standing ovation. I can't fight the truth. She's the most gifted dancer here. Surely, she'll win it all, including my Danny.

I feel an unpleasant sense of self-betrayal and I'm troubled by the realization of the massive amount of talent C.C.'s up against. *Can she compete at this level?* I know Brooke's having the same thought. Her face gives it away. I can't fault Danny for applauding until his hands tingle. When I search for Mercedes' famous mother, she's gone. I notice Skylar makes a quick exit to presumably congratulate her friend, and I imagine Danny itches to follow.

No one has much to say. What can you add to something like that? The quiet's unnerving. The soloists that follow are good but not great. So far, Whitney and Mercedes are definitely in the lead, but C.C. still has a chance. After all, she's the queen of tap and just needs to be over-the-top sensational. I want to tell her to let herself go and allow the spotlight to work its magic.

"C.C.'s next," I say, "I think I'm gonna be sick."

"Stay positive," Brooke says. "She's ready, and she'll nail it."

"She's a born performer," Jarrell reminds us, "and with this level of competition, it will push her that much harder." We huddle close and cross our fingers. My silent prayer asks that she excel and be happy with her performance. *God, please bless her on this stage tonight, and, Daniella, if you could smile upon her, I'd be grateful.*

Without warning, the lights restore to full power. The announcement is clearly meant to torture us: "Ladies and gentlemen, we will now have a ten-minute break."

"*Nooo!*" I say. "I can't take it!" I slump in my seat.

"Poor C.C. must be on pins and needles," Brooke says.

"Why don't you go and check on her, Brooke? I'll stay here with Danny and Jarrell. Maybe Zach's with her, keeping her calm," I say.

"On my way," Brooke says. She sprints from the ballroom.

"Give her a hug from us!" I shout.

"How much longer?" I ask Danny.

"Two minutes less than the last time you asked," he says.

"I'm seriously going to explode. These have to be the longest seconds of my life."

"Relax, Libby," Jarrell says. "The judges are returning. I'm sure they'll start any time now. Here's Brooke."

"How is she?" I ask.

"She's cool, calm, and collected," Brooke says. "Miss Aimée's with her, and everything's under control. Don't worry, Libby. Zach's there to wish her luck, too. We've all seen her routine, and she can perform it in her sleep."

"C.C.'s as ready as she'll ever be," Miss Aimée reports when she returns to the ballroom. "I'll sit with her parents and grandfather. Don't forget to cheer," she teases.

When Zach takes a seat between us, I ask, "Are you sure she's fine?"

He squeezes my hand. "Yes, she's more than fine. She's got this."

Guy Fisher's announcement gives me chills. "Now performing, Miss Cynthia Cunningham from L'Esprit Dance Studios, Chicago, Illinois."

The moment C.C. steps into the spotlight and strikes her opening pose, my foolish worries evaporate. If anyone's looking for center stage, it's currently owned by a sassy, long-legged dancer with bouncy, red curls and flashing, green eyes. When her midnight-blue costume catches the light, its hundreds of hand-sewn crystals sparkle like a million diamonds in the evening sky. I love the music she and Miss Aimée chose. Justin Timberlake's "Can't Stop the Feeling" has a swiftly changing tempo that showcases C.C.'s skill and artistry. Her flying feet, perfect riffs, syncopations, and distinct taps blend to form impossible combinations. C.C., in her element and having fun, is truly a vision to behold. She knows how to perform for an audience and seduces the judges with her astounding talent and enthusiasm. Her solo's exceptional, but it's her vibrant personality that lights up the stage. Her joy is contagious and brighter than any spotlight. No Dancer of the Year contestant ever projected such passion and showmanship. She's a rare and gifted performer, and I was wrong to ever doubt her. C.C.'s technique and confidence are skyrocketing tonight. I'm sure she's never been more radiant.

Every dancer's solo tells a story. Unlike Mercedes' where everyone sat in quiet awe, C.C.'s invites the audience to join her party. Spontaneously led by L'Esprit, the audience claps along, raising the energy level in the room. Even the judges join in. It's hugely unfair that ten minutes can last forever but C.C.'s two-minute routine passes like the blink of an eye. Of course, it's probably a good thing her number didn't last longer, or we'd all be dead from forgetting to breathe. A fast-paced series of turns followed by a flying cartwheel takes her to the edge of the stage and the end of her piece. When I sneak a peek at the judges, they sit bolt upright with jaws dropped.

All the spectators join L'Esprit in raucous applause. We shout until our voices give out. Brooke, Jarrell, and I follow Miss Aimée and C.C.'s family to the dressing area, but Danny and Zach stay behind. Zach, anxious to check C.C.'s score, heads to the judges' table. Danny's pulled away by his L.A. studio friends who want to celebrate with him and Mercedes. "Tell C.C. she was fabulous," he says. I promise I will.

We hug C.C. until she begs us to stop. "C.C., you blew the roof off this place! That was your best performance ever. But we have one question. When the heck did you learn to do a flying cartwheel? We never saw that coming!"

C.C. laughs. "A girl can't divulge all her secrets!"

Everyone talks at once, but I'm most impressed by her grandfather. He stands alone, patiently waiting. When we give C.C. space, she falls into his arms and no words are spoken. That's the voice of pride and love. Their bond has always been special to behold.

After the last soloist performs and the judges' scores are tallied, Guy invites the competitors to the stage. "I'm sure

Howard and Clare wholeheartedly agree this is, by far, the most talented group of dancers our convention has ever seen. Well done, one and all," Guy says.

Where most soloists including Whitney, Danny, and Jarrell nervously squirm, C.C. stands rigid as if paralyzed, and Mercedes, cocky as usual, looks bored by the inconvenient formality.

"The scores were extremely close, and this was a tough decision for our judges," Guy says.

"Just tell us already," I beg.

"At this time, it's my pleasure to announce, in no particular order, our top eight senior level scorers who are invited to perform at Gala Night and possibly be one step closer to winning the Dancer of the Year title. Please hold your applause until the last soloist is named.

The male dancers are:
Edmond Finney - Carousel of Dance Academy, Houston, TX
Tyler Gust - Art in Motion, Tampa Bay, FL
Jarrell Jackson - L'Esprit Dance Studios, Chicago, IL
Daniel Landry - Star Struck Studios, Los Angeles, CA

The female dancers are:
Cynthia Cunningham - L'Esprit Dance Studios, Chicago, IL
Chantel Robeson - Dropbeat Dance Center, Atlanta, GA
Whitney Ruthers - B-Bop Dance Studios, Chicago, IL
Mercedes Slade - Star Struck Studios, Los Angeles, CA

"Congratulations, soloists!" Guy says as he ducks for cover. We rush the stage screaming. C.C. leaps with glee into our arms, followed by Jarrell. I want to get close to Danny, but Mercedes already has him in her clutches. When Miss Aimée and C.C.'s family finally let her go, she looks for Zach.

I give C.C. her phone just as it buzzes. Her eyes brighten. The text reads, *Look up*. When C.C. lifts her head, Zach's standing on a chair above the packed floor. She deftly catches the kiss he throws and presses it to her heart.

Later in his room, holding his cell a foot from his ear, Vinnie listens to Mercedes' rant. "Dammit, you promised she'd never set foot on the stage for her solo tonight, but she did!"

"I've been following her for days. Her friends and that Z-Dug guy never leave her side. Besides, the hotel's crawling with security."

"And whose fault is that? I'm warning you, Vinnie, make it happen! If C.C. shows up at Gala Night tomorrow, you can kiss your future acting career goodbye."

GUYS AND DOLLS

Guys and Dolls is a Tony Award winning musical comedy set in Depression-era Times Square based on the short stories by Damon Runyon. Choreographed by Michael Kidd, it premiered on Broadway at the 46th Street Theatre in November of 1950 to nearly unanimous positive reviews and won a bevy of awards. The book by Jo Swerling and Abe Burrows spawned numerous revivals and a 1955 movie starring Marlon Brando and Frank Sinatra. *Guys and Dolls* tells the story of a couple of big-city gamblers and the women who loved them. Considered by many to be the perfect musical comedy, the original show ran for 1,200 performances.

Chapter Twenty-Three

The most festive evening of the dance season has arrived. For months, C.C. and Brooke described Gala Night as the ultimate extravaganza of my young life. I believe them because according to all the magazines, Stairway to the Stars Gala Night rates highest overall among the national circuit of competitions. It not only showcases the week's top scoring routines but also includes a surprise appearance by a famous celebrity. Another major feature is the blockbuster routine performed by the STTS teaching staff.

L'Esprit's small group lyrical, choreographed by Miss Aimée to honor Brooke's near-death experience and miraculous recovery last year is one of the routines chosen to be featured. Thrilled that it won awards earlier this week for outstanding choreography and best emotional execution, it includes C.C., Jarrell, me, and two others from our studio. It comes up early in the first part of the program, shortly before C.C.'s solo. Brooke and I have her costume set in a backstage alcove, and I'll be ready to help her make the quick change.

Because Brooke will be watching, and we want to make our studio proud, we're determined to focus on our performance. It's an intense piece, and we never take God's gift of our friend's healing for granted. I remember during her illness, the Allen family refused to curse the darkness. Instead, they embraced the light and inspired everyone to stay strong and keep the faith.

I can hardly wait to witness the expression on Grandpa Bailey's face when C.C. does her solo again tonight. I bet she'll be even more dazzling than last night. Nothing makes him happier than to see her light up a stage. He likes to say she doesn't need to chase the spotlight; it chases her. I'm told the hosts of the glitzy and glamourous evening are Howard and Clare. Mr. Guy Fisher will do the announcing, and Elena will begin the gala— like she does each year—with the traditional parade of studios. Dancers and family members arrive formally dressed. Many of the female dancers stand on the special red carpet outside the ballroom in their worn-only-once prom gowns. Most of the moms, including mine, wear fancy ensembles. Dads and brothers are handsome in suits and ties.

"Honored guests and male judges always dress in tuxedos," Brooke says.

"That's nothing," C.C. explains. "Wait until you see the women. The celebrities and judges are decked-out like they're going to a Hollywood bash. You'll see the most fashionable guys and dolls in town."

Although my pale-pink, floor-length number is embellished with beading at the neckline and waist, it's simple and subtle. "Hopefully, this dress is pretty enough to catch Danny's eye." I say.

"Libby, you have nothing to worry about. Danny's only interested in you," Brooke says.

"Yeah, but after seeing how he drooled over Mercedes' solo yesterday and knowing she'll perform it again tonight, I'm not so sure."

"With any luck, she'll get tangled in the web she weaves and eaten by Hagrid's giant pet spider, Aragog," C.C. laughs.

In preparation for the parade, the studios arrange themselves in alphabetical order. We find Miss Aimée and the other L'Esprit dancers in the middle of the pack. Whitney and Tia chat at the front of the line with Miss Bea. Carol Ruthers huddles among the other B-Bop families, her arms tightly crossed. Carol's aloof demeanor darkens when she spots C.C., Brooke, and me. I imagine she still suspects we played a part in Whitney's disappearance a few days ago. Either that, or she's completely threatened by C.C.'s chances of winning the title over her darling daughter.

"Never mind her," my mom whispers. "She's nothing but trouble."

We avoid eye contact. "I'm with you, Mrs. Nobleton," C.C. says.

"Well then, so am I," Jarrell says. He places a protective arm around Brooke, and we quicken our pace feeling the prick of Mrs. Ruthers' accusing eyes.

Jarrell's parents, Mr. and Mrs. Jackson, follow suit. But his colorfully dressed, six-foot-tall, audacious Auntie Coco, who's never missed one of Jarrell's performances, stops in her tracks. She flashes Mrs. Ruthers a death-stare worthy of the evil Lord Voldemort. "Is there a problem?" she says.

"Excuse me?" Carol says.

"You heard me, woman," Coco barks. "Pop those eyes back in your skull."

With an exaggerated sigh, Carol shakes her head and turns away. Jarrell, understanding their concern for Brooke, corrals his family. "Chill, Auntie. She doesn't scare us. She's the true definition of a bad dance-mom."

We join Miss Aimée and the rest of our studio, admiring how lovely she and all of our friends look tonight. Accustomed to seeing each other in rehearsal clothes or sweats every day, some of the girls are almost unrecognizable.

"Jenna! Your floral gown is gorgeous," I say. "The sweetheart neckline shows off your teardrop necklace and dangle earrings perfectly."

"I love yours, too, Libby." Jenna turns to face Brooke and C.C. "You guys would look pretty wearing brown paper bags, but, Brooke, that shimmering white dress is a stunning choice. And, C.C., your two-piece gray, satin gown is a knock-out."

Like most teenagers waiting to enter, many use the time for group photos to post on Snapchat and Instagram. I talk with my friends, all the while searching the back of the line for the Star Struck dancers. I spot Skylar in a violet lace, mermaid-style dress that accentuates her slender figure. Mercedes wears a one-of-a-kind designer gown. It reveals one bare shoulder and flows with cascading pastel ruffles that sweep the floor. Only interested in their selfie stick, they pose with duck faces and mile-long lashes, but I see no sign of Danny.

When the doors eventually open to the magnificent hall for the grand reception, dinner, and performances, the Broadway Center Hotel ballroom has been transformed into the most sophisticated venue I've ever seen. This year's theme, written in glittering letters, is displayed on a fancy, wrought iron easel. *Welcome to a Night of Stars & Elegance.*

When the ceremony commences, Elena, in a strapless gold creation, introduces each studio. We proceed into the ballroom one group at a time. Our teachers lead us to reserved tables accompanied by the sound of dubbed applause and camera flashes. Scattered about the room, judges and faculty clap and wave. Just as Brooke and C.C. described, they're dressed to the hilt. "Do you guys see Zach anywhere? I bet he looks hot in his Calvin Klein tux," C.C. says.

"No, not yet," Brooke says.

C.C. frowns.

"Maybe he's with Danny. I haven't seen him either," I say.

As we walk to our seats, my dad's eyes bulge at the sight of Miss Crystal LaMond's revealing outfit. It rivals something only J-Lo would dare wear. It has a plunging neckline and hugs her every curve. Thank goodness for the small handfuls of bling splashed in just the right places. She gives my dad a flirtatious wink. Mom good-naturedly leads him to their table to sit with the other L'Esprit parents. "Will, you can breathe now; the Cunninghams have saved our places," she says.

"I recommend you put your eyeballs back in their sockets, too," Coco chides.

One hundred tables are set with silver linens and midnight-blue napkins. Floral centerpieces, bead-rimmed charger plates, and crystal glassware grace every table. Sparkling chandeliers float above our heads, and soft lights glimmer from behind the draped chiffon that adorns the walls.

"This ballroom's ready for royalty. Could the guests of honor be England's William and Kate?" I ask.

I wait for Brooke and C.C.'s answers, but suddenly they're both admiring someone over my shoulder. I hear a "shhh" and turn to see Danny pressing his index finger to his lips. He holds the most beautiful bouquet of pink roses tucked with baby's breath. "These are for you, Libby. You're the most enchanting belle of the ball," he says.

I blush, and my legs go wobbly. "Oh, Danny! I love them. It's so thoughtful of you. I don't know what to say."

Danny bends forward. "How about, 'Thank you,' and a sweet kiss on the lips?"

Not wanting our first kiss to be in front of my parents and a thousand prying eyes, I shyly respond, "Thank you."

"And . . ." he says, leaning closer.

I hesitate. "Well, I, I could . . ." I look around and catch sight of my dad's raised eyebrows. What's worse, Mercedes and Skylar are watching, too.

"You could what?" Danny says. His eyes twinkle with delight.

"Um . . . promise to kiss your lips in private later?" I lick mine and feel flush all over.

"That'll work, Libby. Kiss me later," he softly whispers in my ear and walks away.

Oh, Danny. I have every intention of keeping my promise.

While other studios continue to be introduced, I reach for my chair. Every cell in my body tingles. My thoughts race. *What just happened?*

APPLAUSE

Applause is a Tony Award winning musical with book by Betty Comden and Adolph Green based on Mary Orr's short story, *The Wisdom of Eve*. Choreographed by Ron Field, the Broadway production opened in March of 1970 at the Palace Theatre. The story centers on aging star, Margo Channing, originally played by Lauren Bacall, who takes a fledgling actress under her wing unaware that she plots to steal her career and her man.

Chapter Twenty-Four

I return to Earth when C.C. and Brooke poke me to pay attention to the all-female international contingent from Mexico. It's fun to see them traditionally dressed in peasant blouses and richly-colored, embroidered skirts that swirl when they walk. Each wears a large, exotic flower in her hair and everyone applauds extra loudly for them.

"Don't they look great?" Brooke says.

"I'm so glad they'll be doing their routine again tonight," C.C. says. "They may not be the most fluent in English, but, Lord knows, they sure can dance!"

"And dance is the only language you need, right?" Brooke says.

"You mean other than the language of love?" I gaze at Danny.

"You and Danny are certainly speaking the same lingo. Drink some water," C.C. says. "Splash a few drops on your face, too. You

167

look a bit overheated." We take our seats, and I gulp a glassful while Brooke and C.C. find humor in fanning me. I bat away their flying napkins, hoping Danny's not watching.

Every place setting holds a fancy menu and program. The highest scoring soloists from the Mini, Junior, and Teen divisions will perform as well as last night's top Senior division soloists in contention for the title. Based on her technical growth this year, I'm not surprised that Whitney qualified. But I wouldn't be shocked if Mrs. Ruthers pulled some strings with Clare and Howard. She probably threatened legal action unless they made amends for what happened to Whitney. Although Whitney's solo is superior, she's lucky Brooke's not competing or there's no way she'd be on tonight's list. We keep our fingers crossed that after last year's winners perform and the grand finale production number ends, Guy Fisher will announce C.C.'s name as this year's female winner. I still can't decide if I want Danny or Jarrell to win the male title. I remind myself that the scores have already been tabulated. Each dancer's fate is sealed; their performance tonight won't change a thing.

"C.C., why are you so uptight? Are you nervous about performing?" Brooke asks.

"No," C.C. says. "I'm disappointed that Zach isn't here. I keep texting him, but he's not answering. He told me he had an audition but that he'd be back in plenty of time for the gala. He promised nothing would keep him away."

"Calm down. Maybe the audition ran over or he's stuck in traffic," I say. "He's crazy about you. He'll get here soon."

"Well then, you think he'd answer at least *one* of my texts," she says.

Our conversation stops when Howard and Clare introduce Guy Fisher. He steps onto the stage resplendent in top hat and tails. In his most grandiose voice, he addresses the audience.

"Ladies and gentlemen, boys and girls, honored guests, welcome to a Night of Stars and Elegance." He twirls before executing a light-footed triple time step. The audience applauds, except for C.C., who constantly scans the door and checks her phone. Guy continues with his humorous banter and opening act, but all Brooke and I can do is worry.

When C.C. goes to search the hall, I nudge Brooke. "Where the heck is Zach?"

"This is so unfair. He needs to get his cute butt over here," Brooke says.

"I was talking to him earlier when he got a text about a callback. He said it was odd because he didn't expect a response so soon," Jarrell says.

"It must be terribly important," I say.

"C.C. can always count on us and the rest of L'Esprit for support, but if I'm feeling let down by Zach, I can only imagine her state of mind," Brooke says.

"Shhh. She's coming," Jarrell says.

"We have a wonderful treat tonight," Guy announces. "I'm proud to present Broadway sensation, a rare recipient of the entertainment industry's EGOT—Emmy, Grammy, Oscar and Tony. She's New York's shining beacon of loveliness, Miss Olivia Hampton-Slade."

He invites her to take the spotlight and perform one of her famous tunes from her smash Tony Award winning musical, *Nothing Comes Easy.* The crowd rockets to their feet, the applause deafening.

"I guess a gal needs to sing for her supper around here." She kisses Guy on the cheek before taking the microphone and center stage. The audience welcomes her with a standing ovation, all except for two. When we prompt her, C.C. has the decency to rise, but Avery stubbornly remains seated and stone-faced. Carter, on the other hand, claps vigorously, ignoring his jealous companion who tugs his arm. He shakes her off and even adds a whistle. Mercedes scowls at the woman half his age but then notices me. She squints and brazenly mouths, *Loser*. I feel a nauseating flash of heat in the pit of my stomach and look away.

"Forget about her," Brooke says. "Mercedes obviously has issues."

"Her dad happens to be one of the wealthiest talent agents in the business. According to Auntie Coco and her favorite gossip column, the Slades split a few years ago over his involvement with the young bombshell," Jarrell says. "I guess Avery Harper not only landed a small part in one of his movies but also the leading role in his bedroom. Rumor has it, Mercedes can't stand her."

"Yuck!" I say. "We had the misfortune of seeing them in action yesterday. Even though Mercedes has been nothing but rude, I can understand her disgust."

"Thank you ladies and gentlemen," Olivia says. "I'm honored to be here this evening and sing one of my favorite songs, but just like the rest of you parents, I couldn't be prouder of my beautiful daughter and her studio. In fact, kudos to all the studios represented here tonight. You're doing phenomenal work. And Howard and Clare, hats off to you. You've outdone yourselves this year," she says. "I have a feeling tonight's gala will be like none other."

Perhaps it's because Zach's missing, but something about her words fills me with dread. Clare Lexford appears uneasy at the sight of Zach Dugan's unoccupied seat. She's probably concerned about how his absence will affect the teachers' number. I see her whispering to Howard and neither seem pleased.

"There's such exceptional talent here," Olivia says. She smiles at Mercedes. "From where I'm standing, Broadway's future has never looked brighter. I'm certain there's another Sutton Foster or Hugh Jackman out there ready and waiting to be discovered." Everyone applauds and screams louder than before.

"You know, this is how I got my start in the business. I'm a former Dancer of the Year titleholder, and it's one of my fondest memories. After I graduated from college, I was lucky enough to get a few jobs in chorus lines with national touring companies before landing my first leading role on Broadway. I even worked in Hollywood." She nods at Carter. "But my true passion has always been live performance. Who knows what opportunities Stairway to the Stars will offer you. I wish you all the luck in the world."

While everyone shouts excitedly, I'm perplexed. *Could the system be rigged? How can C.C. or anyone else possibly win the title over Mercedes Slade?*

"The song I'm about to sing is for lovers, old and new." Olivia winks at Carter and then turns with a mother's admiration toward Mercedes. Danny and the other Star Struck dancers cheer. The men in the audience stretch taller in their seats hoping the Broadway star will look their way. Olivia cues her accompanist and begins to sing. She's superb as she glides across the floor dancing and belting out her sultry song. No mother and daughter ever looked more alike.

"She's fantastic and completely gorgeous. Carter Slade's a fool!" Jarrell says.

She works the room, entrancing everyone with her melodic voice and elegant moves. When the chorus dancers from her hit show join the routine, we sway in our seats. As Olivia reaches the final crescendo, the audience leaps to their feet. The applause intensifies and only then does she take her final bow as the spotlight fades to black.

The pianist continues softly playing as Olivia returns to the main floor. She takes her seat among the other distinguished guests at Clare and Howard's table, but not before giving Carter a shrug, which seems to say . . . *At least the public adores me.* She sips a glass of champagne. I observe her expression sour and wonder if she silently curses the man she was married to. She then appears amused that Carter notices Steven Chen's congratulatory kiss. I chuckle when Olivia reacts unsympathetically as Avery, annoyed by Carter's longing look, kicks him under the table. The Lexfords, judges, and staff shower her with praise for a job well done. I'm irritated by Baxter Banks. *Could he possibly appear more bored? Is that miserable man ever happy? I thought only joyful people danced.*

The faculty table is full except for Zach's place. C.C.'s eyes are glued to his empty chair. She only glances away every few seconds to check her cell. "Where can he possibly be? He still won't answer." C.C. pounds the table in frustration. "If he's not dead, I'm gonna kill him."

THE GOODBYE GIRL

The Goodbye Girl is a musical with book by Neil Simon, based on Simon's original screenplay for the film of the same name. Directed by Michael Kidd and choreographed by Graciela Daniele, it opened in March of 1993 at the Marquis Theatre. The female lead was played by Bernadette Peters and marked Martin Short's Broadway debut. Tepid reviews considered the show a losing hand well-played by Peters and Short.

Chapter Twenty-Five

"*D* inner is served," *Guy announces.* "Our wonderful evening of entertainment will continue promptly at seven. Dancers appearing on stage should plan accordingly."

"Here come the wait staff, Libby. You'll love this! It's a favorite tradition on Gala Night. They perform a choreographed routine while serving our meal," Brooke says.

"It's always hilarious!" Jarrell says.

When the pianist strikes the first chords of "Be Our Guest," the waiters smoothly glide among our tables, balancing domed platters while singing and dancing. They lift the covers on cue and the entrées served taste delicious, but C.C. refuses to take a bite.

"Try and eat something," I say. "You'll need your strength to get through the night."

"I can't. I've lost my appetite," she says.

Brooke offers a buttered roll. Barely taking a nibble, C.C. looks at her phone for the hundredth time.

In the rear of the ballroom, Mercedes argues with the one waiter who performed poorly, having obviously missed every rehearsal.

"I didn't know I'd be walking into the middle of a Broadway production," Vinnie says. Rolling her eyes, she fights the urge to slap him. "You looked ridiculous, and why is *she* still here?" Mercedes whispers through clenched teeth. "You told me it was handled. Do you really want me to text Carter proof of your pool house romp with Avery?"

"Take it easy, Mercedes! The first part of the plan has already been executed, and phase two is underway. Be patient. You'll get what you want, and so help me, I'm not leaving until I get what I want, too. Delete that damn video once and for all and make sure your father has a spot for me in his next film."

"You need to go before my dad and Avery recognize you," Mercedes says.

"Don't worry. They won't. I'm that good of an actor, and right now, I'm a freakin' chameleon."

"What's up with Mercedes and that waiter?" Jarrell asks.

"Maybe she found a hair in her salad," Brooke says.

"Heaven help him if she did. With any luck, she'll let him live," Jarrell says.

When Mercedes returns to her table, she touches Danny's shoulder and whispers something in his ear while staring wickedly at us. They both laugh. When Danny looks my way, I get queasy. *Is he laughing at me?*

Pushing food around her plate, C.C. manages to swallow a bite or two. Jarrell, Brooke, and I know she's seething inside. Although we haven't known Zach long, his missing Gala Night seems completely out of character even for something as significant as an audition. After all, he made a point to tell everyone how happy he was about his solo in the faculty routine and how much he looked forward to C.C.'s performances.

"Maybe he does this sort of thing all the time," C.C. says. "Maybe he's just playing me." She wipes a small tear of frustration from the corner of her eye.

I'm furious. My friend doesn't need this boy drama on the most crucial night of her dance career, and I wonder if Danny is doing the same with me. He and Mercedes sure act cozy. I can't stand the way she constantly flips her hair and touches him. He doesn't seem to mind.

"No, C.C., I don't think Z-Dug's that way. He's too nice a guy," Jarrell says. "If you want my opinion, his feelings for you are real. I'm sure he'll have a good explanation for being late."

Suddenly, two strong arms wrap around C.C. from behind. "You ready for your big night?" For a split second, her face lights up.

"Hi, Mr. Bailey," Brooke says.

Masquerading her disappointment, "You bet I am, Grandpa," C.C. says. "Your being here means the world to me." C.C. stands and hugs him close.

"Cynthia, I wouldn't miss this for anything. I'm telling you, I have a good feeling about tonight. I bet you'll be crowned the next Dancer of the Year. And you know I have a good sense about these things."

"You're not biased, are you?" C.C. asks.

"Not a chance. You'll always be a winner to me."

We wave when Miss Aimée signals us to head to the dressing

rooms. We know our lyrical piece will be up quickly once the show opens.

"C.C., I'll text you the second Zach arrives," Brooke says.

Dressed in costume, we wait with other dancers in the holding area. C.C. checks her phone one last time before slipping it into her dance bag. Based on her expression, I keep my mouth shut.

On the main floor, the staff finishes clearing the dishes, and the houselights dim. Guy Fisher stands in the spotlight. From our vantage point, we can't see the first act, although we know it's a flashy jazz number. It won the high scoring production award with a large group of dancers from Charleston, South Carolina. We get excited when their music starts. We saw them rock it earlier this week, and based on the reaction in the ballroom, they're acing it again. We're disheartened that we won't get to see the Mini-division soloist from Minneapolis who follows them. She's cute as a button in her little navy-blue and white sailor costume and reminds us of the former, adorable child star, Shirley Temple.

C.C. high-fives the small dancer. "You go Little Miss Mini Ha Ha from Minnesota!"

"Thank you, Cthee, Cthee," the little tapper replies with her two front teeth missing. "Good luck thoo you, thoo."

For several minutes, we stretch and mark our lyrical routine. C.C.'s "the show must go on" attitude puts Jarrell's mind at ease. He huddles our group for a pep talk and searches our faces. "You dance nerds know I'm sad that this is probably the last time our original cast will perform together." He hesitates and clears his throat. "We've trained long and hard because this is something special to everyone at L'Esprit. As the only graduate of the group, I'm honored to have danced alongside each of you. I can't possibly imagine what it will be like to study somewhere else. I wish I never had to leave."

"We feel the same," Jenna says.

"This means more to me than any title. It's the culmination of my life growing up at L'Esprit. It represents not only the healing power of dance, but also of love and friendships. When I think of all we've been through and how we almost lost Brooke . . ." Jarrell trembles, unable to finish.

C.C. gathers strength. "Thankfully we didn't lose her. Even though we already won top honors for our small group lyrical, Jarrell and I want to slay tonight's performance. I can't tell you how proud I am of this number. Not only was it choreographed by our favorite teacher, it was dedicated to Brooke. We came together during an extremely difficult time and made it a symbol of our passion for dance and faith in God's healing grace."

"No other group of dancers will ever feel this way, because they never lived through what we did. Remember when we first presented it at L'Esprit?" Jarrell says. "The audience was moved like nothing we'd ever seen. Don't let go of what a gift pouring yourself into an artistic endeavor can do for others, and what receiving their appreciation can do for you."

C.C. looks at Jarrell. "I assure you, whatever else I'm feeling tonight, I'll give it my all."

"We don't perform for accolades—we do it for our love of Brooke, Miss Aimée, and each other," Jarrell says.

Our time on stage passes in an emotional blur. When we strike the final pose, our emotions are indescribable. Even Olivia Hampton-Slade rises to her feet. Brooke chokes back tears. Miss Aimée and Mr. Trent beam with pride. Deep down,

I know I've never danced this piece better. And I can tell the rest of our group feels the same.

I dress quickly and help C.C. change into her solo costume. She checks her cell phone, but there's still no new message from Zach. "I can't believe he's missing everything." She stomps her foot. "He's gonna miss my solo, too. I'm crushed. Why did he send this?"

She shows me his last text from 4:16 p.m. *Can't wait to see you dance tonight! See you soon. XOXO Z.*

"I don't know, but you've got to put Z-Dug out of your head." With C.C. this frazzled, I fear she might bomb her solo. I toss her the tiny screwdriver from her dance bag. "Don't forget to tighten your taps. And remember: you can do this with or without him."

"You're right. I can and I will! We have nearly thirty minutes before our solos are up. Tell Jarrell I'll be out soon to stretch." When I remind her that all of L'Esprit and her family are here for her, she stands tall, chin up, shoulders back. "Thanks, Libby. I want this, and I'm ready."

In the hall, Jarrell reviews choreography. "C.C. will be out in a few minutes," I say. "Break a leg, Jarrell! Remember, it's yours for the taking. I'll be in the front rooting for you! Oh, I almost forgot, Brooke told me to give you this." I kiss his cheek, and he grins.

As I head to the ballroom, I pass Danny and Mercedes who are preparing for their upcoming performance. Marking his dance, Danny never notices me, but Mercedes' cold shoulder keeps me moving. I don't stop to wish him luck.

I'm deflated, but Brooke builds me up. "You guys were awesome. Seriously, that dance touches me beyond words. I love it more every time I see it. Everyone literally went nuts. Your body lines were impeccable, and when my sweet Jarrell held you in his arms, the lift was exquisite. I still can't believe I was its inspiration. Did you give him a good luck kiss from me? Is C.C. ready for her solo?"

"Yes, to both questions."

"Zach still hasn't been sighted, and I'm really worried, Libby."

"Me, too. I haven't seen C.C. this wound up since you were in the hospital."

"She needs our positive vibes right now."

"She's not a quitter. She'll power through," I say, keeping my doubts to myself.

The next several numbers are sensational. When Danny's studio is up, he, Mercedes, and Skylar, along with other L.A. Star Struck dancers, perform a breath-taking ballet that won best senior level technique. It's a classical piece, and I'm forced to endure Danny and Mercedes' partnering. Their chemistry is undeniable. They even manage the impossible task of impressing Baxter Banks. Their studio must have an awesome ballet department to produce such skilled technicians.

Jarrell's next, and Brooke and I scream at the top of our lungs. The other L'Esprit fans whistle and shout. Although the audience goes insane and no one else sees it, when his music begins, Brooke and I notice he's slightly off his game. He seems winded and late on his entrance. "Oh no, Jarrell isn't as grounded and confident as he was last night."

"I see it, too," I whisper. "He's doing fine but not as well as usual. Why does he keep looking toward the wings?"

"He loves his solo, but he's behind on the music. Something's off. He seems distracted." A few more counts into the routine, Jarrell pulls himself together and dances with his typical style and precision. "As they say, 'It's not how you start, it's how you finish,'" Brooke says.

We both stand and clap, relieved that his performance ended strongly and his mishaps were minor. When Guy Fisher steps into the spotlight, he praises Jarrell's exceptional showmanship. "That young man is, without a doubt, Broadway-bound. I certainly don't envy the judges' job of selecting one guy and one girl for the title."

Brooke and I get the jitters when we realize C.C.'s solo is coming up fast, but before another routine finishes, a side door into the ballroom suddenly opens. A backstage attendant rapidly approaches Miss Aimée. Jarrell, wearing his L'Esprit hoodie over his costume, races to our table.

Guy, following his script, announces: "Next up, in contention for female Dancer of the Year, performing to "Can't Stop the Feeling," her award-winning tap solo, is Miss Cynthia (C.C.) Cunningham from L'Esprit Dance Studios, Chicago, Illinois."

Our L'Esprit family cheers wildly, but when her music plays, the spotlight's empty. C.C.'s the goodbye girl.

THE PHANTOM OF THE OPERA

The Phantom of the Opera is a multiple Tony Award winning musical with book by Andrew Lloyd Webber and Richard Stilgoe, music by Webber, and choreography by Gillian Lynne. Based on the French novel *Le Fantôme de l'Opéra* by Gaston Leroux. It opened at the Majestic Theatre on Broadway in January of 1988 and became the longest running show in Broadway history. It celebrated its 10,000[th] performance in 2012, the first production ever to do so. The famous set designs by Maria Björnson which include the falling chandelier, subterranean gondola, and sweeping staircase earned her multiple awards. In the show, the phantom behind the mask lures the female lead, Christine, to his lair beneath the opera house.

Chapter Twenty-Six

"**W**here is she?" *Brooke says,* visibly shaken.

"That's what I've been trying to tell you," Jarrell insists. "Nobody knows. She's not backstage."

I scan the room. "What do you mean? It's not like the Phantom of the Opera took her. She's gotta be here."

"I'm just saying, I never saw her. I looked everywhere. The crew paged her a dozen times. I was forced to run onstage for my solo at the last second."

C.C.'s music stops. After an awkward silence, Guy announces a slight change in the program and introduces the next act.

Howard and Clare appear mildly annoyed by the disruption. All of L'Esprit and C.C.'s family turn to each other confused. When the backstage messenger leaves, Miss Aimée scurries to our table in the dark and confirms Jarrell's story. C.C.'s missing from the line-up, and no one has a clue where she's gone.

"Libby, were you the last person to see C.C.?"

"Yes, Miss Aimée, I think I was. We were in the stairwell for her costume change. She was going to tighten her taps and join Jarrell to stretch before their solos."

"She never came out, Miss Aimée," Jarrell says.

"Did she indicate that anything was wrong? Is there something unusual going on with her tonight?"

"Um, yes. I mean no. I don't know, Miss Aimée."

"If you know anything at all, you've got to tell me. I'm worried sick, and I know her family must be, too."

Above the soloist's music, she repeats herself in a louder, more agitated whisper. "Well, Libby?" Scared, I look at Brooke and Jarrell. "The three of you," she demands, "in the hall. Now!" I've never seen her so mad. We leave the ballroom, aware of rude glances. Our pounding hearts mimic Miss Aimée's angry footsteps.

With our backs against the wall, Miss Aimée pleads. "One of you tell me what's going on, because her family will be out here any second, and they'll want answers."

Brooke fights to keep quiet and looks at Jarrell.

"Dammit, one of you start talking!" Miss Aimée demands.

"We don't exactly know what's happened, but she's been upset all evening because of Zach Dugan," I say. Brooke shoots me a warning expression.

"Z-Dug? What does he have to do with this?" Miss Aimée barks.

"Maybe nothing, but he promised C.C. he'd be here to support her, and he never made it," I say.

"He had an audition or something this afternoon but said

he'd return in plenty of time," Brooke says reluctantly. "C.C. was miserable when he didn't respond to any of her texts."

"Texts? Promised? Why? Is something going on with the two of them that I should know about?" she asks.

We feel horrible betraying our friend. C.C. trusted us to keep their budding romance a secret. "They like each other a lot. Maybe he called her, and she went to meet him," I say.

"Yeah. Maybe they just lost track of time," Jarrell says.

"This makes no sense! C.C. would never skip out of her solo for a guy, even if it is Zachary Dugan. She's too responsible," Miss Aimée says. "Let's hope it's nothing more serious, like Whitney experienced."

"What do you mean, 'more serious?'" Brooke asks. "You don't think she was taken like Whitney claimed, do you?"

"Security didn't want to create a panic, so we were told not to discuss it in too much detail, but Whitney's claims are true. Something criminal did happen to her."

I cringe, thinking the worst.

"Girls, go to that stairwell immediately," Miss Aimée says. "Look for any sign of C.C. And Jarrell, go and get Trent." She looks past us. "Here comes Preston Bailey with Mr. and Mrs. Cunningham. I have to keep them calm."

Brooke and I sprint backstage, searching every face for C.C.'s. We reach the stairwell where I last saw her and don't know if it's good or bad that her dance bag sits on the floor wide open. I rifle through it and notice her cover-up is missing, but oddly her cellphone isn't.

"How strange. She would never go anywhere without this," I say, holding up her phone. Brooke snatches it from me and reads the most recent text. "It's from Zach!"

Wonderland is a musical with book by Jack Murphy and Gregory Boyd, lyrics by Murphy, music by Frank Wildhorn, and choreography by Marguerite Derricks. The story is based on the 1865 novel, *Alice's Adventures in Wonderland* written by English author, Charles Lutwidge Dodgson under the pseudonym Lewis Carroll. Rewritten numerous times, the show premiered on Broadway at the Marquis Theatre in April of 2011. It's one of the few new musicals that failed to receive a nomination for any major theatre award. Due to poor reviews, it closed one month later after only 33 performances. Wonderland tells the story of a modern-day woman who goes on a life-changing adventure below the streets of New York City.

Chapter Twenty-Seven

Thirty minutes earlier

*A*ll is forgiven when C.C. reads Z-Dug's text. *Meet me on the 7th floor veranda. I have something special for you before you dance your solo. Hurry!*

What girl can resist an invitation like that? Remembering the flowers Danny gave Libby, C.C. asks herself if his surprise will be a bouquet or something small and simple like a kiss. She doesn't care. If he stole a daisy from a table centerpiece, she'd be just as excited. C.C. knows she shouldn't go alone but decides he's worth the risk.

C.C. throws her arms into her L'Esprit black and pink hoodie, mistaking the weight in her pocket as her cell. She slips out of the stairwell unseen, certain that if she hurries, she'll make it back in plenty of time to warm-up with Jarrell before their solos.

As C.C. steps off the elevator, she sees the elaborate doors that lead to the open veranda. The romantic oasis is dimly lit and sparsely occupied. Awestruck by the magnificent backdrop of the city's skyline and a million glistening lights, she spots Zach enjoying the view at the furthest end of the railing. She stops to admire him. For a tiny instant, C.C. wonders what she's doing here and experiences a flicker of disappointment when she realizes he's not wearing his tuxedo or holding flowers. His brimmed hat almost completely covers his hair and sits at a cocked angle. She curiously notes the snug fit of his leather jacket across his athletic shoulders.

C.C. steps closer to Zach, and in one swift motion he grabs her. "Do exactly as I say if you don't want to get hurt. You're coming with me. One sound and I swear, I'll toss you over this railing."

Oh my God, oh my God, oh my God. "Who are you? Where's Zach?" C.C. begs.

"No questions. You'll see your precious lover-boy soon enough. Now, keep your head down and for the last time, SHUT UP!"

C.C. struggles to break free from the man pretending to be Zach. When he pokes her ribs with something blunt and cold, she stiffens. When he jabs her a second time, shock sets in. *He's got a gun!* His upper body strength leaves C.C. with no choice but to comply. The man holds her with a vise-like grip and steers her into a nearby service elevator, pinning her into the corner. The slow descent feels like a ride into hell. The stranger seems eerily familiar, and a sense of recognition nags at C.C.'s tormented mind.

Having previously disabled the elevator's security camera, the man knows it plays a harmless, continuous loop in the main control room. When the doors open at the lowest level of the sub-basement, he carefully checks to make sure they're alone before hustling her to a cement block utility room in an abandoned section of the parking structure. The small, dark space reeks of paint and gas fumes. A scraping sound tells C.C. there's something or someone else trapped inside. When her abductor hits the light switch, C.C. nearly faints. Z-Dug's tied to a sturdy, wooden chair, his mouth gagged, his hands bound behind his back with zip ties. An ugly, purple welt forms on his chin, and blood oozes from a cut above his left eye.

"Now you two lovebirds can spend some quality time together," the man says. Pulling up an identical chair, he offers it to C.C. "Have a seat, Miss Cunningham. Don't make this harder than it has to be."

"You know my name? Who are you? What do you want?"

"I said no questions. Here's the deal. Sit down like a good girl, and I'll tie you two together. That's not so bad, is it? Follow my orders and you won't end up looking like him," he says, waving his gun in the air.

C.C. looks at Zach and can't imagine how he got here. *This is beyond crazy.* Zach's eyes beg, *Cooperate.* C.C., instead, twists out of her captor's clutches and reaches for the door. Zach's moan causes her to hesitate and in that split second, the man, with the force of a killer, pulls her hair backward and tosses her onto the empty chair. Before she can react, he yanks plastic zip ties around her wrists and gags her mouth.

"I warned you. Don't make me do something you'll regret," he says.

C.C. kicks furiously. The man easily side-steps her futile attempt to escape. With a wicked laugh, he straps her ankles to the chair. He flicks off the light and leaves. The heavy door closes with an echoing thud. C.C.'s absolutely certain that the click of the lock is the scariest sound she's ever heard. In silent darkness, she cries. *Am I in Wonderland? Into what horrid rabbit hole have we fallen?*

LITTLE SHOP OF HORRORS

The Little Shop of Horrors is a critically acclaimed Off-Broadway horror-comedy, rock-musical written by Howard Ashman and composer, Alan Menken. It's based on the 1960 cult horror film of the same name. The production made its Broadway debut at the Virginia Theatre in October of 2003. In it, a hapless florist's clerk buys and nourishes a Venus flytrap-like plant. The plant, the star of the show, played by a series of increasingly large puppets, originally designed by Muppeteer Martin P. Robinson, ultimately grows big enough to devour everything in its path. In the finale, the gigantic plant extends over the audience to snap its hungry jaws.

Chapter Twenty-Eight

"*Aimée, what's going on? Where's our daughter?*"

Troubled by the panic in Curtis and Julia Cunningham's eyes, Aimée wishes she could give them a straight answer. Sadly, she can only offer a less-than encouraging response. "I simply don't know. I'm told Zach Dugan is missing, too. They may or may not be together. No one knows for certain. I'm as concerned and confused as you are."

The conversation escalates when Preston Bailey joins the group. "There's no way she left on her own," he says. "I always feared this day would come."

"Why do you say that, Mr. Bailey?" Trent asks.

"Isn't it obvious? I'm an extremely wealthy man, and she's my only grandchild. Maybe someone took her for ransom. Didn't a different redhead disappear earlier this week?" His shaky fingers swipe his forehead.

"Oh, Dad, you haven't received any threats or messages, have you?" Julia Cunningham asks, her voice quivering.

"No, but that's not to say that I won't," he says. "When you were growing up, I always worried about you for the same reason."

"Dear God, Preston. Are you thinking the other girl was a botched attempt to get our daughter?" Curtis Cunningham asks.

Brooke and I race in. I give C.C.'s phone to Miss Aimée, and she reads Zach's last text aloud.

"Oh, that darn girl! Did she honestly give up a chance to win something she's trained for her whole life over a silly boy?" C.C.'s mother says.

"I know she's never cared about anyone this way before," Brooke says. "But I also don't believe she'd take off and not come back. I want to think she's safe with Z-Dug, but deep down I'm afraid for her."

"Me, too." Miss Aimée says. "C.C.'s too trustworthy to sneak away with a guy. Leaving without permission or a buddy is, in and of itself, a terrible lapse of judgement and a serious infraction of the rules."

"The thought of that young hip-hop punk making a play for my daughter somewhere in this hotel infuriates me. I'll beat the dance moves right out of that kid if he's the reason C.C.'s missing," Curtis Cunningham says, ready to explode.

"Let's not jump to conclusions," Mr. Trent says. "We all know C.C. This is totally out of character for her, and with

Whitney's disappearance earlier this week, we can't take any chances. Hotel security should be alerted in case there's something sinister at play."

"I'll inform the Lexfords," Miss Aimée says.

She winds her way through the maze of tables and dreads breaking the news to Clare and Howard. She stoops between the couple. "We have a problem," she whispers. "My student, Cynthia Cunningham, can't be located."

Expecting Clare's typical, drama-infused reaction, the announcement that another top contender for Dancer of the Year is missing is instead met with a dazed expression. "What did you say?" Clare whispers.

"I said we can't find C.C." Possibly due to the free-flowing champagne, Aimée guesses, rather than gala-ending hysterics, the Lexfords and Elena meekly stand and follow.

Once outside the ballroom, Miss Aimée and Mr. Trent explain the sequence of events. Elena speaks into the nearest house phone and asks to be connected to the Chief of Security. "They're on the way," she says.

Stepping forward, I ask, "What should we do?"

"I'm sorry," Miss Aimée says. "Our studio must be wondering what's happening. Go to your table and behave normally. We don't want unnecessary rumors spreading. Let's not ruin the show for anyone else, especially if she was simply swept away by Zach. Don't say anything until we have more details."

Brooke and I must look as uncomfortable as we feel. "Girls, we don't know that any harm has come to her," Mr. Trent assures.

"What if someone asks us where she is or where you guys are?" Brooke asks.

"Make something up. Say you think she's sick and went to her room. Tell them we went to check on her."

"This year's convention is rapidly turning into the Little Shop of Horrors. I told you, Howard, our nightmare's just beginning," Clare sighs.

CAROUSEL

Carousel, an award-winning musical from the team of Rodgers and Hammerstein II, is a successful follow-up to their blockbuster hit, *Oklahoma. Carousel* was adapted from Ferenc Molnár's 1909 play *Liliom.* Choreographed by Agnes de Mille, it opened at the Majestic Theatre in April of 1945. It's been repeatedly revived on stage and was made into a film in 1956. An immediate hit with critics and audiences, *Time Magazine* named *Carousel* the best musical of the twentieth century. Most critics agreed that Miss de Mille's American dance patterns made *Carousel* as much about dance as song. The storyline involves the main characters' lives spinning out of control, facing life and death. According to *New York Times* reviewer, Brooks Atkinson, *Carousel* is "a conspicuously superior musical play." Its theme of love and devotion is timeless and universal.

Chapter Twenty-Nine

*T*he hotel's *Chief of Security,* Ray Watts, fears another possible abduction ala Whitney Ruthers and springs into action. After alerting all available personnel, he instructs Clare, Howard, and Elena to return to the gala and keep it running smoothly. "Act as if nothing's wrong." He orders Trent and Jarrell to accompany his Deputy, Officer Clark, to the seventh-floor balcony. "You two know Miss Cunningham well. Take a look around. Report to me at once if anything appears unusual. We have first-rate surveillance equipment. If they've left the hotel, we'll know. I'll instruct my staff to scan the videos."

The Cunninghams, overwrought with emotion, are sequestered with Preston Bailey in the Chief's office. "I apologize for the accommodations," Watts says, "but I recommend you remain here until we figure this out. Keep an eye on your phones in case you receive a ransom call. Jane, my assistant, will stay with you and be in constant communication with me."

"We understand," Julia Cunningham says, her voice and body trembling. "Please find her."

"We'll do a sweep of the hotel first. If nothing turns up, I'll place a call to NYPD Detectives Grabowski and Rizzo. They're the lead investigators on the Ruthers' case and our backup if needed. Remember, it's entirely possible she and Zach are together having an innocent flirtation, merely caught up in the moment."

"You don't know our daughter," Curtis Cunningham says. "There's absolutely no way she would miss something this important over a mere flirtation."

"That's right," says Preston Bailey. "I want the detectives contacted immediately. In fact, I want the FBI. I'll make the call myself."

"Sir," says Watts, "that seems a bit premature. Have you received a request for ransom?"

"No," bellows Bailey. "But if it's the worst-case scenario, we're losing precious time."

"If you insist, I'll contact the detectives and have them speak with you as soon as they arrive. Right now, I'll take Aimée to the veranda, and we won't stop until every inch of the hotel is searched and secured. I promise you, if Zach and C.C. are here, we'll find them."

Aimée stops to hug Curtis and Julia and gives Preston Bailey a kiss on the cheek. "I've known C.C. since she was a toddler. There has to be more to this than meets the eye. Stay strong."

In the elevator with Chief Watts, Aimée decides that he's a person who knows his business. The Black man is completely bald, clean-shaven, and in his mid-fifties. He stands six-feet tall and looks to be about 195 pounds of pure muscle. She's curious to know if the gun strapped to his hip is loaded. "How long have you been the hotel's Chief of Security?" Aimée asks.

"I've spent my whole career in law enforcement, and I've been with the Broadway Center Hotel long enough to have seen just about everything." Having observed her sideward glance, he adds, "In case you're wondering, my sidearm is real, loaded, and I know how to use it." He radiates confidence, and Aimée's spirits rise with the ascending elevator. "Don't worry," he says. "No one's getting lost on my watch. We'll find them. That's a fact you can take to the bank."

The elevator doors part, and Aimée flies into Trent's arms.

"How's it looking up here?" Chief Watts asks. "What's that, Son?"

Jarrell reluctantly points to the floor near the edge of the balcony's railing. "Oh, no!" Aimée gasps. "That's C.C.'s headpiece for her solo costume. She was here. What does this mean? Where can she be?" Aimée breaks free of Trent to search the sidewalk below.

"Stop, Aimée. Officer Clark already checked. She's not down there," Trent says. He pulls her against his chest, chasing the gruesome thought away.

Watts' walkie-talkie crackles to life. "Chief, we've isolated something on the veranda's security video. It's grainy and the angle is limited, but you should come down and take a look.

The family identified their daughter. She's with a male, but his identity's uncertain. He keeps his head down and his hat casts a shadow over his face. We're checking the elevator footage now."

"Great job, Jane. Thanks. Send up Officer Tillman."

"Right away, Chief."

Clark bags C.C.'s headpiece and hands it to Watts. "Jarrell, this is a key piece of evidence. Good work. I would appreciate it if you'd return to the gala and join your studio. I'll have someone from my staff escort you. Say nothing about this to anyone. You never know who's listening. Can you do that, Son?"

"Yes, sir." *I'll go, but I can't promise to stay silent.*

"Go and remember: not a word."

Jarrell's certain that his sad face and slumped shoulders will invite speculation.

"Trent, I need you to accompany Officer Clark to Zach's room. Check if they're there. Aimée, this is Officer Tillman. You two do the same. Inspect C.C.'s room. If we're lucky, that's where we'll find them."

The walkie-talkie buzzes again. "Chief, Grabowski and Rizzo are here."

"Copy that. I'm on my way."

Jarrell rejoins us at our table. He fakes a smile to Clare and Howard and anyone else looking our way. The Lexfords play along with the charade.

My phone vibrates. It's a text from Danny. *Sorry to hear C.C.'s sick. I'm up next. Wish me luck. Kiss me later.*

If C.C. weren't missing, I'd be the happiest girl on the planet. All I can do is reply with a shamrock and kissy face emoticon. Jarrell sits next to me. "Please tell me that's Zach or C.C. you're texting."

"No, it's Danny. He dances soon."

"Jarrell, do you have any news?" Brooke asks.

Jarrell speaks quietly. His look of anguish terrifies us. "I was told not to talk, but I found her headpiece, and security confirmed her identity on surveillance with a guy."

"Was it Zach?" I say.

"That's the mystery. They can't be sure."

"Headpiece? Are you sure it's hers? I helped bobby pin it myself. That thing was practically bolted to her head," I argue.

"It's C.C.'s. I saw her initials."

"They have to be together. Maybe they got tangled up in another hot kiss and . . ."

"And what, Libby? I've known her a lot longer than you! She'd never skip out on her solo and just disappear. She'd never frighten me this way."

"Brooke, we know you're worried. We are, too. But it's not Libby's fault," Jarrell says. "We've got to stick together on this spinning carousel of madness."

"I'm sorry. Honestly, I am. I shouldn't snap at you. I'm screaming inside and hate sitting here pretending everything's okay when my best friend is missing!"

"I totally get it, Brooke, you've both been friends forever. I'm only trying to stay positive. I didn't mean to hurt your feelings."

"Has anyone questioned you two?" Jarrell asks.

"Yes. We stuck to Mr. Trent's script. I even lied to Danny because Mercedes was eavesdropping."

"Oh, that hateful girl! She'd love it if C.C. blew off the competition and ruined her reputation by being with Zach," Brooke says.

When the lights dim, Danny's solo begins. He's beautiful on stage, but one of my favorite people in the world has mysteriously vanished. I'm reminded of Daniella's disappearance at L'Esprit before she died, and pray that history doesn't repeat itself. Appreciating Danny's performance right now is impossible.

"Dear Lord, please help us find our friend. Keep her safe," Brooke prays. "C.C., where are you?"

"We'll get through this nightmare together," Jarrell wraps his arm around Brooke.

"Have they checked Zach's room?" I whisper.

"Or ours?" Brooke says.

"Security's on their way. I know it sounds terrible, and I'm sorry, but I heard Chief Watts say that the longer they're missing, the less likelihood there is of finding them safe."

"Did you have to tell us that?" Brooke stifles a sob.

"Then they better find them soon," I say.

"Mr. Trent and Miss Aimée want me to text and let them know how fast the show's moving and whether or not you've heard from C.C." From under the cover of the table, Jarrell sends the bad news. *No sign of C.C. or Zach. Teacher's piece up in 8 numbers.*

We watch the rest of Danny's routine through watery eyes and a haze of fear.

CLUE THE MUSICAL

Clue The Musical is an Off-Broadway musical with book and choreography by Peter DePietro. Based on the board game and the 1985 film, *Clue* opened Off-Broadway at the Players Theatre in December of 1997. Relying on audience participation and the clue cards drawn, the show has 216 possible endings. Reviews were mixed to unfavorable. The *New York Daily News* called it "excruciatingly unfunny" and quipped, "Inflicting such embarrassing material on a group of able-bodied actors and then supplying them with a variety of deadly weapons is a dangerous provocation." The show closed after only 29 performances.

Chapter Thirty

*T*rent and Officer Clark agree that Zach's unoccupied room offers just one clue, his empty garment bag. "It looks like Zach changed into his tuxedo expecting to attend the gala," Trent says.

After a quick but thorough search, Clark says, "I don't see any signs that they were here." "The bed hasn't even been touched." Trent winces when the officer adds, "If they were fooling around, it's unlikely that they'd take time to fix it."

"C.C.'s not that kind of girl." The doubt written on the officer's face infuriates Trent.

"I'm sorry," Clark says. "I know you believe that, but strange things go on in this hotel all the time. Teenagers pull plenty of crap you'd never imagine. Although, I'll admit, Stairway to the Stars dancers are typically better behaved than most. I'd hate to shock you, but I could tell you stories."

Trent, annoyed with the chatty officer, heads for the door. "I've been a part of countless dance conventions around the world in better hotels than the Broadway Center. I'd stake my life on it: C.C. would never deliberately violate the rules."

The bang of the hotel room door masks the officer's mumbled reply, "I'm sure she's pure as the driven snow."

"What's that?" Trent asks.

"Nothing. Let's go report to the Chief."

Several floors above, Officer Tillman's loud knock on C.C.'s door startles Aimée. "Miss Cunningham!" shouts Tillman. "Police! Open up. We're coming in." Waiting a heartbeat, he uses his room pass and cautions Aimée. "When I open the door, step carefully. If she's not in there, we don't want to disturb anything. In fact, it might be a good idea if you let me look around first."

While Aimée waits, her imagination runs wild. When the officer returns, his announcement dashes even the slightest hope. "C.C. isn't here. Come on in. Does everything look in order?"

She scans the cluttered space. "I guess," she says. "The mess of clothes, costumes, and shoes scattered about is exactly what I'd expect in a room shared by three teenage girls for nearly a week."

"I'm sorry," Tillman says. "I can tell you're disappointed and nervous. Fear not, Aimée. We'll find her. At least now we know where she isn't. We're done here. Let's not keep the Chief waiting."

In the Chief's office, C.C.'s family crowds together—scared out of their minds, angrier and more uncertain with each tick of the clock. After conferring with his officers, Chief Watts recaps the situation. "Here's what we know. Officer Clark found Mr. Dugan's empty tuxedo garment bag in his room. Surveillance video at 8:45 p.m. proves that C.C. was seen on the seventh-floor veranda in the company of an unidentified male dressed in street clothes. Although her costume headpiece was found, we have no footage showing where the two went from there. We're concerned some of our cameras may have been compromised. If she's been kidnapped, no ransom call has been received." C.C.'s grandfather concurs with a slight nod of his head.

"Other than that, our search came up empty, and although the pair is missing, they may or may not be together. Detectives Grabowski and Rizzo have been fully briefed. We are continuing the hunt, floor-to-floor. It's our belief that Miss Cunningham and Mr. Dugan are somewhere in the hotel. I'm sorry I don't have more information."

C.C.'s family, unable to fully comprehend the unbelievable turn of events, sits helpless and shocked.

Deep in the sub-basement, back to back in the airless utility room, C.C. and Z-Dug reach for each other's hands. Their fingers entwine, and he squeezes hers enough to let her know that he's okay. C.C. desperately wiggles her wrists and feels Zach doing the same. As she violently twists and turns in her chair, she feels the poke of a small object in her pocket. *Wait. That's not my phone; it's the screwdriver!* She remembers placing it there, intending to tighten her taps. *Oh, God. My solo! I'm sure I've missed it by now. My family and Miss Aimée must be frantic. This is bad. We have to break out of here!*

Victor / Victoria is a musical comedy with book by Blake Edwards, choreography by Rob Marshall, and music by Henry Mancini. Unfortunately, Mancini died before he could complete the score. The musical, based on Edwards' 1982 film of the same name, was a remake of the 1933 German film *Viktor und Viktoria*. The show opened at the Marquis Theatre in October of 1995. The musical starring Julie Andrews (Edwards' wife) was riddled in controversy when she made headlines for refusing the show's lone Tony nomination stating solidarity with the cast and crew whom she felt were egregiously overlooked. She also refused to perform at the Tony Award ceremony which was considered lackluster that year due in part to her absence. The story follows an impersonator who falls in love with the male lead. Is the impersonator a man or a woman? No one knows. *Variety's* unkind reviews read, "It's just no fun at all . . . an entirely joyless affair."

Chapter Thirty-One

⭐

After a small ensemble of contemporary dancers perform, Mercedes knows her solo's next. Alone in the dressing room, she applies one last coat of bright, ruby lipstick. The sudden vision of an elderly man beside her image in the mirror spooks her. Before she can scream, he covers her mouth. "The deed is done," the man says. "Your rival is tucked away and out of sight for the rest of the night."

Mercedes pulls his hand off her face and spins around. She studies him closely. "Geez Vinnie, you nearly gave me a heart attack. You really are a chameleon!" She frowns as she wipes the smudges from the corners of her mouth. "Did you have to mess up my lipstick?"

"I had to sneak past security to get to you, and I knew you wouldn't recognize me from my last impersonation of a waiter in the ballroom."

"The buzz of bewilderment was awesome when C.C. missed her solo!" Mercedes says. "And the look of irritation on the judges' faces, priceless. I'm almost home free as long as you, Vinnie, keep your part of the bargain."

"No worries, doll. Get rid of your phone's incriminating video clip, and I'm on the next flight to L.A."

"Oh, but our deal isn't finished yet."

"C'mon Mercedes, what else do you want from me? You put my job and future acting career on the line. I've delivered exactly what you demanded. Your feared competitor is out of the way."

"Hold your horses. Don't forget, Vinnie, the idea of a hitman was yours."

"Actually, if you recall, it was Skylar's. And anyway, it was a joke. You twisted it into your own evil scheme. I don't intend to get screwed over by you."

"Well, I'm not the one who fooled around with Avery in the pool house, am I? I'll delete your X-rated video but not until I win the damn title."

"Poor Mercedes Slade, you're a she-devil with an angel's face. What did Mommy and Daddy ever do to you to make you so vindictive? I can't help it if you don't win."

"Oh, I'll win! But I want you here to ensure C.C. doesn't show up first. Look on the bright side. This has been awesome training for your career. Consider how many different characters you played this week: a creepy plane passenger, NY tourist, bellhop, stranger in the park, waiter, and now this crotchety, old dude." She points her index finger in a circle around his face. "This is your most clever disguise yet." She laughs. "Why I bet you could even be the next Victor / Victoria on Broadway. Just wait until the show's over, then you can leave, and I'll lay the groundwork with Carter to give you a chance in one of his films. Maybe he'll even let you audition for a role in Johnny Shallows' upcoming movie. Daddy may not like to spend much time with me, but he certainly loves to give me what I want, and you know it."

"All right then, I'll double-check on the captives."

"What do you mean, captives? There's more than one? Vinnie, what have you done?"

"Let's just say I needed the perfect bait to set the trap."

Mercedes extends her palm. "That's enough. I don't wanna know."

"Fine. I'll wait in the ballroom until you get your precious tiara, but then dammit, delete the video once and for all and let me get on with my life!"

A crew member enters the room and calls Mercedes backstage. "Sir, you can't be in here," she says.

Mercedes quickly takes a whack at her acting skills. "Oh, I'm sorry, ma'am. This is my grandfather. He came to wish me luck."

"Well, Miss Slade, you need to take your place in the line-up, and he needs to return to his seat." She motions them both to move along.

"Oh, Gramps, a kiss for luck before you go?" Mercedes says with a demure smile.

Vinnie grudgingly obliges. When the runner turns her back,

he smacks Mercedes soundly on her butt. "You are a miserable brat," he whispers.

"Thanks, Gramps. I love you, too."

Exhausted by their struggle, C.C. and Zach let their heads touch. He gently nuzzles the back of hers. Even though C.C.'s terrified, she's grateful that she isn't alone and knows she can trust Zach to keep her safe.

This is all my fault. Zach was just the lure to hook me. But why? Who is that guy, and why do I feel as if I've seen him before?

Zach rubs her head harder. When her gag slips, she understands what he's trying to do. C.C. moves back and forth until both their gags loosen. Spitting the cloths from their mouths, they sputter and cough.

"I'm so sorry," C.C. cries.

"C.C. stop! You're all I care about right now. I swear, I'll kill him with my bare hands if he did anything to hurt you. Who is that creep?"

"Creep! That's it, I've seen him before. Maybe he's the guy Libby's been warning me about. I think he's been hanging around the hotel, and I'm almost sure he's the shadowy guy from the park. Don't you remember? I know I've smelled him before."

"What do you mean?"

"His cologne. It's overpowering!"

"What do you think he wants?"

"No idea, but he will never get away with this. If we could just break these zip ties," she says, twisting her wrists. "I have a screwdriver. It's tiny, but it might work. Try to pull my jacket toward you. See if you can reach your fingers into my pocket."

"Right or left?"

"My right. Please be careful. If it falls, I don't know what we'll do."

C.C. scoots her hips far to the right and feels his small tugs.

Slowly, Zach probes with his fingers until he finds the cold metal of the tool. He eases it into his hand and shouts for joy. "Got it!"

"Do you think it'll work?"

"It has to. It may take a little time, but it's our only chance."

"I know you can do it, Z."

The forceful rattle of the doorknob stops Zach cold.

RUMORS

Rumors is a Tony Award winning murderous farce by Neil Simon. The play, starring Tony-winner Christine Baranski, opened at the Broadhurst Theatre in November of 1988. Dinner, gunshots, police interrogations, and an incredible development in the basement ensue.

Chapter Thirty-Two

☆

When Mercedes enters the faintly lit wings, I'm sure she's disappointed that Danny isn't there, yet she pulls out all the stops when the audience erupts at the first sound of her electrifying music.

Danny sits at my side, his face fraught with concern. "What's wrong? Was my solo that bad?" He's shocked by the tears in my eyes and even more so when I tell him the truth about C.C.

"You mean she's missing?" He senses my panic and reaches for my hand. "I'm so sorry. I'm sure they'll find her soon. Try not to worry."

When Mercedes spots Danny holding me, her jealous fury ignites her performance. She dances her solo more seductively and with more aggression than she did the night before. The audience reacts with uncontrolled fervor to her jaw-dropping routine. When Mercedes leaps off the stage and slips away like the black-widow spider she portrays, even the judges stand and applaud. Olivia claps the longest for her incredibly gifted daughter and shares an embrace with Clare and Howard. Danny's focus remains solely on me.

"Hubba, hubba. Is she sensational or what?" Guy Fisher remarks. "Mercedes Slade, you stole the show. That routine was a masterpiece of precision and originality. Take fifteen minutes everyone. Our fabulous teachers' number, reigning champion's duet, and grand finale—followed by the Dancer of the Year presentation—will be up right after this short break. You won't want to miss a single second."

As the houselights brighten, Brooke and I do what we can to compose ourselves. Many L'Esprit dancers and parents rush our table seeking answers about C.C.'s whereabouts. Whitney's earlier incident has everyone on edge, and rumors fly.

"Is C.C. okay?" Jenna asks.

"We heard she's sick. Is that right?" A concerned dancer wants to know.

"Can she still perform her solo if she makes it back soon?" another parent asks.

We're relieved when Mr. Trent and Miss Aimée arrive. "Settle down, dancers. We're not exactly sure what's happening," Mr. Trent says.

"Is she in her room?" several moms ask.

My parents, aware that something's terribly amiss, ask, "Is she with her family?"

"We believe C.C.'s in the building," Mr. Trent says. "I'm sure everything will get sorted out soon."

"But what about the title? Is she automatically disqualified from the competition?" another dancer questions.

"No, no. They'll use her solo score from last night. Remember, tonight's just for show. Competition results have already been tabulated," Miss Aimée says.

"Let's all pray she makes it back in time for the DOTY production number," Mom says.

Listening to everyone speak at once, I close my eyes. *Hopefully C.C.'s disappearance isn't held against her. She's worked so hard for this night. But, if she's with Zach, she'll be in deep trouble. I'd rather he be the reason than something worse. Mostly, I want her to be safe. Dear Heavenly Father, help us find her.* When I open my eyes, inquiries continue to bombard Miss Aimée and Mr. Trent.

"And if she does win and isn't here to accept her award, what happens then?" someone asks.

I imagine Miss Aimée fears if she's not back in time, the judges will present her award to the next dancer in line. "Even if she's not here, the show must go on!" she says.

"This is bizarre. Has anyone seen her?" Jenna says.

Just then, the houselights flicker and Guy makes an announcement: "All STTS faculty members please proceed to the backstage area."

"Take your seats. I'll be dancing soon, and I expect to hear you cheering," Mr. Trent says.

Miss Aimée and Mr. Trent walk away as if they haven't a care in the world, but I know they're dying inside.

MEAN GIRLS

Mean Girls is a new musical adaptation of the 2004 film of the same name with book by Tina Fey, direction and choreography by Casey Nicholaw. The show premiered on Broadway in April of 2018 at the August Wilson Theatre. *New York Magazine* called it "hilarious, witty, worldly, and wise." *Mean Girls* is based on the *New York Times* Best Seller, *Queen Bees and Wannabes* by Rosalind Wiseman. In the book, you learn you can't cross a queen bee without getting stung.

Chapter Thirty-Three

L'Esprit's dancers return to their seats, and we're soon surrounded. Skylar taps Danny's shoulder. "What'd ya think of Mercedes' performance tonight? Was she or was she not on fire?"

"Yep. She's always great," he says.

"I wasn't sure you even saw me," Mercedes says. "How about a congratulatory hug?"

He offers her one arm, but Mercedes envelops him in both of hers. "We did it, Danny! We aced our solos."

"Yeah, I guess we all did," he says. He pulls away and looks across the table. "Whitney, you were awesome tonight, too." Brooke, Jarrell, and I agree.

The truth almost kills me, and I nearly choke on my words. "Mercedes and Whitney, both your solos were amazing."

Mercedes gives me a "tell me something I don't know" nod, but Whitney's sincerity surprises us. "Thanks, guys. That means a lot. Danny and Jarrell, I loved yours, too. I don't know how the judges will ever decide."

"I guess everyone did their best, except for poor C.C.," Mercedes says. "What happened to your friend, Libby? Did the level of competition scare her away?"

"In your dreams," I say.

"We noticed Z-Dug never made it tonight either. Do you suppose they skipped out to have a little 'alone time' together?" Mercedes says, motioning with air quotes.

"Everyone can tell he's hot for redheads. I bet even Whitney changed her hair color for him," Skylar says. Whitney visibly shrinks.

"She's changed her hair color lots of times. Big deal!" Tia says.

"Oh, Tia, you of all people should know what some girls will do to get a boy's attention. After all, you're the one who got knocked up and had to drop out of dance to have a baby. Isn't that right, Whitney?" Mercedes says.

"Yeah. Congrats on that," Skylar says.

Mortified, Tia fights tears. We sit awkwardly silent. "How could you?" she whispers to Whitney.

None of us, except possibly Jarrell who suspected it all along, knew the real reason Tia dropped out of high school and regionals. Breaking the silence, we offer our congratulations. "That's wonderful, Tia. A baby is always a blessing, no matter the circumstance," I say.

A small teardrop rolls down her cheek as she feels the full weight of Whitney's betrayal. "Thanks for telling the world, Whitney." Furious, she gives her friend an icy look before turning to face me. "Yes, thank you, Libby. You're absolutely right. My baby, Madeline, is a gift from above."

"I guess we all have our little secrets. Maybe Zach and C.C. are playing house like you did, Tia." Mercedes and Skylar laugh.

I bite my tongue, but Brooke speaks up. "What's your problem? Why do you have to be such mean girls? What makes you think they're messing around somewhere? Do you know something we don't?"

"If she's not sick, and not with Zach, I hate to think of the alternative. We'd never want a repeat of Whitney's unexplained episode," Mercedes says, grabbing Whitney by the arm. "We need to change into our costumes for the finale." Whitney looks nauseous. She glances at Tia who stands alone, her cheeks burning. Too late, Whitney realizes buddying up with Mercedes and Skylar was a huge mistake.

"Break a leg, Mercedes," Skylar says before returning to her seat.

"You guys should come, too," Mercedes says to Jarrell and Danny. "I'm sure Trent and Steven will have some quick formation adjustments since C.C.'s MIA."

"Go. We'll catch up," Danny says. In total disbelief, we watch the pair walk away. "Mercedes and Skylar were way out of line," Danny says. "Don't listen to them, Tia. You were brave to have your baby. It couldn't have been easy for you."

"We're sorry, too, Tia. You're welcome to sit with us," I say.

"No thanks, I'll watch with my mom and B-Bop friends," she says and walks away.

"I really do feel sorry for her, but with C.C. missing, none of this matters right now," Jarrell says.

"You and Danny have worked so hard to be here, and this is it: your senior year," Brooke says. "Go dance."

"C.C. wouldn't want you to give up," I say.

The boys leave, and Miss Aimée returns. She's never looked more stressed. Clare and Howard study her carefully from across the room. Aimée signals with a quick shake of her head that there's nothing new to report. C.C.'s officially vanished without a trace.

Guy Fisher once again takes the spotlight. "Ladies and gentlemen, it's that glorious time of the evening, the highly anticipated faculty routine is next." With a sweeping motion of his right arm, he steps offstage. When the first chords of their music play, the crowd rises to their feet, celebrating to the beat.

Brooke and I view the show-stopping number, praying for a miracle. Just yesterday, Zach playfully bragged about how excited he was to perform his solo section. But no such luck. He's not there.

Mr. Trent dances beyond expectation and improvises mind-blowing moves to fill in for Zach's absence. Even Mr. Banks turns several flawless fouetts in a row. It may have been a trick of the lighting, but I swear I saw him crack a smile. Myra Gold shakes her groove-thing with some assistance from Guy Fisher who gets in the act by partnering with her across the stage. Crystal LaMond literally works every part of her limber body from the tip of her head to her talented toes. Every teacher dances full-out. Being professionals, their number is phenomenal, but Brooke and I know how much better it would be with Zach. After sharing a few high-fives and final bows, they exit the stage.

When the audience settles down, last year's dance champions are introduced. They dance an exceptional contemporary piece. According to the program, they choreographed it themselves. The lyrics tell a story about missing someone you love and the pain of separation. The song hits too close to home for Brooke and me, and we both want to run out of the ballroom screaming C.C.'s name.

I cry, "We should be out there looking for her!"

"I agree," Brooke sniffles.

Miss Aimée squeezes our hands. "Girls, we have to let security handle this. I know it's hard, but we can't get in their way. I don't need either of you disappearing, too."

"I can't stand it, Miss Aimée. I'm so frightened. What if something terrible has happened to her?" I say.

In the darkness, C.C. and Zach wait, barely breathing. The door violently rattles one more time, then nothing.

"Do you think it's him?" C.C. softly speaks.

"Yes," Zach whispers. "Probably testing to make sure the door is still locked. Whatever he's planning, he's not finished."

IT AIN'T NOTHIN' BUT THE BLUES

It Ain't Nothin' But the Blues is a Tony nominated musical revue written by C. Bevel, L. Gaithers, R. Myler, R. Taylor, and D. Wheetman, based on an original idea by Taylor with choreography by Donald McKayle. Mr. McKayle was among the first Black men to break the racial barrier by means of modern dance. The show opened on Broadway at the Ambassador Theatre in September of 1999. The revue traces the history of "blues" music with more than three dozen songs.

Chapter Thirty-Four

☆

The lights in the ballroom flicker with the announcement of the long-awaited DOTY production. Several spotlights playfully crisscross in front of the sparkling backdrop, and the noise level raises several decibels as the individual studios acknowledge their favorite dancers.

"C.C. was supposed to be featured in the choreography," I say.

"Yes, Trent told me how impressed Steven was with her technique and showmanship," Miss Aimée says.

"What will happen now?" Brooke asks.

"They'll fill in the empty spots as best they can and keep going, just like we did when you were in the hospital, Brooke," she says.

"Got it! Even if our friend has disappeared and we don't know if she's dead or alive, the show must go on." Brooke quietly weeps. Miss Aimée holds her.

On cue, Guy Fisher announces the finale. "Put your hands together. You're about to witness the most spectacular routine of the convention. I'm telling you folks, it's sensational. With Steven Chen and Trent Michaels collaborating, let's just say you're about to be wowed. Ladies and gentlemen, I proudly present this year's Dancer of the Year contestants."

The frenzied cheers grow louder. The studios begin calling the names of their favorite dancers.

"You've got this, Mercedes and Danny!" Skylar shrieks.

"You're the best, Whitney!" The B-Bop dancers scream, all except Tia, who sulks with her head lowered.

"We love you, Jarrell," several L'Esprit dancers shout. I feel horrible because I can't match their enthusiasm.

"Tonight's winners represent Stairway to the Stars for an entire year and inspire greatness in each of us," Guy says. Again, screams fill the ballroom. "The performers you're about to see include our top male and female dancers from across the country who qualified at one of our regional competitions this year. The soloists showcased earlier this evening scored highest last night. But that doesn't necessarily mean they'll be crowned the winner. Any one of these fifty outstanding dancers could be awarded the coveted prize. The highest combination of their interview, audition, and solo scores, along with their classroom evaluations, will determine our new titleholders."

Guy seems to be stalling for time. I imagine Mercedes was right—Trent and Steven are busy making last minute formation and partnering changes because of C.C.'s absence. When Guy gets the thumbs up from backstage, he says, "I think they're ready. They're dressed to impress and eager to set this stage on fire. Performing 'Varsity Drag,' allow me to present the dancers vying for the prestigious title."

Brooke and I share a genuine, albeit fleeting, sense of happiness as Jarrell and Danny lead the pack. Everyone sells the rousing routine, dancing full-out. It kills us to know C.C. should be up there owning her piece of the stage. This routine was made for her. Our stomachs turn when Mercedes steps to center. She steals the spotlight from where we know C.C. belongs. It's hard to witness Jarrell and Danny partnering with the Star Struck diva. They play to the audience as though they love every second. I can tell Mercedes sure does. Even Whitney has a more integral part of the choreography as she travels downstage. C.C. told us Whitney was originally cast in the back row. The routine exceeds expectations. Dynamite dancers with lightning-fast feet dance up and down plexiglass steps that look slick as ice. They perform neck-snapping turns and impressive lifts as the routine builds. No one can tell that there's a hole anywhere because it's quickly filled by another dancer, but the hole in our hearts can only be filled by our friend. *Where on Earth are you, C.C.?*

L'Esprit's concern rises as others share our disappointment and frustration. C.C.'s truly vanished from the spotlight. I worry gossip will spread that she skipped out because of the threat Mercedes poses. *Darn you, Mercedes, for putting that notion in my brain.*

Brooke sets her eyes on Jarrell while I steady mine on Danny. He absolutely has the 'it' factor. He's simply too talented and handsome for his own good. Every DOTY contestant performs brilliantly, but Danny owns the show. I can't believe they learned and perfected this fantastic routine during a few brief sessions. I've no doubt it should be Danny and C.C. winning the title. Mercedes is awesome, but she's no C.C. Surely the judges would have learned that in the interview process, or by observing her work ethic and how she treats fellow dancers. Mercedes can't be the type of person the Lexfords want to represent STTS. *This is so unfair! I'm terrified. God forbid, what if C.C. wins but is never found?*

It's strange how your mind leaps from one random thought to another when you're half-crazed. One second, I want to remain positive and imagine that she and Zach will appear to announce they've been hired to dance in a movie together. That'd be a happy ending. In the next, I'm sure she's been abducted for ransom or something worse. I curse myself for watching too many scary stories on the Investigative Discovery Channel. Either way, time's running out. With each tick of the clock, I think of what Jarrell often says when he's down: "It ain't nothin' but the blues." If she doesn't show up soon, it will be too late.

MOVIN' OUT

Movin' Out is a Tony Award winning jukebox musical featuring the songs of Billy Joel, conceived and choreographed by Twyla Tharp. It premiered on Broadway at the Richard Rodgers Theatre in October of 2002. Although doomed by critics on the road, with Twyla Tharp's firm grip, the show garnered Broadway reviewers' praise, "True-heart original!" "Setting a new standard for the rock musical!" "Spectacular!" Unlike the traditional musical, *Movin' Out* is essentially a series of dances linked by a thin plot, and none of the dancers sing. The show, in essence, is a rock ballet.

Chapter Thirty-Five

*D*eep *underground, Zach's frazzled nerves* scream when the tiny screwdriver nearly slips from his blood-deprived fingers. While he performs the slow, painstaking task of sawing and prying the ties apart, he begs for guidance from every saint he can remember from his grade school days at Holy Angels Academy. In the disorientating dark, C.C. prays and blinks away tears. It surprises her how much missing her solo and a chance to win the title mean to her. She aches at the realization that she has upset her teacher, family, and friends.

"Talk to me, C.C. What do you think this is really about?"

"I don't know. Maybe he wants money. My grandfather is

Preston Bailey. He's a multimillionaire. After my parents, I'm his only heir. I guess he could be holding me for ransom."

"What? You're an heiress? Well, la-de-dah! I thought he was after me. This is depressing," Zach teases.

When Zach jerks forward to avoid her pinching fingers, they hear a loud snap.

"It worked! Good job! That was just the move I needed to break through."

"You're my hero, Zach."

"You're the ingenious one. What other girl travels with a screwdriver in her pocket? I'll have us freed if I have to chew our way out. Although, if I have to be trapped in a dark dungeon, I'm happy it's with you."

"Same here. No offense, it's just that the timing stinks."

"I don't suppose you have a Swiss army knife hidden somewhere?"

"Sorry. No. But I'll never leave home without one or a flashlight again."

The endless scraping continues. Just as C.C. doubts her prayers will be answered, Zach breaks through his second zip tie and frees his ankles. He immediately works on hers. He tugs and stretches the plastic until C.C.'s able to slip her tiny hands and ankles out. They fumble in the dark for the light switch and are blinded by the harsh glare of the overhead fluorescent bulb. The sight of her bruised wrists pains him, and he gently kisses each one. He holds her against his body with a ferocity that C.C. never knew existed. "Now," he says, "let's figure out how to bust through this steel door." Zach fishes in his wallet for a credit card. "I've seen this in the movies, but I've never actually tried it; have you?"

"Step aside. Let an expert show you how it's done. Before long, we'll be movin' out!" C.C. takes Zach's Visa card and carefully slides it between the lock and door frame. It takes a few tries, but the blessed sound of the click is unmistakable.

"You are an extraordinary woman of many hidden talents. Someday I'd like to learn how you acquired *that* particular skill."

C.C. beams. The pounding of her heart and raging adrenaline cause her to tremble. When she collapses against Zach, he scoops her in his arms. His tender lips calm her fears, and the intense kiss she returns ignites an eternal flame in his heart.

SHOWBOAT

Showboat is a musical in two acts with book and lyrics by Oscar Hammerstein II and music by Jerome Kern. It's based on Edna Ferber's best-selling novel of the same name. The show opened at the Ziegfeld Theatre in December of 1927. *Showboat* was a watershed moment in the history of American musical theatre marrying for the first-time, spectacle and seriousness. Compared to the trivial, unrealistic operettas, light musical comedies, and "Follies"-type musical revues of the 1890s and early 20th century; *Showboat*—completely integrated song, humor, and production numbers into a single artistic entity—creating a new genre.

Chapter Thirty-Six

Dazed, I'm consumed with thoughts of C.C. and Zach. "Libby, pay attention," Brooke says. "The production routine is finished. Let's cross our fingers for Jarrell and Danny."

Two crew members prepare the awards table and wheel an oversized mockup of a *Dance Star Magazine* to center stage. The massive magazine cover silhouettes male and female dancers where the faces of the first-place winners will soon appear. Clare, Howard, and Elena weave their way through the hopeful DOTY dancers crowded on stage and congratulate last year's titleholders. Contestants line up, anxiously awaiting the judges' decision. The convention's photographer stands ready to record the momentous event.

Guy grandly thanks the dancers and their families for another fabulous season. "I can't take the suspense. I'm told the results are extremely close with individual placements separated by mere fractions of a point." When the crowd quiets down, he continues with the highly-anticipated news. "This is it. Here we go! Our fifth-place finalists are Miss Kari Koontz from Vortex Dance Center in Phoenix, Arizona and Matthew Trellax from Creative Edge Dance Studio in Raleigh, North Carolina."

The pair bounds forward to receive their national honors. Along with hugs from Elena and the Lexfords, they're each given navy-blue championship jackets, scholarship envelopes, and Olympic-size embossed medals. Guy presents their teachers with colorful floral bouquets before ducking out of the way of their tearful celebrations and photographs. The audience erupts with spirited applause, but none louder than their hometown studios.

The tension builds as Guy announces, "Placing fourth are Chantel Robeson of Dropbeat Dance Center in Atlanta, Georgia and Edmond Finney from Carousel of Dance Academy in Houston, Texas." The two proud dancers step up and accept their awards.

Brooke and I share an awkward glance with Miss Aimée when Whitney Ruthers is awarded third-place with the immensely talented Tyler Gust from Tampa Bay, Florida. Whitney's disappointment is apparent; her smile doesn't quite reach her eyes. To her credit, she puts on a happy face as she accepts her award. Miss Bea, beyond jubilant, practically skips through the ballroom to join Whitney. Of course, Mrs. Ruthers hoots with pride as she approaches the front of the stage, her iPhone ready to Snapchat the universe about her daughter's newsworthy accomplishment. When she passes our table, we sense her frustration that Whitney wasn't named champion. She glares at us and mumbles.

"Did she just say what I think she did?" Brooke asks.

"Why? What did you hear?"

"I swear she said, 'Cunningham better not win.' I can't believe the nerve of that woman," Brooke frowns.

We forget our irritation when Mr. Lexford taps Guy's shoulder for a whispered conversation. The room becomes dead silent. Brooke and I sit frozen in our seats.

"Maybe C.C.'s back," I say.

Howard takes the microphone. "Please excuse the interruption. I know you're eager to learn the names of our top four dancers, but I simply have to mention what an unprecedented competition season it's been. Never in all our years have Clare and I seen such an extraordinary level of talent, nor have our runners-up and grand champions come from the same two studios." Star Struck and L'Esprit are certain it's their dynamic duos and scream uncontrollably. Jarrell and Danny remain professional, but Mercedes perks up as if she's already wearing the crown. She puffs her chest and lifts her chin with nauseating conceit.

On stage, Jarrell and Danny share a laugh and friendly handshake.

"Whether you're the pilot or my wingman, it's been a real honor, Jarrell."

"Same here, friend. Just wish C.C. could be here."

Those that never saw C.C. perform can only imagine Mercedes taking home the title. Of course, L'Esprit roots for C.C., especially Brooke and me. But when Guy speaks, his words take the wind out of our sails.

"Unfortunately, our female runner-up was unable to participate in the final portion of our gala this evening due to an unexpected situation. Our thoughts are with her and her family, but we still want to honor her by name. Taking second-place are Cynthia Cunningham and Jarrell Jackson from L'Esprit Dance Studios, Chicago, Illinois. And congratulations to Miss Aimée Harris, their teacher."

Although a major letdown, we applaud raucously. Jarrell's Auntie Coco does a little happy dance and shouts, "You'll always be first in my book, Jarrell!"

Miss Aimée hugs Jarrell and accepts C.C.'s award on her behalf. We continue to praise Jarrell, but we're distracted by the buzz of the spectators over C.C.'s absence. Brooke and I put on our brightest smiles for Jarrell's sake. The Lexfords, in certain turmoil, do the same. Their "everything is beautiful at the ballet" act is Academy Award worthy. After all, everybody's in the dark. I only hope that avoiding bad publicity isn't more important than finding our friend. If it were up to me, I would've shut this convention down and locked all the exits.

Brooke waves to Jarrell and blows him a kiss. Jarrell's lop-sided grin is devoid of joy and he looks lost as he poses for photos without C.C. at his side. Mercedes shines in anticipation of hearing her name. She maneuvers closer to Danny, and I'm not sure what she covets more: the title or him.

When the confetti canons boom, Mercedes and Danny are officially announced this year's Stairway to the Stars top male and female Dancers of the Year. Mercedes pulls Danny into the spotlight. The giant kiss she plants on his lips lasts way too long, and I'm crushed when he fails to resist. I can't help but look away.

"Congratulations you two, well-earned! You must be ecstatic," Guy says.

Mercedes snatches the microphone, "I am! I mean we both are. We actually won, Danny. It's a dream come true! We took first-place! We're the grand champions, and it feels FAN-TAS-TIC!"

Brooke rolls her eyes, "Get the obnoxious showboat off the stage."

Guy tries to wrestle the mic from Mercedes' grip, but she steps away from him and blabbers on. "For as long as we can remember, our greatest wish has been to stand side-by-side as the celebrated titleholders. We love this convention, our teacher, and our studio so much. And we love each other. Can you believe it, Danny? We won! We're grand champions."

Star Struck goes wild. Skylar hops up and down, unable to contain her excitement. Like a surging tsunami, the L.A. dancers edge their way through the massive audience toward the newly crowned winners. Avery's enraged when Carter and Olivia push her aside to share a victory embrace. Mercedes and Danny's similar display of affection leaves me sad and confused.

Skylar, intent on taking tons of pictures, shoves her way forward, holding Mercedes' one-of-a-kind, bedazzled iPhone. She stops at our table. "Don't Mercedes and Danny make the best couple, Libby? They really do love each other, you know. And Brooke, such a sore loss for your boyfriend. Shame about C.C., too. Rumor has it she ran off with Z-Dug. Redheads can be such tramps, can't they?"

Neither of us can take another second. When Skylar "accidently" trips over Brooke's foot, Brooke moves to slap her, but I hold her back. I can't say we feel badly when Skylar's knees weep with rug burns.

"Real mature, ladies. This isn't a grade-school playground." Skylar picks herself up off the floor. "Face it! C.C. wouldn't have won even if she cared enough to be here. You two are even bigger losers than she is." When she stomps away, she bumps squarely into the chest of an older gentleman. He pushes past

Skylar and fumbles to reattach his mustache. Carter looks at him suspiciously.

"Hey, watch it mister!" Skylar says, searching the man's face. His eyes look familiar and much too clear for someone of his advanced age. He says nothing.

"Wait a minute," she tugs his arm. "Do I know you?" Again, he doesn't say a word. His eyes are drawn to the jeweled cell phone she's holding.

Above the cheers and celebration, a high-pitched voice cuts through the chaos. "PLEASE! SOMEBODY HELP US!"

DEATHTRAP

Deathtrap is a comedy-thriller written by Ira Levin. It opened at the Music Box Theatre in February of 1978 to mixed reviews from the *New York Times.* One critic wrote that it contained effrontery everywhere and fun straight through. However, another panned the play. *Deathtrap* was adapted into a film of the same name in 1982. The show combines components of a thriller, horror, murder, deceit, innocent dialogue with hidden sinister meaning, and plot reversal with unexpected turns of events. *Deathtrap* holds the record for the longest running comedy-thriller on Broadway.

Chapter Thirty-Seven

The DOTYs on stage notice the commotion and point to the rear of the ballroom. Brooke and I climb on our chairs for a better view. Suddenly, the kitchen doors swing open, and spectators split like the parting of the Red Sea. Two terrified and disheveled individuals burst into the ballroom.

"It's Zach and C.C.!" Brooke cries.

"WE WERE KIDNAPPED!" Zach shouts.

Chief Watts' walkie-talkie squeaks and sputters. "Chief, you're needed at the gala. Bring C.C.'s family ASAP." Watts speculates about the urgency of the message as he sprints to the elevator, closely followed by the Cunninghams and Preston Bailey.

Blinded by the spotlight, Mercedes ignores the disruption. She continues talking until Danny grabs the microphone. He squints past the light. "Zach, C.C., is that you?"

Clare and Howard, shocked by the disturbance, stare at each other in disbelief.

"It's them!" Jarrell says before leaping off the stage.

"What's going on?" Howard demands. Clare wobbles as if ready to faint, but Guy reacts quickly and steadies her in his arms.

Miss Aimée blocks the glare of the lights. "Can you see them, Howard?" she gasps. "Please tell me it's C.C."

Guy takes charge of the situation. "Stop the show!"

Mercedes' eyes double in size. "No! This is *my* night, *my* prize! I earned it. I deserve it!"

As Brooke and I race toward C.C., the stranger, who's been fixated on the phone in Skylar's hand, lunges for it.

"Get him!" Skylar says. "He's stealing Mercedes' cell!" She dashes after the man and reaches for the phone, but the stranger yanks it away and bolts for the door. Skylar doesn't give up. She jumps onto the nearest chair then dashes across the table in two long strides, scattering dishes, flatware, and glasses in her wake. She flies through the air and lands on the man's back. As they fall to the floor, she clutches his head. Skylar shrieks when she realizes she's holding a handful of gray hair. "It's a wig!" she screams.

The man scrambles to escape, but it's my bad luck when I block his path. When he knocks me down, the force of our collision causes Mercedes' iPhone to soar. At the same instant, another one drops from his pocket. Skylar dives for it. In a split second, the man pulls me to my feet, swoops an arm around my neck, and roughly pokes something sharp into my back. "You're coming with me," he says.

Brooke screams. "He's taking Libby!"

I shake my head and mouth, "*He's got a gun.*"

"Wait. This isn't Mercedes' phone!" Skylar shouts.

Brooke recognizes it instantly. "That's Zach's!"

"Get him!" Skylar yells.

"Who cares about the stupid phone? He has Libby!" Brooke cries.

The outburst gets the full attention of Carter, Olivia, and Avery. Skylar studies the face of the man whose gray mustache dangles precariously. Having a crush on him for as long as she can remember, she recognizes his eyes and scent. "Wait, Vinnie, is that you?"

Dragging me along, the man panics and tightens his grip.

"I knew it! It is you, Vinnie!" Skylar yelps. "What's going on? Why are you ruining Mercedes' big night?"

"You ignorant fool! You're the one ruining everything!"

"Vincent Wilde!" Carter barks. "What the hell are you doing here, and why are you wearing that ridiculous disguise? Have you lost your mind? Release that poor girl!"

Avery laughs. "Carter, it's so hard to find good help these days." She winks at Vinnie.

Guy Fisher makes his demands clear. "Turn up the houselights at once! Quiet everyone!"

Mercedes witnesses her plan unravel. Sensing Vinnie's about to get caught and confess, she shouts over the mic, "Skylar, give me my phone!"

Skylar shrugs. "I don't have it." She points to Vinnie, who waves it above his head.

"Is this what you're looking for?" he shouts while police and security surround us.

Suddenly, my father appears out of nowhere.

"No, Dad! He's got a gun!" I shout.

Without fear or forethought, my dad blindsides the man to the ground with a football tackle move from his high school days. As they wrestle to their feet, Detectives Grabowski and Rizzo close in. "Everybody, stay where you are!" Grabowski shouts.

A single gunshot rings out and I see my dad tumble backward. Caught in a deathtrap, the crowd drops to the floor, tipping over chairs and tables for cover. The crash of tumbling plates, flower-filled vases, and pillar candles create a cacophony that adds to the horror.

"Stay down!" Rizzo yells.

Jarrell peeks above the table. Armed officers stand with weapons drawn. The scene is surreal.

I let out an ear-piercing scream at the agonizing sight of my dad's motionless body. Blood gushes from his head. I'm momentarily frozen in place by the violent scene and miss my chance to escape. I ache to crawl to him, but held once more in my captor's clutches, I cannot. "No!" I wail, "What have you done?"

From across the room, C.C. points and screams. "That's him. That's the guy who took us! He's got Libby." Zach's held by officers who thwart his attempt to rush the man.

My mom and Brooke cry on their knees next to my dad's body. "Why are you doing this to us?" C.C. says, her voice weak with grief.

The gunman holds me with his weapon digging into to my back. "Mercedes Slade," he yells, "if I'm going down, I'm not going alone!"

SHEAR MADNESS

Shear Madness is a non-musical play. Marilyn Abrams and Bruce Jordan acquired the German rights and created *Shear Madness* from Paul Pörtner's murder mystery, *Scherenschnitt*. It opened in New York City at the New World Stages Off-Broadway Theatre in November of 2015. *Shear Madness*, set in a hairstyling salon, is considered one of the longest-running non-musical plays in the world. The production, a hilarious whodunit, has a wacky cast of characters that improvise nightly with humorous references to current events and audience interaction that gives the show a different ending every night.

Chapter Thirty-Eight

A n *officer speaks quietly into* a small handheld device. "Man down. Active shooter. Broadway Center Hotel grand ballroom. All units respond. Repeat, all units." Thunderstruck, everyone glares at Mercedes—except for the NYPD, who remain zeroed in on me and my gunman.

"Arrest this guy!" Carter shouts. "This is sheer madness."

"Your precious girl had to win," the man says. "She wanted Cunningham out of the way. She devised a scheme and blackmailed me to do her dirty work."

"How dare you! Mercedes is innocent," Olivia snarls.

Inflamed, Carter shouts, "Vincent Wilde, are you nuts? Our

daughter is the best dancer here! Why would she need to do that?"

"She's starved for your attention. Admit it. You don't notice anyone unless they're mega-stars making you a boatload of money."

"Mercedes, is this true?" Carter asks.

"I can prove it," Vinnie says. "Her recent texts and video will show she's the mastermind behind eliminating C.C. from the competition."

Avery shakes her head. "I told you, Carter, your daughter's nothing but a spoiled brat."

"Oh, shut up, Avery!" Carter and Olivia screech in unison.

"I swear, Daddy. I have no idea what he's talking about. Everyone, please, you have to believe me. I didn't even know he was here," Mercedes says. "If he took C.C., it must have been for money."

As the police move closer, the man called Vinnie presses the pistol to my head and hands me Mercedes' phone. "Stay back!" he shouts to the officers. "Give us the password, or I'll shoot this girl, too."

Danny panics. "What's wrong with you, Mercedes? Do it! Give him the damn passcode."

"I never told you to kill anyone!" Mercedes cries.

"Miss, give it to him. You don't want to make the situation worse," Detective Grabowski warns.

Mercedes sobs in the spotlight.

The gunman points his weapon across the room at Carter and Olivia. "I swear, Mercedes, tell me now, or I'll shoot your parents, too."

"Shoot me instead. My life is over." Mercedes falls to her knees. Danny crouches at her side.

"Last chance," Vinnie says.

"Go to hell! You're the guilty one. You went too far, Vinnie. This was never the plan!" Mercedes says.

"You don't want anyone else to get hurt," Danny says. "I have faith in you. Please give Libby the passcode." Mercedes nods to Skylar.

"I think I know what it is," Skylar says. "Try S-T-A-R, I mean 7-8-2-7."

With shaky fingers, I punch in the four-digit passcode, and her cell phone opens.

Vinnie nudges me. "Go into her photo albums and select videos." Feeling the butt of the gun against my temple, I do exactly as he says. He looks at Avery in disgust. "You really made the rounds, didn't you? How many others were there?"

"I have no idea what you're talking about!" Avery insists.

"Forward all of these to her father," he demands. I hit send.

The room waits in silence.

Carter's cell phone pings. When the videos play, sound and all, he visibly sags. "Oh Mercedes, why? What were you thinking? And Avery, we're done!"

"Me? I had nothing to do with this!" Avery protests.

"Maybe not tonight's drama, but you're as guilty as sin. It looks like you've had something to do with just about everyone on my staff. Like I said, we're finished! Figure out how to fly commercial because I never want to see you again. And Vincent, I know desperate people do desperate things, but this is insane! Put the gun down. Let the girl go."

As the police bar his escape, I sense his desperation and fear for my life. Surprisingly, he shoves me aside with a mumbled apology that only I can hear. When Grabowski gets close enough to recognize the weapon as a harmless Smith & Wesson stage prop, he pounces. Vinnie knows it's over and gives up without a fight. He's quickly handcuffed and led away. With an expression of pure contempt, he looks at Carter. "I regret ever meeting the sorry lot of you. Why don't you ask Mercedes if chasing the spotlight was worth it?" Rizzo confiscates the gun along with Mercedes' and Zach's cell phones, and shouts to the crowd, "The gun's fake; the threat's over!"

I collapse at my father's side. "Dad, wake up. Please don't die," I beg.

The rise and fall of his chest and the arrival of the paramedics fill me with relief. "Libby," Mom says, "it'll be all right. My husband's name is Will," she tells them, and they immediately assess his condition.

"Will, can you hear us?" one asks.

"Looks like he has a possible dislocated shoulder and a nasty laceration on the back of his head that will require stitches. Don't worry, ladies, head wounds often look worse than they actually are," the EMT says. I flinch when the other paramedic lifts Dad's lids to examine his eyes. They're a weird shade of gray. "Add a possible concussion to that," he says.

Dad wakens slowly. He touches his head and grimaces when he moves his arm. "What happened? Have I been shot?"

"No, Sir. There's no indication of a bullet wound."

"Will, when you fell during the scuffle with that madman, you hit your head on the edge of a table and knocked yourself out," my mom says.

"But he had a gun! I heard the shot and saw the flash."

"You did, Will, but it was only a stage prop. It couldn't fire a bullet."

After passing the standard concussion protocol, he's allowed to sit up.

"Libby, sweetheart, are you okay?"

"I'm fine." My voice quivers. "It's you we're worried about."

From the stage, Mercedes begs, "You have to believe me, Danny. I didn't mean for things to turn out this way."

"Don't play innocent, Mercedes, and don't you dare ever kiss me again. We always have the choice to do the right thing, and none of this was right. My heart breaks for you. You're so gifted and won the title fair and square, but you blew it. For what? Chasing the Spotlight? Well, now you're stuck in it like a deer in the headlights. You wanted fame and attention. Tonight, you found it. You should be more careful what you wish for."

Danny hurries to my side and holds me close. "I was so scared. I don't know what I'd do if something happened to you." Soon we're surrounded by Zach, C.C., Brooke, and Jarrell. We share hugs and Danny's sweet kisses assure me everything will be okay.

Past hundreds of onlookers—suffering humiliation beyond belief—Mercedes and the Slades are escorted to Watts' office for interrogation. To make matters worse, Carol Ruthers, with the Lexfords in tow, appears. "Are these the people responsible for hurting my daughter? I demand justice for Whitney."

"Mercedes, who is this woman, and what is she talking about?" Carter says.

"Oh, Dad, there's so much more to this story than I bargained for."

Carter, envisioning a possible lawsuit, wisely advises his daughter to keep her mouth shut.

Carol looks at Clare and Howard. "Certainly, this teenage delinquent won't be allowed to keep the title, and if all the rumors are true, C.C doesn't deserve it either!"

"This evening has been traumatic for all of us," Howard says. "Please give us time to get the full story and sort things out. We promise to be fair."

Like casualties of war, we're loaded into ambulances that transport us to the nearest hospital. Never in my wildest dreams did I imagine that Gala Night would end so dramatically. In the emergency room, the detectives take our statements and suggest we press charges. Thankfully, none of our injuries are life-threatening, and soon we're released.

It's nearly two in the morning when we return to our hotel room where we're met by Mr. Trent and Miss Aimée. We huddle together, relieved to have survived this horrible night. Will any of us truly recover? Despite our tangled nerves and undeniable resentment toward Mercedes and her evil partner in crime, we pray that the Slades will find the help that they need. Call me a bleeding heart, but a small part of me feels sorry for Mercedes and the death of her dream.

My mother cradles me in her arms. Dad, with his head bandaged and his shoulder immobilized in a sling, finally convinces her to let me breathe. "Oh, Libz, we're both so thankful you're alive."

I shudder. "I'll never forget that gut-wrenching fear when I thought," my words catch in my throat, "you were dead, Dad." I tenderly stroke his cheek. "Thank God the gun wasn't real."

"People live through far worse every day. We're the lucky ones. We have each other and our faith."

"Amen!" Mr. Trent says. He wipes C.C.'s mascara-streaked face and kisses the top of her mangled mop of curls. "All I can say is: praise the Lord no one was seriously hurt."

Convinced we're safe, our families retire to their suites. Miss Aimée and Mr. Trent are the last to leave. "You girls sure you want to be left alone?" Mr. Trent asks.

"Yes, we'll be all right," C.C. says.

"You've been through so much, I'm sure this wasn't the competition week any of you were expecting." Miss Aimée reaches out, and we rush into her open embrace. We stand in a puddled mess of relief and regret, unable to speak.

Finally, our tears stop. "Everything was just about perfect until the gala," I say, "but I'm blessed to have shared my first competition's highs and lows with true friends at my side."

"It always helps to stay positive," Brooke says.

"Speaking of good things," I say, "maybe C.C. will be named the rightful winner."

"That's true," Brooke says. "With all the commotion, I hadn't even stopped to consider it. The Lexford's won't let someone like Mercedes Slade keep the title. Will they? As the first-place runner-up, shouldn't C.C. be named the official replacement?" We beam with renewed hope.

"Not that it seems to matter in the same way it did just hours ago, but is that true, Miss Aimée?" C.C. asks. "Do you think I'll be awarded the title?"

Miss Aimée bites her lower lip and looks to Trent. He hesitates and shakes his head ever so slightly. "C.C., we can't say for certain what will happen or how the Lexfords will decide which way is better for their organization to proceed. Remember, each of you and your parents signed an agreement form, and unfortunately, C.C., whether you were falsely coaxed to go or not, you did leave unannounced and without a partner, a clear and serious violation of the rules."

"The most important thing is that you're okay and able to dance another day," Miss Aimée says.

"We'll just have to be patient, keep our spirits up, and let you recover from tonight's insanity," Mr. Trent says.

"All we can do is wait?" Brooke says.

"It's out of our control, and I'll accept the outcome either way. Z-Dug or not, I let my emotions get the best of me, and I shouldn't have left. I made the situation far worse, especially for my family and you guys. I'm truly sorry," C.C. says through a fresh torrent of tears.

Seeing C.C. brokenhearted tears us apart. She's the one we always count on to be strong. We hold her until her sobbing stops.

"It makes me furious," Brooke says. "What happened to you and Zach is totally awful and unfair."

"It is," Miss Aimée agrees. "It should have never happened, but it did. God doesn't promise life will be fair. All we can do is learn our lessons and keep moving forward."

"Title or no title, C.C., we've always been beyond proud of you as a dancer, and we're even prouder of your maturity and the ownership you're taking for your actions. Remember, one bad decision doesn't define you," Mr. Trent says.

The two of them sandwich C.C. with one last hug. "Get some rest if you can," Miss Aimée says. "It's been a long, hellish night."

Left alone, we slip on our pj's and slide beneath the covers. Rather than talking, we individually text with Danny, Z-Dug, and Jarrell. I hate to admit it, but I'm jealous that Jarrell and Brooke will be together in Chicago for the remainder of the summer. C.C. and Zach at least had the chance to say goodbye at the hospital. It feels like a cruel punishment that I may never see Danny again. His flight leaves before sunrise.

After growing close to the boys in such a short time, I worry that C.C. and I will struggle letting them go. I'll have to trust that everything we experienced—from falling in love to nearly dying—will all make sense someday, because right now, it doesn't. I fall asleep with tears on my pillow. I miss Danny already.

ON YOUR FEET

On Your Feet is a jukebox musical with book by Alexander Dinelaris and choreography by Sergio Trujillo. The production opened to positive reviews and box office success at the Marquis Theatre in November of 2015. Showcasing the Cuban-fusion pop music made famous by 26-time Grammy Award winning husband and wife team, Gloria and Emilio Estefan, it tells the story of two people who believe in their talent and each other.

Chapter Thirty-Nine

S*unday dawns with a blue* sky and the promise of a fresh, new day. Although Danny's farewell text early this morning was sweet, and he says he'll always stay in touch, my smile hides a thousand tears. Preston Bailey has one request. He asks that we join him at St. Patrick's Cathedral for morning Mass. I imagine it's to praise the Lord that we survived last night's reign of terror. C.C. tells us the cathedral had been her grandmother's favorite place in New York. The magnificent structure, built in 1879, takes up an entire city block. As hard as I try to concentrate on the celebration at the main altar, my eyes drift upward to the church's awe-inspiring architecture. I'm transfixed by the high, stone arches that look as though they're reaching heavenward and the vibrant stained-glass windows that surround us.

Even in July, when so many locals vacate the city in search of cool breezes, there isn't anything about New York that I don't love. I'm drawn back into the service when the congregation connects to recite *The Lord's Prayer*. C.C., Brooke, and I clasp each other's hands, bonded by the knowledge that ours is a special petition of thanksgiving for C.C. and Zach's safe return. I shudder to think of what might have been. When we offer each other the Sign of Peace, it serves as the start of closure, especially for C.C. whose darkly bruised wrists are a painful reminder of her horrid capture and escape.

After the final blessing, we reverently tour the cathedral, admiring the small chapels, religious paintings, and artifacts that adorn the holy space. As others file in for the next Mass, our group reluctantly leaves. We step outside into the glorious sunshine of Fifth Avenue where our Sunday morning stroll takes us past Tiffany's, one of New York's most famous jewelry stores. Too intimidated to enter, we gawk at the precious diamonds and gems displayed in the window. We each sigh, dreaming of the day we might be gifted with an iconic blue box. We're surprised when Mr. Trent steps from the shop. Completely caught off guard, he hides a Tiffany bag behind his back.

"You're out bright and early," he says somewhat flustered.

"Just saying goodbye to the city before we leave," Dad says. I notice him wink at Trent.

With a wave and silly grin, Mr. Trent, looking like a kid caught with his hand in the cookie jar, hails a cab and hops in.

"Looks like Miss Aimée's in for something special," I say.

We continue to soak in the sights and sounds of New York. On our way back to the Broadway Center Hotel, we pass Rockefeller Center, the NBC Studios, and Radio City Music Hall.

"Libby, did you ever think about auditioning for the Rockettes?" C.C. says.

My mother laughs and retells her favorite story about my strong kicks before I was born and how her doctor dubbed me, "his little Rockette." I beg my mother to stop, but everyone agrees auditioning would be a worthy goal.

"Yes, you should all do it," chimes Preston. "You three have the talent, the looks, and the legs for it."

"So do a million other dancers, Grandpa," C.C. laughs.

"But you three are exceptional," he says. "And you're mine! All this walking is making me hungry. I'm going to forego my traditional Waldorf Hotel brunch and treat you to a spot that I think you'll find much more agreeable. Follow me."

Our trek ends at Ellen's Stardust Diner on Broadway and 51st. "This is a unique place," Mr. Bailey says. "All the servers are aspiring performers. They periodically break into song with hopes of being discovered. It's called the restaurant for drama and dreamers."

When the diner's manager stops at our table, he greets C.C.'s grandpa like an old friend. Proudly, he tells us that several performers have signed contracts and are appearing on Broadway. "In fact," he says, "one young man's down the street at the Winter Garden Theatre, dancing and singing in the *School of Rock*."

We're enthralled by the Broadway-bound talent when they perform for us. "C'mon everyone, on your feet," Mr. Bailey says. We reach into our pockets to contribute to the tip bucket cleverly named Phill-Up. We learn that the money collected is divided among the servers for dancing, acting, and singing lessons. Our parents tip generously, and even though C.C.'s grandpa tries to hide his offering, I see his folded hundred-dollar bill tucked inside.

"Girls, if Broadway's truly our goal, we need to consider voice and acting lessons," C.C. says. I'm glad to see her thinking of her future again.

Before heading back, we detour past the Winter Garden Theatre and pose for pictures alongside giant posters of the musical's cast. Acting goofy, we play air guitars and pretend we're in the show. C.C. insists on having her grandfather in a shot, and I know it's the one she'll post on social media. Before moving on, we study the poster with great care, trying to guess the lucky waiter from the Stardust Diner.

At the hotel, we separate from our parents and promise to begin the daunting task of packing. They act as though they can't wait for us to get to our room, and my intuition tells me something's up.

DREAMGIRLS

Dreamgirls is a Tony Award winning musical with lyrics and book by Tom Eyen, choreography by Michael Bennett and Michael Peters. It premiered on Broadway at the Imperial Theatre in December of 1981. *Dreamgirls*, staged with a mostly African-American cast, proved to be a star-making vehicle for several of its performers. In 2006, it was adapted into a motion picture of the same name starring, among others, Beyoncé Knowles, Jennifer Hudson, and Anika Noni Rose. The musical follows the story of a young female singing trio from Chicago called the Dreams who become superstars. According to critic Frank Rich, of the *New York Times*, ". . . it's a beautiful and heartbreaking new musical." In it, we see the high toll of guilt and self-hatred that's inflicted on those who sell their artistic souls to the highest bidder. *Dreamgirls* is about the price of success.

Chapter Forty

*H*uge boxes wrapped with pink satin bows rest on our beds. Three ivory-colored envelopes are addressed with our names in fancy script. "What is this?" Brooke asks.

"No idea, but here's a note," I say.

For my three dancing Dreamgirls,
Love, Grandpa Bailey

"Isn't he the best?" C.C. says. She tears apart her special envelope. "Look! We're invited to a Farewell New York party given by Miss Aimée and Mr. Trent," she says.

"What? Where? When?" I ask, ripping mine open.

"Today," says C.C., "at The Cloisters. I told you I saw them getting into a cab earlier this week. This must be what they were planning."

"What's in the boxes?" Brooke asks.

The bows have our names attached, and we open them in one swift motion. Lavender tissue flies everywhere and we squeal at the sight of the contents. Inside are three of the most gorgeous dresses we've ever seen.

"I love mine," Brooke says.

"Me, too," I say.

"Me, three," laughs C.C.

Holding them in front of us, we whirl and twirl in circles. Each dress is a subtle shade of lilac and although all are short, they're each designed differently. Brooke's is a strapless, full skirted creation. C.C.'s has one bare shoulder and is super straight, and mine is a lacey halter top fit and flare. We love them and can't wait to try them on. Just then our cells buzz. We recognize the caller IDs.

"We're outside your room," our parents say. "Let us in." They confess they've been listening at the door and are clearly exited for us.

"This is too much," I say, hugging my mom and dad. C.C. does the same while Brooke stands off to the side. Her joy for us is bittersweet. However, when her phone dings, she hurries to the door and pulls it open. There stand Brooke's parents, holding up her favorite gem-encrusted sandals. "We're told you might need these," her mom says. Brooke falls into their arms, and no one dares to move or speak.

We carefully lay our dresses on the beds, and our mothers help us check our accessories and shoes. When it's decided that we have everything we need, we're told to meet in the lobby at 3:45 sharp. At 4 p.m. town cars arranged by C.C.s grandfather will arrive to drive us to The Cloisters.

"But what about our flight home tonight?" I ask.

"One more surprise," my mom says. "We're staying another night and flying out in the morning. But that doesn't mean you shouldn't use this time to pack everything you don't need. It'll be an early flight tomorrow instead of a late one tonight."

We talk nonstop while stuffing our suitcases. When C.C. double-checks her costume bag, she gets quiet. "Don't be sad, C.C. All dancers get melancholy when the dance year and competition season end. It's unlikely that these fun and fancy costumes will ever be worn again, but you've done them proud," Brooke says.

Finally, unable to ignore the elephant in the room, and painfully aware of the undecided Dancer of the Year title, we offer C.C. a chance to open up. I'm encouraged by the tiny, fleeting smile that passes over her face and we share a giggle when Brooke recounts, in vivid detail, Skylar hiking up her gown to make a mad dash across the tabletops.

"I thought poor Mrs. Lexford was going to have a conniption," Brooke says.

"She'll be okay," I say, "I have a feeling the Lexfords are a lot tougher than they look."

"You're probably right, Libby. But I'm not ready to relive Gala Night, not yet anyway. Miss Aimée and my parents are giving me a pass until we get home, and I don't know what will happen then."

"C.C.," I press on, "I guess you did break the rules by agreeing to meet Zach, but you were both tricked. Surely, the competition will take that into consideration. Won't they?"

"Bottom line," C.C. says, "I'll take responsibility for my actions and accept whatever punishment I deserve. Right now, I'm just happy to be alive. I've been told to let it go, and that's exactly what I'm trying to do. Let's have fun tonight. I only wish Zach and Danny were still here. We didn't even have a proper goodbye."

"I feel so bad for the two of you," Brooke says. "Jarrell will have to escort all three of us to the party. I'm positive he won't mind."

I DO! I DO!

I Do! I Do! is a Tony Award winning musical with book and lyrics by Tom Jones based on the Jan de Hartog play *The Fourposter*. Choreographed by Gower Champion, it opened at the 46th Street Theatre in December of 1966. *I Do! I Do!* was an ideal investment in that it had inexpensive sets and costumes, as well as a small cast. The film adaptation, written by Champion, was announced but following the commercial failure of several movie musicals, the project was abandoned. The two-character story spans fifty years and focuses on the ups and downs of marriage. Courtesy of Gower Champion, the stars perform an engaging soft-shoe to end all soft-shoes, because it is done with no shoes at all.

Chapter Forty-One

We *gather in the Broadway* Center Hotel lobby—our dads handsome in lightweight, summer suits—our moms pretty in designer fashions from Bloomingdale's. "Be sure to thank Grandpa Bailey for your dresses," Mrs. Cunningham says.

"We helped pick them out, but Mr. Bailey generously insisted on charging them to his credit card," Mom says.

When C.C.'s grandpa sees us, he grins ear-to-ear. "Perfect," he says. "Absolutely perfect!" We spin and show off our dresses before ganging up to shower him with hugs and profuse thanks. We are, indeed, a very fashionable group.

Shiny, black town cars arrive at precisely four o'clock. When C.C. invites her grandpa to ride with her, he declines. "C.C., my dear, I'm as anxious to get to The Cloisters as you and your friends, but one of these town cars is reserved for me and a special guest."

"You're being very mysterious, Grandfather," C.C. says with a pretend scowl. "You know I hate being kept in the dark."

"Don't worry," he promises, "I'll be there after a slight detour."

We watch his driver pull away from the curb. "That was odd," C.C. says.

"Maybe he has a date."

"Good grief, Libby! What a thought. Although it wouldn't surprise me. I swear he looks and acts younger every day."

"He's an extraordinary man. You're so lucky."

"I agree. I know, too, that you dearly miss your grandfather. I'm sure he was just as wonderful."

"Thank you. You're a sweet friend for understanding." C.C., Brooke, and I hug before we enter our car.

"Girls," Dad laughs, "you're going to be together again in less than forty-five minutes."

"It's just what we do," we giggle.

With a final wave, we're ready to go. I notice an extra, unoccupied car. Perhaps the company sent one too many. I put it out of my mind when my dad settles into the comfort of the soft leather seat. "I could get used to this," he says with a heavy sigh.

"Don't worry," I say. "When I'm a famous Broadway diva, I'll send my car for you and Mom every night. No charge."

"Gee, thanks, Libz," he laughs. "You're a real sport."

The drive to The Cloisters takes us to Upper Manhattan. We follow the Hudson River to the New York medieval landmark.

There, we're met by museum staff. They guide us to an inner courtyard where we're offered a variety of refreshments and asked to stay together.

"I don't see Miss Aimée and Mr. Trent," Brooke says.

"Nope," I say. "I'll bet the other town car at the hotel was reserved for them."

The shaded walkway abuts a lush garden decorated with many statues and fountains. The opulence of the museum feels otherworldly. It's as if we've been transported back in time, a feeling I know well.

"This is nice, but isn't it kind of a strange place for a farewell party?" C.C. says.

"I was thinking the same thing," Brooke says.

Just then, our guide announces: "Ladies and gentlemen, at this time kindly follow me to the Langon Chapel."

"Huh? I'm confused. No Miss Aimée, Mr. Trent, or Grandpa Bailey! And now we're going to party in a chapel? I don't get it. We just went to church," I whisper, not wanting to offend our guide.

"Play along," C.C. says. "I have to believe that all will be revealed in due time."

It doesn't take long, and the revelation is a stunner! At the entrance to the Langon Chapel, everything becomes crystal clear. "Holy Mother of Pearl," I say. "This isn't a Farewell to New York party. It's a wedding!"

"Those sneaks!" Brooke says.

"How could we not see this coming?" C.C. cries.

We wait for our parents to confirm or deny our suspicion. C.C.'s mom is the first to break the silence. "Yes, you're right," she admits. "Aimée and Trent are getting married in this beautiful chapel today. They didn't want to distract you from your dance classes and competition this week, so we honored their wishes."

"Phew," Mom says. "I'm glad the cat's out of the bag. Dad and I wanted to tell you so many times, Libby, but we were sworn to secrecy."

"We can't believe you didn't catch on, especially when we saw Trent at Tiffany's this morning," my dad says. "Not to mention the matching, colored dresses," our moms laugh.

"I can't believe it either," I say. "Girls, we're slipping. I suppose with all the chaos yesterday, we missed every sign today."

"C.C., you even said couples get married at The Cloisters," Brooke reminds her.

"I know." C.C. says. "This is unreal. How could we fall for a lame excuse like a farewell party?"

"Sheesh. Look at us. We're even dressed like bridesmaids!" I say.

"You're right," Brooke says. "All we need are flowers."

As if on cue, we're each handed a small bouquet. The lilies of the valley, forget-me-nots, roses, and lilacs instantly remind us of Daniella Devereaux and her love of the fragrant blooms. We shiver in unison.

"Seriously, guys," I say. "I can feel Daniella's presence."

"Me, too!" Brooke says. "After all, she was Miss Aimée's cherished great aunt."

Our parents take their seats, but we three, honored that Miss Aimée chose us to stand by her side, are escorted to the front of the chapel by another member of the museum staff who introduces himself as Mason Evers. We're instructed to walk to the left of the altar. We look around nervously, not knowing what's expected. Our moms motion us to stand tall and still.

"Five-six-seven-eight," C.C. counts. "Heads up, ladies, it's show time."

When the priest enters the sanctuary, C.C. understands her grandpa's covert mission. Approaching the altar is Father

August Caine. He's rotund with a shock of white hair and mischievous blue eyes. He's the pastor of a favorite parish her family visits when in New York.

"That's Father Augie," C.C. says, genuinely happy to see him. "He and my grandpa were college roommates at Fordham University." C.C.'s grandfather takes his seat next to her parents, satisfied that his part of the conspiracy is complete.

"Look," Brooke says. A large, wooden door opens. Out steps Mr. Trent followed by Stephen Chen. If possible, they are more handsome than ever, but it is who's behind them that excites us most. Following in a row, wearing huge smiles and gorgeous light-gray tuxedos with lavender ties, are Jarrell, Danny, and Zach.

"Don't tell me they were in on it, too," C.C. whispers.

"Don't know. Don't care," I say, thrilled by their unexpected appearance.

Brooke shushes us, "The ceremony's about to begin."

When Danny winks at me, I melt. When I wink back, the flash in his sexy eyes sends shivers from the tip of my head to my silver, strappy, high-heeled feet. I wiggle my tingling toes in anticipation of the evening ahead.

Everyone rises to their feet at the soft sound of an angelic harp, emanating from somewhere in the rear of the chapel. All heads turn, and I'm delighted to see my beloved dance teacher from Wisconsin: Miss Aimée's dearest friend, Dana Greenly. I love that she's Miss Aimée's maid of honor. Dressed in a tea-length, chiffon gown of the palest shade of blue, she's lovely— her stroll along the ancient aisle, slow and elegant. At the foot of the altar, she takes her place beside us.

When Miss Aimée appears at the chapel door, she is, to our great surprise, accompanied by Mr. Stan, L'Esprit's trusty caretaker. I'm momentarily fooled into thinking that I'm seeing an angel. She's a vision of pure light wrapped in delicate, white lace. No princess—real or make believe—was ever more radiant. Her walk down the aisle on the steady arm of Mr. Stan makes everyone emotional. He wears a stylish tuxedo, and as the man who's watched over Miss Aimée for most of her life, he's her ideal escort. Miss Aimée locks eyes with Mr. Trent, and her focus never wavers until Mr. Stan places her hand in Trent's. When Mr. Stan bends slightly to kiss Miss Aimée's cheek, I hear a loud sniffle. Mrs. Summers, the elderly floral shopkeeper and our dear friend from L'Esprit, gently dabs her eyes with a dainty handkerchief and waves. Happy to see them both again, I wonder when they arrived and who's taking care of L'Esprit. But of course, they'd be here. She and Mr. Stan are the closest thing to family that Miss Aimée has ever known.

Lucky for us, our dresses have small hidden pockets where our moms had the foresight to place a few tissues. Like Mrs. Summers, we're never getting out of here with dry eyes.

When Mr. Trent and Miss Aimée take their place before Father Augie, I notice that Miss Aimée's gown is even more spectacular when viewed from behind. Low-cut and stunning, its silhouette flatters her figure, and I love that the exquisite design exposes her graceful dancer's back.

With all the visual distractions, I don't hear much of the traditional exchange of vows except for my favorite part: "I do! I do!" But those they've personally written are spoken with such fervor, I hang onto every word like an eavesdropper to an intensely private conversation.

Trent fights back tears when he says, "I promise you, Aimée, I am yours for eternity."

Miss Aimée gently touches his face. "You, Trent, are my life, my love, now and forever."

By the conclusion of the ceremony, my friends and I are emotional wrecks. High school sweethearts, Trent and Aimée spent years chasing careers. Now their love has come full circle. The bride and groom approach the unity candle. The instant they join hands and touch the flame to the wick, a brilliant light fills the chapel illuminating the stone walls with a golden glow. We stare in awe.

Seated in the last row, Mason Evers wishes he had someone to high-five. This is exactly what he envisioned. To his knowledge, the phenomenon has only happened twice in the past, and the elements must align precisely. *Bravo*, he tells himself. *I knew there was something special about this couple.* When he witnesses the same dancing orbs he'd seen at their earlier meeting, he's certain that with four, loving entities as guides, theirs is a marriage made in Heaven. Besides, when Preston Bailey, one of the museum's most generous benefactors, asks to reserve the chapel and close The Cloisters for a private event, one goes the extra mile.

In the brief golden glow of the chapel, Aimée sees the orbs and intuitively recognizes the spirits of A.J. Dalton, his beloved wife, Daniella, and her own deceased mother and father. Bowing her head, she receives their blessings and promises that even though she's given her heart to Trent, there will always be a special place in it for each of them.

"Trent, do you see them?"

"Who?"

"The orbs, our guardian angels."

"No, my love. But I knew you'd want them here. I'm glad they received my invitation." The depth of Aimée's love overflows, and her joyous tears mix with ours.

"May I present Mr. and Mrs. Trent Michaels," Father Augie says. "You may kiss your bride."

The guests applaud as the blissful pair makes their way down the aisle, accompanied by the enchanting strains of a harp and violin. Miss Dana and Steven Chen follow next. When the guys each offer us an arm, we're over the moon to be reunited. I hear Zach promise never to leave C.C's side. "You're stuck with me," he says. His adoring eyes seal the deal.

"I wouldn't have it any other way." She snuggles closer and wraps her arm around his.

I don't know how much happiness a place can hold, but these stone walls are ready to burst.

CRAZY FOR YOU

Crazy for You is a Tony Award winning romantic-comedy musical with book by Ken Ludwig and choreography by Susan Stroman, based on Gershwins' 1930 musical, *Girl Crazy*. It opened on Broadway at the Shubert Theatre in February of 1992 to rave reviews. The *New York Times* called it "fresh and confident, riotously entertaining, a classic blend of music, laughter, dancing, sentiment, and showmanship." A man with a yen for show business decides to put on a show to save a dying theatre and is reunited in the finale with the girl he loves.

Chapter Forty-Two

The reception is a romantic and elegant affair. Mom employs her professional skills as the official wedding photographer. I can tell she's in her glory using The Cloisters as a timeless backdrop. When we each pose with our dates, Mom doesn't have to coax me to smile. In fact, I don't think I'll ever stop.

We take turns congratulating the bride and groom, and I even give Mr. Trent a peck on the cheek, something I couldn't imagine doing a year ago. I'm reminded of how fortunate I am to have been accepted into L'Esprit's inner circle.

When introduced to Mr. Trent's parents, we can plainly see where he gets his outrageous good looks. Warm and welcoming, our families become fast friends. C.C., with Zach's arm firmly around her waist, chats up Steven Chen. If any one of us is Broadway-bound someday, it's her. I laugh when Danny, still in awe of Mr. Trent, stumbles over his words when congratulating him. I never knew boys could blush, too.

"Danny," my dad says, "Libby means everything to us. Kate and I know you care about her. Last night your actions proved how important she is to you. Thank you for helping to protect her. Anytime you're in Chicago, you're welcome in our home."

"Thanks, Mr. Nobleton. I appreciate that more than you know. I've never met anyone as kind and sweet as your daughter. I'm just thankful everyone's safe."

"As the saying goes, 'all's well that ends well.' The evening's young, and so are you two. Go make the most of it."

"C'mon, Danny," I say. "Let's walk." He takes my hand. As we stroll away, I say, "I'm sure L.A.'s great, but you'd love Chicago, too."

"That sounds like an invitation."

"It could be. We all go home tomorrow. When will I see you again?"

"I guess that's up to you."

"Well, what are your plans now that you're a famous Dancer of the Year and a high school graduate?"

"I hope to follow in Mr. Trent's footsteps. I've been accepted at Juilliard. My goal has always been to dance with a professional company, I'd love to do both at the same time, if that's even possible."

"Whatever you do, I know you'll crush it. Can we at least text or maybe FaceTime once in a while?"

"Libby."

"What?"

"Stop talking."

He leads me behind one of the ancient arches that line the stone walkway. "You know I'm crazy for you."

When he pulls me against his body and our lips meet for the first time, sparks fly and my spirit soars. This time I'm the one blushing. "I promise you, Libby, I'll *always* stay in touch." I shiver when his soft breath tickles my neck. We follow the path, suspended in an oasis of serenity created by the courtyard's medieval European gardens and trickling fountains. My heart tells me this is where I'm meant to be. When we tear our gaze away from the sweeping vista of the Hudson River, our eyes search each other's. *Are we both feeling this undeniable connection?*

I swear he reads my mind. "Trust it. This is real." Danny's lips gently press against mine. The kiss we share stirs the deepest corners of my soul, and I never want to let him go.

We reluctantly rejoin the party. Round tables are set with white china, glistening crystal, and fancy silk napkins, but I hardly notice. The night is charmed, and I can tell that Brooke and C.C. share my feelings. We toast the bride and groom and laugh at Steven's best man speech. Referring to their college days, he jokes that Trent was always a slow learner. Everyone knew he would marry Aimée, but no one expected him to let a decade pass before he made it happen.

Dinner is served to the accompaniment of a gifted pianist. He's a virtuoso, deftly playing everything from popular show tunes to classic Sinatra to Taylor Swift. When our plates are cleared and the wedding cake is ceremoniously cut, we surround the makeshift dance floor. Miss Aimée and Mr. Trent waltz slowly to "The Way You Look Tonight" and are joined by Miss Dana and Steven. Mr. Stan and Mrs. Summers make the cutest couple dancing together as if it's the most natural thing in the world. We guess about what we should call Miss Aimée now that she's a married woman. Jarrell decides she should be Mrs. Trent or Mrs. Aimée, but we vote him down. She'll always be Miss Aimée to us.

After the horror of last night, you couldn't find a giddier bunch. Finally, we invade the dance floor, kick off our shoes, and rock it out until the last song plays. It's a slow, beautiful ballad that has every guest swaying and wishing this magical night would last forever.

But all good things must end. Our dads look immensely relieved when Miss Aimée tosses her bouquet, and it's caught in one swift motion by Mrs. Summers. Mr. Stan wears an enormous grin. Could there be another wedding in L'Esprit's future? After all, Mrs. Summers has been a widow for an awfully long time.

With grateful hearts, Miss Aimée and Mr. Trent say goodbye to us and all the other guests. As they slip into a waiting limo, Mom tells us they're honeymooning in Paris. C.C. and Zach kiss passionately, not caring who sees them, insisting distance won't change a thing. When Brooke and Jarrell announce they're officially a couple, everyone cheers.

We all laugh when someone shouts to Jarrell, "It's about time!"

With one last kiss, Danny and I seal our promise to see each other soon. If this is a dream, I never want to wake up. I only have one question . . . *How soon is soon?*

Epilogue

Months Later ...

Howard and Clare Lexford

Desperate for a peaceful getaway, the couple boards a flight to a remote Caribbean island. Soured by the miserable Gala Night from hell, they ponder selling their convention to the highest bidder. Over pitchers of frosted piña coladas, Howard convinces Clare he could be happy teaching line dancing to the locals, and Clare teases Howard that she could be content if the only things flowing were the endless supply of liquor and her shapeless moo moo.

Vincent Wilde

Vinnie pursues his performance career by directing and starring in the popular musical, *Guys and Dolls*. His ingenious disguise skills come in handy when playing the female lead. His vivacious portrayal of Miss Adelaide is enthusiastically received by jeering fellow inmates at his current residence, a medium security prison in upstate New York.

Mercedes Slade

Under house arrest and the strict supervision of her parents, who, to her delight, have reconciled, Mercedes undergoes an intense course of family counseling and personal therapy. Her 250-hour sentence of community service for participating in the plot to kidnap C.C. is spent on the streets of Beverly Hills, where Skylar Wilkins and other classmates revel in walking by and scoffing. Dressed in a humiliating, neon-orange vest, Mercedes hands out pamphlets touting the evils of teenage fame obsession. Her *real* punishment, however, takes the form of a letter from the Stairway to the Stars organization officially stripping her of the coveted Dancer of the Year title.

Whitney Ruthers

Whitney and Tia, best friends again, admire the cover of the latest issue of *Dance Star Magazine* that she shares with Danny. To her credit, Whitney's full-length, Fosse-style pose is impressive. The wordy article about her and B-Bop is either exceptionally flattering or a bit stomach-churning depending on how much the reader knows. Since being named the Stairway to the Star's female Dancer of the Year, Whitney has softened a bit. Her mother Carol, however, has set the bar for insufferable arrogance, never missing a chance to remind Miss Aimée of L'Esprit's loss. Miss Bea floats on air, basking in the glory of Whitney's success and B-Bop Studio's unprecedented waitlist.

C.C., Brooke, and Libby

The girls, now high school seniors, resume full-time schedules of homework, dance classes, and their positions as L'Esprit's assistant teachers. Jarrell's daily updates from NIU (Northern Illinois University) School of Theatre and Dance keep the girls excited for each audition he wins and role he lands. Over time, with the help of family and friends, C.C.'s nightmares fade. Libby and Will hug each other fiercely every day, thankful to be alive. The girls' best medicine is frequent weekend visits from Zach, Jarrell, and Danny, where the inseparable couples fall deeper in love and dream of the future.

Trent and Aimée

All of L'Esprit celebrates when Trent and Aimée share the glorious news of a baby girl, due to arrive with the first lilacs of spring. Her name: *Daniella*.

Broadway, Musical Theatre, and the Tony Awards

Broadway theatre refers to the theatrical performances presented in the forty-one professional theatres with 500 or more seats located in the theatre district of Lincoln Center and Midtown Manhattan. Along with London's West End theatre, Broadway is widely considered to represent the highest level of commercial theatre in the English-speaking world. The great majority of Broadway shows are musicals. Broadway's first long-run musical was a fifty-performance hit called *The Elves* in 1857. Musical Theatre consists of performances integrating song, acting, and dance. The book or script of a musical refers to its story, character development, and dramatic structure, including spoken dialogue and stage direction.

The first Tony Awards, originally known as the Antoinette Perry Awards for Excellence in Theatre, were presented during a 1947 ceremony at the Waldorf-Astoria Hotel in New York City to recognize achievement in live Broadway productions. Brock Pemberton, a theatrical producer, director, and founder of the Tony Awards was the professional partner of Antoinette Perry who founded the American Theatre Wing. The Tonys received their name when Pemberton handed out an award and called it a Toni, referring to the nickname of Perry. The winners were written on a scroll and rather than a trophy, the prize was either an initialed, sterling silver compact for the women or an engraved, gold money clip or cigarette case for the men. In 1947, the first award ever given in the category of choreography, Agnes de Mille won for *Brigadoon* and Michael Kidd for *Finian's Rainbow*.

Theatre Dictionary

IN is down, DOWN is front
OUT is up, UP is back
OFF is out, ON is in
RIGHT is left, LEFT is right
A DROP shouldn't and a
BLOCK AND FALL does neither
A PROP doesn't and a
COVE has no water,
TRIPPING is okay
A RUNNING CREW rarely gets anywhere,
A PURCHASE LINE will buy you nothing
A TRAP will not catch anything
STRIKE is work (in fact, lots of work)
And a GREEN ROOM, thankfully, usually isn't
Now that you're fully versed in theatrical terms,
BREAK A LEG---but not really!

Theatre Superstitions

- Never say 'Macbeth' in a theatre
- Don't say "good luck," instead say "break a leg"
- Leave a ghost light on at night in the theatre
- No peacock feathers, mirrors, real money, real jewelry or lit candles on stage, they're considered bad luck
- Don't wear blue
- Sleep with your script under your pillow
- Whistling backstage is considered a jinx
- Flowers should be given after the show, not before
- A bad dress rehearsal means the show will be a hit

Acknowledgements

As always, our dancing hearts wish to thank God for blessing our partnership through every step of this creative collaboration.

We're grateful to our faithful family and friends for their support and encouragement. Your frequently asked "how's the second book coming?" kept us motivated and on track.

To every dancer we ever taught—know that every studio hour spent, every convention attended, and every conversation and hug ever shared, you are our inspiration. We love you all!

To our talented dream team at Ten16 Press: Editor, Jenna Zerbel, who cheerfully guided us with excellent suggestions and welcome critiques. Art Director, Kaeley Dunteman, for her amazing creative skills and extreme patience. Interior Designer, Lauren Blue, for her clear and imaginative vision. We are grateful to each of you. Special thanks and praise to the delightful owner of Ten16 Press, the idea machine behind it all, Shannon Ishizaki.

And to our readers, for your patience, enthusiasm, and kindness, we sincerely appreciate you beyond words. Your generous response to Book One of the Dance Legacy Series, *The Legend of L'Esprit*, winner of a National Indie Excellence Award for young adult fiction, means the world to us.

We hope you enjoy this series.

Always have Faith

and

Happy Reading,

Doris and Pandy

We love to hear from our readers.
Visit us at: www.DancersatHeart.com
Contact us at: DancersatHeart@gmail.com